CW01455060

CLIMBING
KILIMANJARO

CLIMBING KILIMANJARO

JIM CUMMINS

authorHOUSE®

AuthorHouse™ UK Ltd.
1663 Liberty Drive
Bloomington, IN 47403 USA
www.authorhouse.co.uk
Phone: 0800.197.4150

© 2014 Jim Cummins. All rights reserved.

No part of this book may be reproduced, stored in a retrieval system, or
transmitted by any means without the written permission of the author.

Published by AuthorHouse 03/11/2014

ISBN: 978-1-4918-9782-9 (sc)
ISBN: 978-1-4918-9783-6 (e)

Any people depicted in stock imagery provided by Thinkstock are models,
and such images are being used for illustrative purposes only.
Certain stock imagery © Thinkstock.

Because of the dynamic nature of the Internet, any web addresses or
links contained in this book may have changed since publication and
may no longer be valid. The views expressed in this work are solely those
of the author and do not necessarily reflect the views of the publisher,
and the publisher hereby disclaims any responsibility for them.

Contents

Introduction

We began our climb for the Summit of Mount Kilimanjaro at 11.30 pm, the Temperature in the camp we just left was –5c and we expect it to be –18c to –20c at the Summit, we are told the climb to the Summit will take 7 ½ to 8 hours arriving around Sunrise, because of the extreme cold we should only spend 15 or 20 minutes at the Summit and get moving downhill, the Descent to our next Camp will take another 7 ½ to 8 hours, that's a total of about 16 hours to our next camp, in between there is no Food, no Drink, no Camp where we can take a rest so we must carry everything we need for about 16 hours to get us up and down safely, I am 67 years old and my Wife Pat is 63, we are by far the oldest in our Group. We have already been climbing for 4 Days and it will take 3 more Days to get us up to the top of Kilimanjaro and back down to where we meet our Bus, you may ask how we find ourselves in this situation when we are retired and at a stage in our lives where most people would look for a more relaxing past time, well we are keen Hill walkers and Kilimanjaro is the ultimate climb for someone like us, it's the highest freestanding Mountain in the world and the highest Mountain in all of Africa and has been at the top of my list of things to do before I die, my wife Pat is a recent convert to Hill walking but is no less enthusiastic about it. For many years now I have been recording important events in my life, and my Wife and some family members have been encouraging me to write a book about it, my account of our Kilimanjaro climb brought more encouragement so I put it all together and this is the story of my Journey from Kildare to Kilimanjaro

Chapter 1

Climbing Kilimanjaro

Only those who risk going too far can find out how far they can go. T S Elliot

<u>Day 1</u>

Why climb Kilimanjaro.

- It's the world's highest freestanding mountain, meaning it's not part of any mountain range.
- It's the highest mountain in the world that can be climbed by ordinary climbers and without having to use ice picks, ropes or any technical equipment.
- At 5895 meters (19340 feet) it's the tallest mountain in Africa.
- It's so big it creates its own weather patterns from humid tropical Rainforests at the bottom to Arctic conditions and glaciers at the top.
- It's made up of 2 extinct Volcanoes, and one dormant Volcano which is known as Kibo, Kibo also has the summit of Kilimanjaro called "Uhuru" and is said to be the highest dormant volcano in the world.
- Because of its height size and location on the equator you will pass through 5 climate zones on your way to the summit.
    1. Cultivation and farm land.
    2. Rainforest.
    3. Heath and moorland.
    4. Desert.
    5. The summit which has Arctic conditions and has 3 glaciers.

My hobby is Hill walking and having done many charity treks abroad, I had been thinking of trying Kilimanjaro as far back as 2008 but then I slipped into a Bog Hole in the Slieve Bloom Mountains and injured my Achilles Tendon and was out of action for 2 years, having tried Physiotherapy, Laser, Acupuncture, with only temporary relief, I finally had surgery and resumed hill walking in 2010.

I signed up to go with Pat Falvey in 2011 and went for a training weekend in March, what they do is try to simulate the last part of the climb to the summit of Kilimanjaro where you are walking right through the day and night for about 16 hours without rest, they can show what it's like to climb a mountain in darkness and test your level of fitness, but they can't prepare you for the cold and they can't prepare you for walking at high altitude where you have less than 50% of the oxygen we are used to at sea level. Pat Falvey is an explorer who has travelled worldwide and has personally climbed Kilimanjaro about 50 times using almost all the routes up and down what he calls his favourite Mountain. However he will not be leading our trip as he is preparing to walk to the North Pole, our leader will be Lorraine Gordon who is a very experienced Walker and a lovely person to be with.

My son Robert and his partner Aisling were going to come and do the climb with me but they had also planned to compete in a Ironman Triathlon and the dates clashed, so they opted for the triathlon, around that time my Wife pat said to me," do you think I could do Kilimanjaro". I was shocked at the idea but I was also impressed with her progress as a walker, so I said to her, let's see about preparing you and see how you get on.

I took her up all the high mountains in Wicklow and then we went to Scotland and climbed Ben Nevis the highest Mountain in the UK, at 1344 meters it was the highest Mountain we had climbed so far, in June we went to Killarney for another training weekend similar to the last day/night on Kilimanjaro and the verdict from Pat Falveys team was that my wife Pat was ready to take on Kilimanjaro. We bought inflatable mattresses and sleeping bags suitable for sleeping in a tent at −20c as well as thermals and jackets suitable for prolonged walking periods at −20c or worse. All was going well until August when Pat found a Lump on her Brest, our travel plans were all in doubt but when all her tests were done she got the all clear with just a few weeks to spare.

The day before we were due to leave I got a cold, I went to Dr. Ahern and he gave me Antibiotics to take if I got a chest infection. It's a long journey to Tanzania and we have a rest day before starting the big climb, the day we began climbing I was sneezing, coughing, had a running nose, a chest infection and had started taking Antibiotics, not a good way to start a climb unlike anything I had ever done before.

The end of day one, at 3000m and still in the rainforest

Climbing Kilimanjaro

There are only 2 mistakes one can make on the way to the truth, Not going all the way, and not starting. "Buddha".

Day 2

Before we can start the climb we are taken to our tour operators' office to have our Rucksacks weighed, they have to be carried up the mountain by porters and must not weigh more than 15 kg. The plan is that we will take 5 days to reach the summit and 2 days to descend so we have to bring enough clothes etc. to last 7 days while we will spend 6 nights in tents on the Mountain. We also have to bring our vital medication, I recently started taking tablets for high blood pressure and Pat takes medication for her Thyroid, for her Heart and for Arthritis, we both have to take Malarone which is an Anti Malaria tablet, there is no cure for Malaria so you try to avoid getting it by taking Malarone. For my chest infection I am on Antibiotics 3 times a day and Pat gives me Paracetamol every 4 hours to keep my cold at bay, I hope we have some time left for walking between our Pill popping sessions.

We are taken by Bus to the Rainforest where our walk begins and as we arrive it starts raining so we put on our raingear. We start walking at 11 am and it's not very hot but it is humid and with our raingear on we sweat all the way to Mechame camp where we arrive at about 5pm. The track through the forest is a dirt track and is slippery but not dangerous so we got through the day with no accidents.

Mechame camp is at 3000m altitude but it's still in the Rainforest, Pat and I are in good shape as we check in but very glad to see the end of the first day walking, when the sun goes down the temperature drops quickly to −3c so we are glad we bought good quality sleeping bags and inflatable mattresses, Pat had no problem keeping up with me and the rest of the group and her level of confidence has improved greatly, today's walk was 18km and all uphill.

We don't sleep so good this first night as our sleeping bags are too tight, there is a 2nd zip which allows the sleeping bag to expand but we can't figure out how to use it, we laughed so much we exhausted ourselves and just gave up.

I started Hill Walking in late 2004 when I joined up with Barretstown which is a charity that provides holidays for children who have Cancer; they had an ad in a Sunday paper looking for volunteers to take up a challenge by walking 100 km through Jungle and Mountains in Brazil. They arranged training weekends where we were taken to the Wicklow Mountains by a very experienced and qualified guide called Robert Farrelly, a most unusual man in his 30s, he has a beard and long hair down to his Backside, Robert neither drinks or smokes but loves Jaffa Cakes and always brings a packet which he shares at lunch time on the Mountains.

The main organizer in Barretstown was Helen O'Malley who came up with the idea of treks abroad as a way of fundraising for Barretstown who need about 6 million euro each year to keep their centre going, the idea behind Barretstown originally came from Actor Paul Newman who founded The Hole in the Wall Gang in Connecticut USA, the idea to extend the organization to Ireland came from an Irish Doctor working in the USA who was a friend of actor Richard Harris who was also a friend of Paul Newman, Paul agreed with the idea and came to Ireland to meet the then Taoiseach (Prime Minister) Albert Reynolds to see what assistance the Irish Government would give to the project. At that time Barretstown Castle was owned by the State having been granted it as a gift by Galen Weston when he decided to move his home to Canada, Galen Weston had been the target of the IRA when they planned to kidnap him at his home and hold him for ransom. The plan went disastrously wrong for the IRA because the Gardai had got a tip off and were waiting in the bushes when the gang arrived in the dark, a gun battle ensued in which one of the raiders was killed, another was captured and others escaped to fight another battle. Before Galen Weston the property was owned by Elizabeth Arden the creator of a cosmetics empire, when she lived there she had the front Door to the castle painted in the same bright red colour as one of her Lipsticks and it's still in that colour today. The state had this castle with 500 acres of good land which they had very little use for so they gave it to the charity on a 99 year lease for one £1.00 Per Year, the 1st Hole in The Wall Camp outside the USA was opened and it was given the name "Barretstown". Paul Newman gave $1,000,000 of his own money and many Irish business people gave large contributions. The new charity opened its Doors in 1994.

Day two with our neighbour Myles O'Brien and our Leader Lorraine Gordon

Climbing Kilimanjaro

The marvelous richness of human experience would lose something of rewarding joy if there were not limitations to overcome. The hilltop hour would not be half so wonderful if there were no dark valleys to traverse. Helen Keller

Day 3

We are awake long before our wakeup call at 6.30, our porters Simon and Amadeus bring us a cup of hot tea and a Basin of Water with which we are supposed to wash ourselves, on the Mountain there is no running Water, no Shower, no shaving until it's all over and we get back to our Hotel, we decide that trying to wash in a Basin of Water in a Tent where you have no room to move and can't stand up is not very practical and we decide to make do with wet wipes instead. Breakfast is ready at 7.30 in a big Tent complete with fold up tables and chairs, all of which have to be carried from camp to camp by porters which are young men in their 20s.

8.30 we start walking, still in the Rainforest for about 2 hours where the trees are smaller, there is a very fine lichen hanging from the trees about 6 foot long, some of it is green and some of it silver, it creates a ghostly dreamlike atmosphere, we keep moving and I regret not having taken pictures of the scene. We leave the forest and come into moorland which is covered by heather like shrubs, at 3800m the trees and shrubs get smaller still, walking gets harder as we gain altitude and have less oxygen to breath in, it is difficult terrain, upwards all day long over large boulders for 5 hours 30 minutes to Shira Camp at 3800m, the campsite is littered with loose rocks so we have to take care as we move about after dark with only our head light to show the way.

Our porters are here before us and have our tents ready to move into; so far only one Woman has suffered from altitude sickness, sick stomach. She is a very negative person who complains constantly so we just keep clear of her. I am not sick but I am exhausted after the days walk, I wonder is it my chest infection or the effect of the antibiotics, or is it altitude sickness. Strong winds battered our tent for a few hours and it was hard to sleep, about 4.30 we got up to go to the toilet and, the wind has stopped but there is heavy frost on the ground. The temperature is –3c.

Hypothermia one of the dangers on a trip like this is exposure to extreme cold which could result in Hypothermia, which is defined as having a core body temperature of less than 35 degrees C or 95 degrees F. As the temperature falls, the body shunts Blood away from the skin to the vital organs like heart, lungs, kidneys and brain. The heart and brain are more sensitive to cold, and the electrical activity in these organs slows in response to cold, if the body temperature continues to decrease, organs begin to fail and eventually death will occur. *Prevention of hypothermia;* when walking in mountains warm windproof and waterproof clothing including head gear and gloves must be carried and put on in time. Be aware of weather forecasts, Carry adequate supplies of food and water. Do not hesitate to retreat if you believe conditions are likely to lead to hypothermia

Day 3 with our Guide Gasper and John the postman from Baltinglass

Climbing Kilimanjaro

The longest journey begins with the first step, Old Chinese proverb.

Day 4

I still have my chest infection, still coughing, the sneezing and running nose have ceased, we talk to our leader Lorraine and our African Head Guide Freddie, I tell them I want to start on Diamox as I may be suffering from Altitude Sickness, Freddie and Lorraine agree and we all hope the Diamox does not clash with the Antibiotics and make things worse. So far Pat has no problems and is coping well with the walking and the altitude, however this morning she took Malarone before Breakfast and got quite sick, after that she took them after breakfast and had no more problems.

We know today is a long haul, our next camp is only 50m higher than last night's camp but to get there we have to ascend a very high peak called Lava Towers at 4630m and back down through a long hot valley. after walking about 3 hours I feel very weak, I lose my balance and stumble a lot, I fall over rocks that are right in front of me, Pat is behind me and keeps asking if I am ok and I keep saying yes. But I can't keep going and have to stop and sit on a rock, our Irish guide Lorraine and Douglas one of our African guides stop with me and Douglas takes my bag to carry it for me, I am in no condition to disagree with him but when I see Pat still carrying her own Bag while mine is carried for me I feel terrible about that.

Pat was crying as she walked behind me as she worried that I might not be able to complete the walk that meant so much to me and having got half way up the Mountain. When we made it to the high point of 4630m Douglas is holding my left arm and Lorraine is holding my right arm as the rest of our group wait for us. I am embarrassed at having to be helped in and I said to Lorraine, please Lorraine, I don't want to be carried in, she understood and let my arm go. We think my problem is a clash between the Antibiotics and the Diamox so I ceased taking the antibiotics, we know it's not a good idea but I have to either stop taking the Antibiotics or the Diamox.

As it is all downhill from now on I take my bag back from Douglas, it's a very difficult and sometimes dangerous descent so the pace is very slow, after 2 hours we are down in a valley which is truly an amazing sight, even more so because a heavy fog has descended on us, Giant Groundsels (Senecious) over 6 meters tall, When the leaves die they don't fall off but wrap themselves round the trunk to protect itself from frost and snow. There is Giant Lobelias 5 feet tall and other plants and shrubs we had never seen before.

The heat in the valley gets the better of me and I have to stop again, Douglas takes my bag again and carries it for the rest of the journey to Baranco Camp, we have been walking for 10 hours and I am completely exhausted, as soon as we eat I go straight to bed and stay there until morning.

When we were planning this trip I said to Pat, "there's only one reason for doing this trip and that is to get to the summit of Kilimanjaro", so if one of us gets sick and can't continue the other one of us should go on and let the sick one go back with a guide, I said that I would go on in that situation, but as each day passes I know now that I could not go on and leave Pat if she were sick and unable to continue, Pat said there is no way she would go on without me if I were sick.

I met a Canadian in Baranco Camp who was in a group which included a 79 year old man and a 73 year old man, they were spending a full day at this camp as part of their acclimatization process, and I never saw them again to find out if they made it to the summit. I am the oldest in our group at 67 and Pat is next at 62.

Climbing Kilimanjaro

Forget yourself by becoming interested in others. Every day do a good deed that will put a smile on someone's face. Dale Carnegie

Day 5

Feeling much better this morning, had a good night's sleep, Breakfast of Porridge, Eggs and Bacon, our Campsites should not really be called Camps at all, each site has a hut where an official Person records everyone who passes through the Camp, other than that there are a few small huts with a hole in the floor which acts as a toilet, most have no door so I stand guard when Pat uses it. Sites are littered with rocks and our porters have to clear spaces to set up our tents, about 10 small and 2 large tents for dining in as well as tents for our guides and porters to eat and sleep in.

The mountain is controlled by the Government of Tanzania and all fees paid go to the government, however like many African Countries Tanzania is incredibly poor and very little goes back to provide facilities for those who climb the mountain, our African guide Freddie said about 57,000 tourists enter the mountain each year but not all make it to the Summit. Most nights our tent is on a bit of a slope and the first thing we do is work out what direction we will lie in as we don't want to be rolling over on top of each other when we go to sleep. We go to bed about 8.30 and are awake before 6am. Our tents are of remarkable quality, light as a feather but when they are properly secured they can withstand strong winds and heavy rain and it's amazing the difference in temperature inside and outside, it's −3c outside but cosy inside.

We start walking at 8.30 and very soon are confronted with an almost sheer cliff about 200m high called "The Baranco Wall" which we have to get up and over. Because I had a bad day yesterday our guides won't let me carry my bag up the wall and it's taken by Alfred who secures it on top of his own bag. This is fine for me but I feel terrible watching Pat still carrying her own bag while mine is carried for me, the path up the cliff face is barely wide enough for one person and at one point the only way forward is to stand facing the cliff face and shuffle along sideways for about 10 feet, we have to climb over boulders that are 5 or 6 feet tall and most of us have to be pushed and pulled at some point, one time Pat got stuck and said to Keith Sheridan, give me a push Keith, he did and pushed her head right up into the backside of Myles O'Brien who was in front of her. It took us almost 2 hours to climb the wall and soon we could see our next Campsite, however to get to it we had to go down into a steep Valley and up the other side, as we descend we come to a very steep decline which is covered in loose gravel and is difficult to keep control and avoid falling, I look ahead just as Alfred our Guide grabbed Pat by the Hand and they took off in a sort of controlled slide at high speed, this continued for quite a distance and they managed to stop just in time as they approached a cliff edge. It took us another 3 hours to reach Karanga Camp where our porters had a lovely meal of Chicken and Chips ready for us. The altitude is taking its toll, one Woman has a sick stomach all the time, another has Diarrhoea, one man is Coeliac and can only have gluten free foods, our Tour Company knew of this and had suitable meals arranged for him but he can't always eat them and he seems to be suffering from a serious loss of energy although he never complains, his bag is being carried by one of our guides, another man is suffering, mainly because he is unfit, he expected he might only be able to keep going for 2 days but he has surprised himself and the rest of us at how well is doing. Another man complains and uses foul language all the time so we keep as far away from him as we can, we don't need negative thoughts getting into our heads at this time. Today we are above the clouds and it's lovely to look down on the Sunrise and Sunset as you would from an Aeroplane.

Africans would have known about the snow on Kilimanjaro for hundreds of years but it remained unknown to the rest of the world until 1848 when a German missionary Johannes Rebmann saw it from the Kenyan side, however Europeans would not believe him saying "you can't have snow on the Equator" it was confirmed in 1861 by another German Baron Von Der Decken who encountered a blizzard at 4270m, in 1889 a German Geographer Dr Ludwig Meyer reached the highest point on Kibo Crater at 5895m which today is called "Uhuru" which in Swahili means Freedom Peak. In 1927 a English Woman, Sheila McDonald became the first woman to reach the Summit; Africans say that when you are on Uhuru you are on the roof of Africa, it became better known when Ernest Hemingway wrote "The Snows of Kilimanjaro" which became a film classic in 1961.

Climbing Kilimanjaro

> *You are never too old to set a new goal or dream a new one.*
> *C E Lewis*

Day 6

Today we have a 4/5 hour trek through a desert of sand and rocks to Barafu Camp. Even in remote places like this, Artists will find a way to display their talents, in areas where there is nothing but loose rocks some people take time to create little monuments and structures, one of them was so good we thought it was a man sitting on a rock until we were almost beside it. On the long climb to Barafu Camp at 4600m, we see young men with 25 litre drums walking away from the camp and others walking to the camp with 25 liter drums filled with water being carried on their heads, this is because there is no water within 10 km of the camp and those young men take it from the nearest river for their supplies, most of our group opted for bottled water from the Supermarket which we had to pay extra for and it had to be carried all the way each day, it took 15 extra porters just to carry our bottled water, Pat is in great form and I feel pretty good too, we arrive at 2pm and lunch is ready for us.

Barafu Camp is the worst of all the camps, more dirt and it's an ordeal just walking around because of all the loose rocks, the toilets are far away and you don't want use them anyway unless it's an emergency, tonight we start our final climb to the summit at 11.30, so we go to bed in the afternoon and sleep for about 2 hours, we then make our final preparations for the big climb. From here on there is no other source of food or water other than what we carry in our bags, we need at least 3 litres of water each, at least 5 energy bars each, we don't get a packed lunch because at this altitude, only sweet foods have any appeal and anyway we can't stop for more than 1 or 2 minutes because of the extreme cold and we can't afford to carry any weight we don't need, we have to turn the water bottles upside down because they freeze at the top first and if the neck is at the top it will freeze and you can't get anything to drink. We normally use a platypus which is a plastic bag with a hose coming from it that allows you to drink as you walk along but this won't work here as the hose is outside the bag and would freeze before we leave the camp.

We will need at least 5 layers of clothes, starting with thermals top and bottom followed by 3 or 4 shirts or t-shirts, a fleece and finally our down filled waterproof jacket which is good for prolonged periods at −25c and heavy duty trousers, we have spare lightweight rain gear in our bags, we put new batteries in our headlights as we can't take any chance of being left in the dark on the narrow track to the summit, we have 3 pairs of gloves each, a woolly cap and a balaclava to protect our face, the temperature in Barafu Camp is −5 and we expect it to be −18 on the way to the top, if there is a wind blowing it will be much worse, we have a lovely evening meal of chicken and chips followed by Water Melon wedges and go back to bed for a while but don't sleep any more, at 9.30 we start getting dressed for the summit.

Everyone who knows my wife Pat is well aware that she is a very organized person, when planning this trip she was ready to go about 2 months before the due date with different batches of clothes separated into plastic bags which were labelled for easy sorting, our medicines were separated into zip lock bags and labelled, so it should be easy to find what we want, however it's not working out like that, every morning and every evening something can't be found, her heart tablets, her phone, we carry out a search and find what's missing and all's well until the next time, apart from that Pat is coping very well, she never complains and is in good form and still act's as Doctor and Nurse for me each day.

Altitude Sickness, What causes it, it starts to affect people above 1500m altitude where the level of oxygen is less than we are used to at Sea level and the main cause is ascending faster than the body can acclimatize, anyone can get it, it makes no difference to, age, gender, level of fitness and there is no way to predict who might or might not get it.

Your body undergoes several changes to deal with reduced levels of oxygen,

- You breathe faster and deeper, you experience shortness of breath, your heart and lungs have to work much harder.
- You exhibit different breathing patterns as you sleep, you awaken more often at night
- Symptoms, you will urinate more often, difficulty sleeping, dizziness, fatigue, headache, loss of appetite, nausea or vomiting.
- Symptoms for more severe Altitude Sickness, bluish discoloration of the skin, chest tightness, confusion, coughing, coughing up blood, decreased consciousness, grey or pale complexion, unable to walk in a straight line, shortness of breath when resting, Death
- Treatment, Descend to a lower altitude as quickly as possible, Get extra oxygen if available, severe cases need to get to hospital, severe cases can result in Death due to Lung problems or swelling of the Brain.

Prevention, climb the mountain gradually; spend extra time at different levels as you ascend, sleep at lower altitudes where possible; take

13

Jim Cummins

diamox the day before starting your climb, Drink lots of water, avoid alcohol, and eat regular meals which are high in carbohydrates

Climbing Kilimanjaro

There ahead, all he could see, as wide as all the World, high, and unbelievably white in the Sun, was the square top of Kilimanjaro. Ernest Hemingway, The Snows of Kilimanjaro

Day7 the Summit

We meet at 11pm for Tea and Biscuits, collect our 3 litres of water each, I take one of Pats bottles to lighten her load so I am now carrying 4 ½ litre's which makes my Bag quite heavy, we make sure to turn them upside down in our bags to prevent the neck from freezing, unfortunately no one told us that our energy bars would also freeze as we go up and the temperature goes down,

11.30 we start our trek to the summit, we are so heavily laden with clothes that we wonder if we can walk at all but we feel very snug and warm even at –5c as we leave Camp. From the start the track is very steep but our African guide Gasper sets a very slow pace, he wants to keep our group together as long as possible. As well as Gasper there are several more guides spread out among our group watching for any signs of trouble with any of our group, the track is up, up all the time but we have to keep moving as there is a constant stream of walkers in front and behind and the track is so narrow that if we stop for a rest we stop everyone that is behind us. After 2 hours Pat has to remove one pair of gloves as they are too tight and hurting her hands, I put on my third pair of gloves because my hands are going numb from the cold.

At 3 hours Pat has to remove one layer of clothes as she is overheating and getting stressed, the lack of oxygen is telling on all of us, our hearts and lungs have to work much harder than normal just to keep us walking slowly.

At 4 hours Gasper can see that Pat is having a bad time and offers to carry her bag, she agrees and he puts her bag on top of his own, her hands are frozen so she puts back on the extra gloves she took off earlier.

At 5 hours both our hands are numb from cold, our gloves and clothes are covered in frost, the water in our bottles is freezing rapidly but we can still get a drink when we need it, I have some gel pads in my bag and when you squeeze them they heat up so we put them in our gloves and use them and they keep our hands warm, they are good for about 30 minutes, at 5 hours our hands are numb again and we use more gel pads which work for another 30 minutes.

When we stop and look back down the mountain there is a continuous line of lights moving slowly like a very long snake as men and women from all over the world make their way to the summit, about every hour we stop and take a few bites from our energy bars but they are frozen and getting very difficult to bite into, then our guide gently tells we must get moving or the cold will get into us and we could be in big trouble, if hypothermia sets in it can be very difficult to bring the body temperature back to normal and only a rapid descent to higher temperatures can bring that about.

At 6 hours Pat puts back on the clothes she had taken off earlier and keeps it on for the rest of the ascent, I am finding it very hard to keep going so Gasper takes my bag and puts it on top of Pats bag, he is now carrying 3 bags and all our water supplies, one water bottle has frozen solid and the others are part frozen but we can still get a drink when we need it, our hands are frozen again and I have no more gels left to warm them, I am reminded of a line from a book called" Kilimanjaro" by Michael Mushabeck in which he describes his climb to the summit, he says, "we moved with utmost caution, one foot in front of the other, hauling ourselves up on what seems like an endless frozen stairway to heaven".

Our head lights are pretty good but sometimes I look left or right and all I see is darkness, does this mean we are on the edge of a cliff, Pat tells me to watch where I am going, I don't tell her we are on the edge of a cliff. I have a balaclava to protect my face but it restricts my breathing so I leave it on for a while and then leave off for a while. Up here no plant grows, no animal lives, the only sign of life is us.

At 6.30am we reach a plateau called Stella Point, the temperature is −18c, although we are still 45 minutes from the summit we know the hardest part is over and we all congratulate each other. The Sun comes up as we approach the summit and there are glaciers on both sides just a few hundred meters from our path, they are an awesome sight to behold and no picture can adequately convey the scene before us, more than 30 meters high, unfortunately they are disappearing at an alarming rate, the ice cap on Kibo the largest Volcano was 12 sq km in 1900, today it is only 2 sq km and may be completely gone by 2025.

Well we did reach the Summit after 8 hours walking and we were among the first in our group to do so, the sense of achievement is almost overpowering, we take pictures to prove to everyone including ourselves that we really did make it. There is a battered old sign on the summit which reads. **Congratulations you are now at Uhuru Peak Tanzania 5895m, Africa's highest point, The World's highest freestanding Mountain and the World's largest Volcano**

We wait for the rest of our group to arrive which they do with the help of our guides, it's still −18 even with the sun shining, and the cold is getting into Pat so we start our descent with our guide Gasper still carrying our bags.

Climbing Kilimanjaro

I never failed; I just discovered 2000 ways that it won't work,
<u>Thomas Edison</u> *when working on the Light Bulb*

Day 8

The descent

It's 8 am when we start our descent, our water supply is already reduced by half, we soon start to shed some layers of clothes and the oxygen levels continue to improve so morale is high, it's amazing that we still have so much energy left, we follow a different route down as the tracks are too narrow for 2 way traffic, it's a very steep descent which should take about 7 to 8 hours with only a short break for lunch on the way. We had been told to have our toe nails cut for the descent as our feet slip forward in our boots thousands of times, toe nails are forced against the front of the boot and it can become very painful, toe nails will turn black and it will take months for new nails to replace them.

It's very steep with loose sand and gravel, it's so steep you can't just walk so we are running or sliding and using our walking poles like ski poles for balance, Pat was having great difficulty and was in danger of having a bad fall so once more Gasper took control, he took hold of Pats arm and controlled her as they slid down at a speed that I could hardly keep pace with, Some of our group fell and had minor injuries. The performance of Gasper and other guides is one of the most memorable parts of the trek for me and Pat, after 4 hours we reach a camp where lunch is waiting for us, we are very tired and glad to have a rest.

The next part of the descent is very different to the last 4 hours, Gasper is gone ahead and we are carrying our own bags again, all the time stepping down over large boulders, this goes on for hours on end and is very hard on the knees and hips, Pat is finding it very hard and moving slowly when we are overtaken by our head African guide Freddie who can see she is in difficulty and takes her by the arm and helps her down from boulder to boulder and continues to do this until we reach Mweeka Camp, Pat said that without Freddie's help this part of the descent would have been almost impossible.

Our African head guide Freddie is a remarkable man, he talks like Nelson Mandela, very soft and calming and you feel you can put yourself in his hands and be safe with him. If someone is very sick Freddie has the last word as to whether they can go on or go back, he's not a Doctor but he knows by looking into your eyes and getting you to talk if you are fit to continue or not. He is 47 years old and has been to the summit of Kilimanjaro 189 times as a guide and before that he worked as a Porter for 15 years starting when he was only 15 years old, Porters only go as far as Barafu camp at 4600m but not to the summit.

Another guide who helped us a lot was Douglas, he has been to the summit 56 times, Gasper has been to the summit 36 times so we are in very good hands with those guys, they give the impression that they have made it their mission to get each of us to the summit and back safely and they will do whatever it takes to succeed in their mission. They are all handpicked by Freddie and they will do anything for him, everyone in our group was greatly impressed by the dedication of our guides and porters.

Our own Lorraine Gordon is tower of strength for everyone and with her colleague Ian they make light of any problem that comes up, Gerry Walsh was supposed to be leading the trek for Pat Falvey but had to pull out at the last minute and Lorraine took his place, we are very pleased with the way we were prepared for this trip and when we talk to friends of ours who tried to climb Kilimanjaro and failed due to bad preparation or trying to reach the Summit too quickly and failing due to Altitude Sickness, we hope to do it again and will use Pat Falvey's Company when we do, Pat Falvey himself has climbed Kilimanjaro about 50 times but he could not be on our trip as he was preparing himself for a trip to the North Pole in 2012

We are back down in the Rainforest at 3080m, Mweeka Camp is the cleanest of them all, it's our last camp and our last Night on the Mountain,

Tomorrow morning we have a 4 hour walk to where we meet our bus that will take us back to our Hotel and a nice Shower.

> *I have decided to stick with love, Hate is too big a burden to bear, Martin Luther King*

Climbing Kilimanjaro

> *Be wise to insure that every word spoken is carried with peace, driven with love and filled with hope, this we know for certain, one day our words will become our last. Courtney James*

Day 9, our last Walk

The plan today is to start our final walk at 9.30, it should take 4 hours or less to meet our Bus which will take us back to our Hotel, after breakfast we finish packing our Rucksacks and leave them ready for the porters who will carry them on their heads to where we meet our Bus.

We are called together in a clearing and Freddie has assembled his entire group of guides and Porters, one of our Girls, Lisa, presents Freddie, our African Head Guide with a collection we have made and which will be divided between all of them, the whole group comes to 60, that's how many people it took to get us, along with all our food, water, tents and cooking equipment up to the Summit and back down safely in 7 days. Freddie says a few words of thanks and then leads his group in singing a special song for us called "Kilimanjaro" which is very nice and is sung very well by the big group.

Our walk for the next few hours is all through the Rainforest, it's all downhill and is very steep, stepping down constantly is hard on the joints and we decide to make our own pace and take our time, on the way I get a good look at some Colobus Monkeys which are a large black and white Monkey with a huge white bushy tail. We are overtaken by our porters, most of them were running with our large bags and equipment on their heads, for them it's the end of the job until called again, when we reach the bottom many of them are already out on the road selling t-shirts and other souvenirs.

That night our tour operator provided a lovely outdoor bar-b-q and our guide Lorraine Gordon asked Freddie to present each of us with a certificate from the Government of Tanzania to prove we had reached the summit of Kilimanjaro. Later we were talking to Lorraine and one of the men from our group and the conversation came round to how difficult married life is in today's world when this man said to us, I am going through a bad patch in my marriage, I'm not going to talk about it but let me show you a text I just sent to my wife, it went like this, *there is a couple in our group in their 60s, the wife is called Puddin, they are married 43 years next anniversary, they are clearly very happy together and are an inspiration to everyone, you ask me what I want from marriage, well I look at them and say, "that's it".* Pat was very moved by this and I thought it was a nice compliment to get.

Next day we went on safari and as we drove away from the town of Moshi our driver said there is Kilimanjaro on your right hand side, when I looked I could see nothing at first but then I saw the summit poking its top out of the clouds, that's all we could see, just the summit and I thought, just imagine, we were up there looking down on the clouds, and with the next turn in the road it was gone.

Me and Pat with our head African guide Freddie (left) and Douglas

more of the gosthly valley

Pat in the middle being pulled up by Myles O'Brien and pushed by Keith Sheridan as we climb the 200 mitre Baranco Wall

happy to see the end of day 4

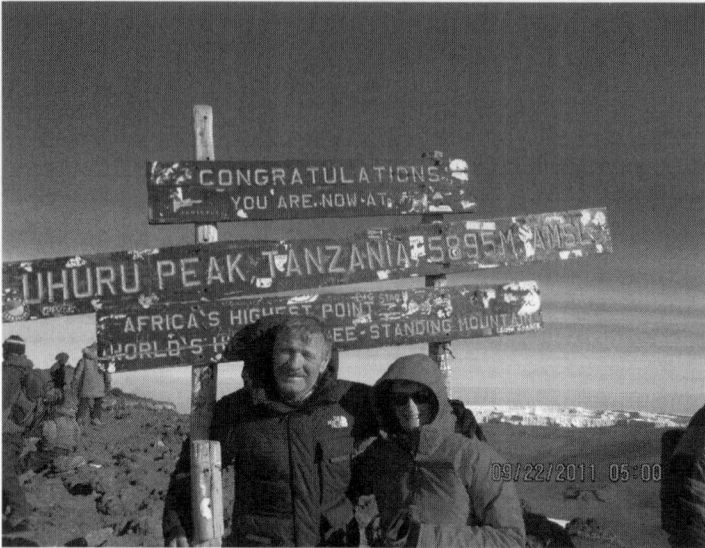

The Summit at last after 8 hours climbing through the
night, even with the sun shining it's still −18c

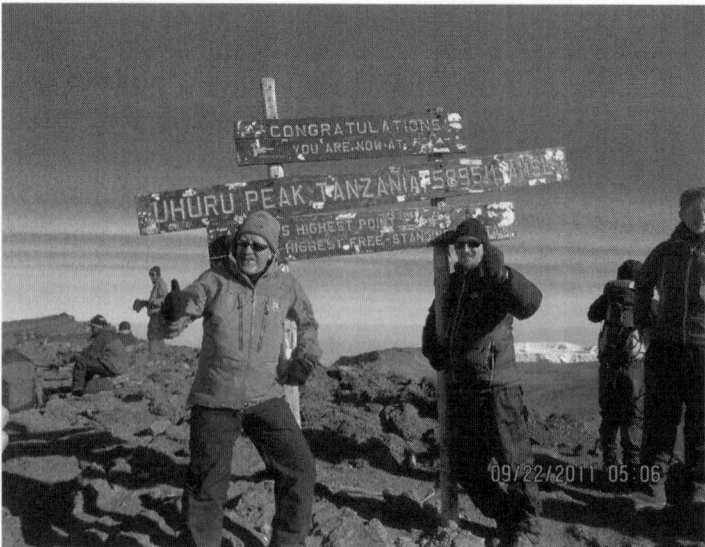

Myles and Keith at the Summit

Pat with our guidee Gasper and one of the
many glaciers in the Background

with our African guides,
l to r Freddie, Alfred and Douglas

up close with the wildlife on safari

Back home and walking in Glendalough

one of the many waterfalls in Glendalough

MOUNT KILIMANJARO-TANZANIA

Senecio kilimanjari	● Uhuru Peak (UP) 5895 m ● Stella Point (SP) 5756 m ● Gilman's Point (GP) 5685 m	*impatiens kilimanjari*

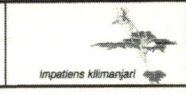

This is to certify that

Mr / Mrs / Miss _____Patricia Cummins_____

has successfully climbed Mt. Kilimanjaro the Highest in

Africa to **Uhuru Peak 5895m** amsl

Date 22/9/011 Time 7.25 AM Age 62

GUIDE **CHIEF PARK WARDEN** **DIRECTOR GENERAL**
Kilimanjaro National Park Tanzania National Parks

P. O. Box 1315
MBULY TOURS & SAFARIS LTD
MOSHI-TANZANIA

CERTIFICATE No. UP 145626

Pats certificate for climbing Mount Kilimanjaro

MOUNT KILIMANJARO-TANZANIA

| | Uhuru Peak (UP) 5895 m | |
| Senecio kilimanjari | Stella Point (SP) 5756 m Gilman's Point (GP) 5685 m | Impatiens kilimanjari |

This is to certify that

Mr / Mrs / Miss _____ *Jim Cummins* _____

has successfully climbed Mt. Kilimanjaro the Highest in

Africa to **Uhuru Peak 5895m** amsl

Date 22/9/011 ..... Time 7.25 AM ..... Age 6.7 .....

| GUIDE | CHIEF PARK WARDEN Kilimanjaro National Park | DIRECTOR GENERAL Tanzania National Parks |

P. O. Box 1315
MOSHI-TANZANIA

CERTIFICATE No. UP 145620

My certificate for Kilimanjaro

Chapter 2—Earliest Memories

I started writing 24th April 1983 with no particular plan other than to record my memories before I lose them. Kildare to Kilimanjaro is the story of my life so far, but it's not one long story, it's made up of more than 100 short stories.

On the day I was born 05 April 1944 World War two was still unresolved, on that day 140 Lancaster Bombers destroyed an Airplane Factory in Toulouse and 270 inhabitants of the Greek Town Kleisoura were executed by the Germans, many items needed for everyday living were being rationed in Ireland and would continue to be rationed long after the War ended, Favourite Songs that Year were, When Irish eyes are smiling and, That's an Irish Lullaby.

My earliest memories go back to when I was making my First Holy Communion; Mom said she would take me to visit her Father Granddad Pender, who lived in Penderstown on the Banks of the Grand Canal in Carbury Co Kildare, it was called Penderstown because so many families named Pender lived there, I really looked forward to this visit but for some reason it never took place to my great disappointed, I have vague memories of Grandma Pender nor can I remember Grandma or Granddad Cummins although I do remember being in their House on the Bog Road. I can remember Granddad Pender calling to our house on his way home from Mass in his Ass (Donkey) and Trap, when he was leaving he would give us a jaunt in the Trap out through the big Gate and then stop and let us off at the small Gate, I must have been very young then.

I remember sleeping in the Settle Bed but I don't know what age I was, I must have been very small because there was 3 or 4 sleeping in it at the same time. That was probably before the extra room was added on, I do remember the extra room being built and I was big enough to help Dad with the work, or at least to get in the way and think I was helping, it was there I learned the Meaning of words like, Rafter, Wall Plate, Purloin and others to do with building work, Uncle John and Teddy Mullaly helped out at different times.

To say we were poor is probably an understatement, we moved into the "new room" as we called it without it even having a ceiling in it, we lay in bed looking straight up at the rafters and above that was the felt so all that was outside the felt was galvanized sheeting, if you think about all the insulation that goes into a modern day house it makes you wonder how we got through the cold nights with so little protection from the elements and it was only when I was about 19 or 20 years old and working for Paddy Flanagan that the Ceiling was put in. One Saturday Paddy and I collected a load of 8" by 4" sheets of hardboard on his truck and we did the job all in one day, Dad may have been working in the factory that day because I don't recall him being there while we did the work.

We had no water supply except what we carried in buckets from the Pump at Pender's Cross half a mile away or from Daly's Well or from McDermott's Pump both of which were on private property, sometimes we would use the Ass and Cart and go to the Pump at Pender's Cross and fill a large Milk Can. When we got home the Milk Can could not be taken from the Cart full of Water so the Water in the Milk Can would be poured into a Barrel at the corner of the House, the Down Pipe from the Roof ran into the Barrel and this Water was used for washing but not for drinking unless we were stuck.

There was a Fireplace in the Kitchen/Dining/Sitting Room and each Bedroom also had a Fireplace but it was normally only the kitchen Fire that was lighting.

Dads Accident: Dad worked as a Boiler Man in the Bord Na Mona Briquette Factory at Lullymore, Carbury County Kildare. On Friday 3rd June 1949, I was 5 years old, Dad was on the Evening Shift when the boiler exploded, he was in the Boiler House with his Back to the Boiler and this explains why Dad suffered such horrible injuries to his Back, the explosion was heard and seen from our house which would be about 2 miles away as the Crow flies, My Brothers Pat and Ned and my Sister

Maura were playing at the back Garden of our House and just as Mom came to check up on them, they all saw a huge Fireball go up from the Factory reaching up to the Sky, then came the sound of the Explosion, Pat said Mom just got on her Bike and tore off towards the Factory and as she approached it she met 2 Ambulances leaving with Dad in one of them. Maura said that her memory of the Fireball and the explosion is as vivid today as it was then although she would have been only 6 years old at the time. The Leinster Leader gave the following report and list of people injured in the explosion.

- **The injured were**
- John Black (30) B.sc. (married) Portstewart, Assistant Manager
- John Cullen, Avoca Wicklow (30, single), drier attendant (extensive burns and scalp wound)
- James Reilly, Coonough, Carbury, married (35) (burns on Face Hands and Legs);
- Patrick Cummins, Rathmore Carbury, married (40) (extensive burns);
- Daniel Grennan, St, Francis Street, Edenderry, married (35), charge hand electrician, (burns on face, hands and arms)
- Michael Sullivan, Lullymore (27, single) (burns on forearm and slight injuries)

In that report they have Dad's age wrong because he was born in 1900 so he would have been 49 at that time. I can remember Dad's regular trips to the hospital in the Bord Na Mona Ambulance, John and Marie who are twins were 3 years old when Dad came home from hospital, I was 5 years old and Mom said that when Dad came home after two months he mistook me for my first cousin Patsy Daly. I believe it was around this time I stuck a fork in Ned's foot and he had to be taken to hospital.

Dad had to attend hospital for 6 months and most times he had to have Skin Grafts and have proud Flesh removed from his Back by burning around the edges of the damaged area which covered his entire Back from the back of his Neck to his Backside, this was very painful but it had to be done. Today it would probably be done under a full Anaesthetic; I wonder what they did to relieve pain in those days. From what I remember of the Scars on Dad's back he must have been close to death after the explosion which occurred in the Boiler House where he worked, Pat thinks he received about £300 or £500 compensation for his injuries and suffering but My Sister Dolores thinks he received no compensation. We do know that he received no pay at all while he was out of work, the local Shop Keeper Charlie Adams gave Mom credit in the shop during this time and it took some years to clear that Bill.

I never remember Dad working anywhere except the Briquette Factory, his wages were £6 a week and the reason I can remember that is because sometimes I had to cycle down to the factory and collect his wages if he were on the night shift and sleeping during the day, the first time I was sent to collect Dad's Wages I turned right instead of left when I got out to the main road, although I thought the Road was strange I was convinced I and taken the correct turn and kept going, it was only when I got to the Power Station in Allenwood about 5 miles away that I knew I had gone wrong and turned back, I never told anyone about my mistake because I felt so stupid for what I had done.

Considering Dad's small wages and the hours he had to work, 8am to 4pm one week, 4pm to midnight another week and then Midnight to 8am another week, six days a week, I have no idea what holidays he got or if he got paid for them, but I often wondered how Mom and Dad brought us through so many hard times and did so without any of us getting into real trouble until we were old enough to look after ourselves.

Dad's illness, Dad was born in the year 1900, he remembered the sinking of the Titanic and was a teenager during the first World War, because he did shift work he would have missed out on a lot of time with his children, although because he and Mom produced Children almost nonstop from the year they got married I'm' sure they would have had little enough time for playing with us, as I remember him he was a quiet Man and I have no memory of him losing his temper or beating any of us, he was a drinker and a smoker which might seem like a luxury considering his circumstances but all Men smoked and drank and Mom also smoked as long as I can remember, the only drink Mom ever had as far as I'm aware was a Baileys and that was very seldom. Dad never fully recovered from his dreadful accident in the Briquette Factory, when we went swimming in the Grand Canal which was about a Mile from our house we often tried to get Dad to come for a swim with us but although he often promised to come he never did, I presume it was because his terrible scars on his Back would have been painful in the cold Water or indeed it might have been embarrassing for him to let anyone but his own Family to see it, his lungs were weak and were made worse by him having to go back to work in the very dusty conditions of the Factory and along with that Dad had always been a smoker, the accident happened when he was 49 years old and he really struggled to keep going up to retiring age at 65, there was no sick pay when he was out of work so he had no choice but to keep going right up to the last day, he was not long retired when he fell and broke his Hip and it was very slow to repair.

One remarkable thing about Dad was that although he had a lifetime of hardship and illness he still had a fine head of black Hair when he died at 72, Considering their circumstances I have no hesitation in saying that both my Parents were really good people and gave good example to their 10 children which helped us to deal with our everyday problems which are miniscule compared to what they had to deal with for most of their married lives. Dad got Cancer and died at home in 1972, aged 72 just seven weeks after our first child Robert was born, we brought Robert down to show him off to Dad when he was 6 weeks old but Dad was so ill and in so much pain that he was hardly able to acknowledge our new Son and he never got to see him again before he died; My Wife Pat and I had been to visit him and had only left at around Midnight, he died at around 3 am and my Mom, Brothers and Sisters were with him at the end. At that time I was working as a Tanker Driver in Conoco, (Jet Petroleum)

My Mother, My Mother was born in 1915, Dad was 15 years old then and my Sister Maura tells me that Dad danced at Moms christening, Mom was working in the Rectory in Carbury when she and Dad started going out together, Dad had been engaged twice to 2 other Women and broke off the engagements and took back the engagement Rings before he started courting Maria Pender, when he proposed to Maria she agreed to marry him but refused to take an engagement Ring saying, you will never take back a ring back from me, so although she had a Wedding Ring she never had an engagement Ring from Dad, Mom was married at age 25 and proceeded to have children one after the other for 7 years starting with Ned, Pat, Maura, Jim (me) Bridget and then there were twins John and Marie. Mom and Dad then took a break from having Babies for a few years They had built their own 2

Room house and later added a second room which was later divided into 2 smaller bed rooms when I was still very young, they then went on to have 3 more children, Brendan, Kathleen and Dolores so there was 5 Boys and 5 Girls, one day soon after giving birth to Twins John and Marie Mom collapsed and fell into the open Fire, Dad was at work and the children were too small to help, Mom managed to pull herself out of the fire and outside the House where she rolled in the Grass to stop her Clothes burning and to cool the parts of her Body that had been burned, Maura said it's believed Mom was anaemic following the birth of the Twins and that was why she collapsed. A few years later Mom had 3 Ribs removed because there was a growth which it was feared might develop into cancer. At this time I was about 12 years old and Dolores was just a Baby and would be the last of 10 children. Following the removal of her Ribs Mom had to wear a large Corset for support and even with that her upper Body was always slightly twisted, she was still unsteady on her Feet and would often fall over for no apparent reason, on one occasion when Mom was in Hospital she overheard one Doctor say to another Doctor, has she ever been tested for MS (Multiple Sclerosis'), there was no more said to Mom about it but the Doctor later told some Family members later that she had MS but that it seemed to have stabilised and if it remained that way then perhaps it's better not to tell her as she seems to be coping ok except for the occasional stagger. I can never recall Mom losing her temper, she was a gentle Person and was dearly loved by all her Children and Grand children and indeed by anyone who knew her. She told me one day that she had no favourites among her 10 children but that if she had it would probably be me, she was very diplomatic and knew how to please everyone at the same time.

In the latter years of Dad's life Mom had been exhausted from taking care of him and when Dad died in 1972 she regained her strength and had a lot more freedom and travelled to visit Pat and his Wife Marie and Children in New York and to Maura, Bridget and Ned and their Children who were all living in Manchester, my Sister Bridget tells me that when Mom came to visit in Manchester she would go to Markets and Car Boot Sales and buy all sort of Pots and Pans and anything that she thought some of us at home could use, on one occasion when Mom was going Home they arranged a Wheelchair because she was unable for the long walk to the Plane, her carryon Bag was on her lap and was filled with all sort of metal Kitchen Implements and Bridget and Maura could still see her when she was stopped at the security checkpoint, first there was one person checking her bag, then there was 2 security Staff, then there was a crowd around her all checking her Pots and Pans, eventually she was allowed go and was wheeled on to the Plane along with her Utensils. Mom also divided herself between her 6 other Children and numerous Grand Children who still lived in Ireland. In the period leading up to Mom's death we all moved home temporarily to be with her as long as possible, we slept on floors and couches and it's amazing that at such a tragic time that so much fun can be had when reminiscing about old times, some of the funniest moments we still talk about was the effect Morphine had on Mom as it was used to try and control the pain from her Cancer, on one occasion when the Doctor was in the room with her she told the Doctor to put out the Horse that was in the Room, on another occasion it was a Dog in the Room. Mom hung on so long that I had gone back to work and was out on one of our Oil tankers when My business Partner Mick Hayden called me on the 2 way Radio and said he would meet me in Templeogue, I thought he had more delivery dockets for me but when I met him he said, your Mom died this morning, Mick took over the Truck and I went home to prepare for the sad event that is a funeral, Mom died from Lung Cancer on Jenny's Birthday 22 November 1988 and was followed in 1990 by my Mother in Law May Boileau who also died from Cancer and my oldest Brother Ned died from Cancer also in 1990.

My mother in law was someone I had come to love just as much as my own Mother and like my own Mother she had a slow lingering Death from Cancer, when her Cancer was at an advanced stage she decided she wanted to visit the Shrine at Knock where the Virgin Mary is said to have appeared to a group of 15 local people ranging in age from 5 years to 74 years old on 21st August 1879, my wife Pat her Father and her Sister Marie took their Mother to Dublin Airport and flew with her to Knock. The reason for flying was that they thought a Car Journey would be very hard on May but as it turned out the Flight on the small Plane was very traumatic, she went in to the Bathroom on the Plane but due to severe turbulence could not open the Door to come out again, her daughter Marie was with her and they were still in the Bathroom as the Plane landed, Pat wanted to go to her assistance but the Air Hostess would not allow her to leave her seat as the Plane was Landing. The flight had been very Distressing for all concerned but particularly for May, they were not looking forward to the return flight but matters were taken out of their hands when the flight was cancelled due to bad weather, the Airline offered transport to Dublin by Bus but when they were told about how ill May was they offered to pay for a Taxi to take her Home. Pat rang me about 10.30 pm to say they were staying in the Longford Arms Hotel which meant they were only half way home, Pat said the Taxi Driver was very good because when he saw how feeble May was he said we will go out by my House and I will change you into my Car which is more comfortable for the long journey. If they had continued all the way home they may not have got home until 2 or 3 in the Morning so they decided to stop in the Longford Arms hotel for the Night. Pat asked me to drive down and take them home in the morning as my Car had reclining Seats and would be more comfortable.

Ned's accident: Apart from Dad's accident, another serious accident would have been in November 1943 when our eldest brother Ned injured his Eye while playing with an old Tyre which had a rusty Wire sticking out of it. Ned somehow managed to stick the Wire into his Eye, he was taken to Hospital where he was kept in for about three weeks and allowed back home. In January 1944 Mom and Dad got worried because Ned's eye was very sore, they took him back to the Eye and Ear hospital and when the Doctor looked at his eye he decided right away that he had to take out the injured eye. Mom stayed that night with her Brother Uncle Willie Pender who lived in Dublin and when she went back to the hospital the next day the operation was over.

Mom had to look after Ned while he was in hospital during the Day but was not allowed to stay the Night and when she was leaving Ned he would throw his arms around her and cling to her pleading with her not to go, it's so different now where parent's are allowed and sometimes encouraged to stay overnight with sick children. That was January 1944 and Ned was three years old, so Mom was six months pregnant on me and Dad had Pat and Maura to look after at home, I presume there was help coming from both Mom's and Dad's family so that Dad could go to work each day. In those days there was almost no means of communication so Mom and Dad would not have been able to talk and comfort each other, I was born three months later on 5th April 1944.

As Ned grew up he was fitted with a glass Eye and it had to be changed each year as he grew bigger, Ned said that when Mom would take him to Fannins in Grafton Street to have his Eye changed, he had a great laugh when the Man in the shop would open a Drawer and when Ned looked into the Drawer there were Eyes of every shape and colour looking up at him.

Dad and Mom on their engagement day

the house I grew up in, after the extension was built

five brothers and Dad at Pats wedding,
l to r, John, Ned, Dad, Pat, Brendan and Me

Chapter 3

School Days: Once there were seven of us going to School at one time, that would have been Ned, Pat, Maura, Jim, Bridget, John and Marie, It was like a mad House for Mom trying to get us all properly dressed, fed and out in time, I was probably the worst of all and was often late for School, Sometimes if I was late I would take a short cut through Bill Holt's Field but this often made things worse as I would get covered in Muck or get stuck in a Hedge and end up with torn clothes from the briars. My best friends in school were James Kenna who I still see at funerals, Cemetery Sunday and the Turf cutting competition, Frank Hannify who I had not seen for about thirty years and then I went to his funeral in Newbridge last year (2011), and Anthony Reilly who became a Mechanic and later spent some time in Goal for dealing in stolen Cars, he had married Nellie Brennan from Ticknevin, she was quite attractive and refined, I nearly had a date once with Nellie thanks to my sister Bridget; I don't recall why it did not take place. Sadly Nellie died in 2011.

Our school was in bad shape towards the end of my School days which I believe ended at age thirteen, there were large holes in the Floor where the boards had rotted away, the desks and seats were in bad shape and very few repairs were ever carried out as they were waiting to get a new School built, however that only came after I had finished School. The first new school was in Ticknevin and this was ready in time for Brendan, Kathleen and Dolores to finish their primary education there.

Families with children attending school were asked to contribute Turf for the school Fires as that was the only means of heating the Buildings, I recall Dad bringing a load of turf on the ass and cart to the School, the Boys School was divided into two Classrooms and each had its own

Fireplace at the front of the Room where the Teacher sat, so the Teacher got the most benefit from the heat and the pupils at the back of the classroom got very little benefit because not only were they farthest away from the fire but they were also beside the door which had no porch and each time it was opened the cold air rushed in and the heat rushed out. There was no electricity and no running Water in any of the buildings, electric power only came to Carbury as I was leaving school, the toilets were a separate Building at the far end of the school yard which made sense because of the smell that came from them, they consisted of a series of wooden seats with a hole in them, no water and no means of washing your hands.

Our School Teachers: Miss Darcy taught the younger boys. She was from County Clare and spent about forty years as a teacher in Carbury until she retired so she would have had a lot of input into our lives in that time. Although she never married she lived in a house which was on the school grounds and was in between the boys and girls school. I understand she returned to County Clare when she retired, Miss O'Rourke was my teacher for some time, as I recall she was much younger and prettier than Miss Darcy, Chris Solan was teacher for the older boys and he is credited with improving Gaelic football in Carbury which led on to the very successful teams of the 1950's, 60's and 70's of which our Brother Pat is considered to be the greatest player ever to come out of Carbury and indeed many would say from County Kildare. When I moved to the big boys school Chris Solan had gone and Patrick O'Connor from Edenderry was my new Teacher until I did my Primary Certificate and left school for good, there was nothing charming or delightful about Mr O'Connor but there was very little I could say against him, I think he did everything that could have been expected for me. His son Vincent was a pupil in my class and he was easily the brightest pupil in the class. I believe he went on to become a Solicitor and had a practice in Edenderry. I recall Miss Abin and Mrs Mitchell as being the girl's teachers, Mrs. Mitchell's husband Tommy Mitchell owned a lot of land which bordered Uncle John's land, he was a very odd man who used to bring home his Hay late at night, I remember seeing him when I was coming home from the pictures at about 11pm with a Cock of hay on his Horse and Bogey, no Light of any sort so it was just as good there was very little traffic then.

Father Hipwell, When I was young the parish Priest Fr. Hipwell always seemed to be cranky and unfriendly, he had a Car but was a terrible Driver, you would hear him before you would see him, revving the engine or grating the gears, sometimes when he would be driving into the Church grounds he would hit the Gate or the Gate Post, I served as an Alter Boy for a short time and when it was my turn to serve at the 8am weekday Mass I would use Mom's or Dad's Bike to go to Church which was about 2 Miles away, one morning I came out ready to go but the only Bike available had a flat Tyre, there was not enough time to fix the puncture and it was too late to walk because Fr. Hipwell wanted Mass to start at 8 am sharp so I decided I would not go at all, later that Day Fr Hipwell came in to our School looking for the Boy who was supposed to serve Mass this Morning, I put my Hand up and was called up to the front of the Class where Fr. Hipwell asked me in a loud voice why I had not turned up for Mass this Morning. I wanted to tell him that my Bike was punctured but was so frightened that I could not speak, he asked the same question again, his voice getting louder and me getting more frightened and still unable to speak, the Priest started shouting at me and his false Teeth fell out on to the Floor, he quickly picked them up and put them back in his Mouth, Mr. O'Connor the Teacher was afraid things were getting too serious and told me to go back to my Seat, after that incident I was so frightened of Fr. Hipwell I gave up serving at Mass although I had enjoyed it up to then.

Horses at school: One year a horse dealer put a lot of Horses in the field behind our School and some of us thought it would be a good idea at lunch time or after school to drive the horses into a corner and if we could catch a few then get on their back and go for a ride, we had some success at this, the only problem was that when you got on the Horses Back there was no Saddle, we had no Reins to stop the Horse and nothing to hold on to but the Horse's Mane.

As soon as you were on the Horse's back someone would hit the Horse a wallop with a Stick and you had to hang on for dear life until the Horse decided to stop himself. We would open a Gate and tie a piece of Rope across it and try to make the Horse jump over it with someone on his back, Frank Hannify jumped on to a Pony that looked quiet tame, he proved to be anything but tame and he bucked and Jumped all over the place and when he could not get rid of Frank he jumped into a Ditch and ran along the bottom of it to the end and then back out again and kept going. Frank had to jump off while going at full speed as he could not stop the Pony. Sadly I was at Frank Hannify's funeral last year (2011). Another day my Brother John was with me and there was a Horse that looked very old and tired, the Horse did not move when we approached him, John had a small Stick in his hand and hit the Horse very lightly but still the Horse did not move, next day when we came back the old Horse was dead right where John had hit him with his Stick, we told John he killed the Horse but John was not too concerned.

Hole in my Pants most of the time I only had one set of clothes for school and for going to Mass on Sundays, this became a problem one sunny Summer Day when I had burst my Pants and had not told Mom about it until I was about to leave for Mass on Sunday Morning, Mom said, I don't Have time to fix it now so you will have to wear your Overcoat to cover it up, I then had to inform Mom that I had also burst the only pair of shoes I owned so Mom said you will have to wear your Rubber Boots (Wellingtons) so I went to Mass on the hottest day of the year wearing my Overcoat and Wellington Boots, when we came out after Mass Jerome Flanagan looked at me and said, Jim, I hope we don't get the weather your expecting.

Eccentrics, every town and village will have a few people who could be classed as, odd or eccentric and Carbury was no different, Patsy Aungier was the local Grave Digger for many years and had long grey hair that must never have been cut because it reached half way down his back, when you got to know Patsy he was a lovely man and had a strange sort of sophistication about him, Nellie Hickey always walked with a limp and wore a Coat that reached to the ground, she had a funny sense of Humour but if she thought you were laughing at her she would soon put you in your place with a tongue lashing, Bill Kelly lived in Ticknevin and always had long hair and a long Beard, Bill was very quiet and kept to himself, he lived in a tiny one roomed House and whenever he was walking past our house we would hide behind the hedge until he had gone by, one day Mom invited Bill in for a cup of Tea and while he drank his tea we all sat staring at him and not saying a word, as he drank his tea there was a small snot on his Beard and when Bill left the Mug he had used was washed but was never used again. Peter Fitzsimons was a tramp who obviously had regular rounds because he would call to our House a few times every Year and Mom would feed him and give him some food to take with him, he went on up to Ticknevin and I believe he slept in Mangans which was a derelict house on the Canal Bank, he was full of chat and seemed to be happy with his lot.

Chapter 4

Washing and cooking

When you consider the standard of living for even for the poorest of families today and compare it with how we grew up there really is no comparison and we were an average Family, the nearest water was a half mile away and had to be carried in Buckets by hand or in a Barrel on the Ass and Cart, we had only a Basin to wash in and a galvanised tub in the middle of the kitchen floor to have a Bath in, the Water had to be heated in Pots on the open Fire, the only heat was from the open Fire which required huge amounts of Turf or Firewood to give out any decent heat, the Bedrooms were cold and damp, Overcoats were used along with Blankets to keep warm in Bed, cooking and baking was done on the open Fire, there was a Crane with adjustable Hooks hanging from it on which the Pots and Kettles were hung, the Crane swung in over the Fire for cooking or out to lift the Pot on and off, there was a Griddle for making Bread, this was a flat Plate about 15 inches in diameter with handles each side for lifting, this was placed directly on to the Fire and the Cake placed directly onto it. The other means of baking was a Baker, this was a cast iron Pot about 6 inches high with a flat bottom and a Lid on top, about 15 inches in diameter, this was placed directly on the Fire or hung from the Crane and when hot enough the Cake was put into it, the Lid was placed on top and some Turf or Firewood from the Fire placed on top of the Lid to provide all round heat and speed up the baking process. Some years later we got a fancy Grate which had been taken out of a big House somewhere, for this to be installed the two sides of the Fireplace were built up and the Grate used much less Turf or wood than the open Fireplace, later still we got a Range with a built in Oven, we had difficulty getting used to the idea that we could have heat without seeing any flames.

Electricity: We grew up without electricity, to imagine what life was like before electricity (and to a lesser extent for many years after we got it) just walk through every room in your house and make a list of everything that needs Electric power or Gas and then ask yourself how difficult life would be without all those items. Our local shopkeeper Charlie Adams installed a Petrol Pump before electricity and it had to be operated with a Handle, a bit like a starting handle for a Car. Paraffin Oil Lamps and Candles provided the only Light in the House, I was about twelve or thirteen years old when the Government introduced a scheme that would bring electric power to all parts of rural Ireland. It was an enormous project and it created many thousands of jobs for both skilled and unskilled workers. Every Pole required a Hole to be dug by Pick and Shovel, each Hole was six foot long by six foot deep by two foot wide and it was a day's work for one man to dig a Hole, the pay was £2 per Hole, some Holes were very difficult, they might have large Rocks or maybe they would take in Water, there was nothing to do but keep on digging and shovelling. The Poles were delivered by Lorry and dropped on the Roadside but then the Men used a Horse to pull the Poles one at a time through the fields to their final destination. Uncle John was one of the men who dug the holes in his fields beside our House, there was one Pole very close to our house, when the Pole was in place and Men hanging the wires from it went home at the end of the Day they left their climbing boots with clamps attached for climbing the poles, I had always wanted to climb one of the poles as I had seen the men do, so I put the boots and clamps on and began to climb. As I went up the pole I imagined myself at the top of the pole, falling backwards and hanging upside down with only the boots holding me in place, I came back down, took off the boots and gave up on that idea and never mentioned it to anyone.

The power was to be switched on at 6pm on Saturday evening and we all waited anxiously for the great moment. We just had one Bulb installed in the Kitchen and at 6 pm someone (I can't remember who had the honour of doing it) switched the Light on, I don't know how many watts the Bulb had but we were all amazed at the amount of Light that came from it. There was no need for Sockets because we had nothing to plug in and could not afford to buy anything, later on we had Lights put in the Bedrooms. I don't remember what the first Plug in items we got was or when we got them, our girls would remember that better than me.

Our first Wireless Before we had electricity Mom bought a Wireless, (Radio in today's language), she bought it without discussing it with Dad and had it delivered and set up while Dad was at work. When Dad came home from work late that night we were all in bed except Mom and she had the Radio turned on with low volume, she said nothing but Dad could hear someone talking, Mom pretended not to hear it and kept up the game until Dad found the Wireless. Mom loved to tell that story for years after the event. This Wireless ran on two batteries, a wet Battery which was about nine inches tall and about four inches square and had a Handle to carry it, it was filled with Acid and had to be charged every three weeks. To get it charged we had to cycle with it to Keogh's in Allenwood which was about 5 miles away on a Bicycle, cost one Shilling, this later became Hayden's Garage which is now closed but still has the Canopy that was over the Petrol Pumps. Charging took four days so we had a second Battery to keep going while it was charging. Later on we could have it charged closer to home in Clarkes of Ballyshannon which later became Tynans.

I went to school with Michael Tynan and met him in later life when he set up his own Car sales and repairs called Michael Tynan Motors at Newlands cross on the Naas Road; he is still there with a very successful Mitsubishi dealership. His older sister Marie was killed by a truck while cycling in O'Connell Street in Dublin when she was only twenty three years old. Michael bought his Heating Oil from me for his Home and Business until we sold our Oil Business; the Wireless also took a dry Battery which was about nine inches by nine square and three inches deep. This could last up to three months and then had to be discarded. Certain programmes became very popular like The Archers, Ballad Makers on Saturday night and my brother Ned was mad about Dan Dare, a science fiction programme.

Our House had a Half Door, this is where the top half of the Door can be left open to let in Fresh Air but the bottom half stays closed to stop children escaping, it's very rare to see them now except in a few rural areas, I'm sure there are some of them in the Bunratty Folk Park where they have reproduced House's as they used to be in olden Days, there was no lock on the Door which tells us that life was very different in those Days.

Larley Adams. Another milestone in our life was when Larley Adams began showing films in the hall which he had originally built as a Grain Store, each Friday and Sunday night, Larley (his proper name was Charles) was a bit of a genius who would have a go at anything, his father owned Adam's Shop in Derrinturn which later became Leo Feely's and is now J & D Fuels having changed hands many times in between. The first film to be shown there was called "Back to Gods Country" starring Rock Hudson, to appreciate our fascination on seeing our first film, (the term movie came much later), you need to consider we had never even seen a Television Set up to this time, and when we see this huge moving Picture of a Man kissing a Woman in front of everyone we were shocked, needless to say there was a full House each Friday and Sunday night. Larley had a go at all sorts of business, he once told me, "you have to speculate to accumulate" he had a milling business where he ground wheat, barley and oats into flour or into feed for animals. This was before electricity came, he had a Fordson Tractor with a Pulley and long Belt running from the Tractor into the Mill and it worked a treat. I worked for Larley for a while when I left School at the milling and also at his Building work on the very first work at the Mushroom Factory along with Bill Pender and John Connolly from Coonogh.

Before that he had built the new house for the Priest Father McDonald, He also built the Bungalow which is still beside the Parish Hall for himself and his family to live in. When we started the boxing club in Carbury Larley was very much involved and was very supportive although he made some money from renting the hall for training twice a week and when we held our first boxing tournament he made money again from renting the hall. I believe his son John was partly disabled but his other son Tony did very well as a film producer in Los Angeles with The Pink Panther and many other well known Films to his credit.

Swimming (Paddling) in the River: We often went swimming, or perhaps paddling would be a more appropriate description, in the River which flows through Uncle John's land, the funniest thing looking back now was that we all swam nude and there would be soft Mud or Silt from the Peat Bogs where the River came from, we would lie in the mud and leave the shape of our body. The worst thing that happened was when Ned convinced me that I should jump for the bank into the river; it was about ten feet high from the Bank to the Water which was about eighteen inches deep and full of Stones. I had a name of being a tough kid (stupid would be more appropriate) and if someone dared me to do something I would not back away from the challenge, my Feet were in a mess but Ned told me I was a great lad and when Mom chastised him over what happened he denied it was his idea.

Accidents: I seemed to be unfortunate as I was always having accidents of one type or another, like the time I almost severed my big Toe on a piece of Glass in the School Playground. It happened at lunchtime but as I could not walk on it Miss Darcy made me wait until school was over and Mick Connolly could give me a lift home on his Crossbar, for years I had numbness in that big Toe but it's okay now.

One Sunday Uncle John was going down to check his cattle in the Field beside our House, I wanted to go with him, he had already left and I ran after him, just past the Shed there was a large Tree Stump, I tripped and fell with my Face hitting the Stump. I think I was knocked out for a moment and then staggered back to the House, my Face must have been a mess because I can still see the shock on Mom's and Maura's face when they saw me. They put me to Bed and sent someone for Dr Healy, I slept for two hours, when I awoke and looked in the Mirror I could hardly believe what I was seeing, one side of my Face was blown up like a Balloon, one Eye was almost closed and both Eyes were very bloodshot. While I was very upset over my accident I was more upset at missing my first football game as I had been picked for the Carbury School Boys Team. Doctor Healy said I should stay home from school and visit him next Thursday at the Dispensary which was in the little Lodge House at George Gill's Avenue. I went to the Doctor the next Thursday and on my way home I stopped at the School where the kids were on their break, I probably just wanted to show off my Face, it still looked terrible even after four days of healing and it caused a bit of a stir outside the School.

I was about thirteen when one day Mom sent me to do some shopping, I was watching someone as I passed Cross's Shop and did not see the VW Beetle parked on my side of the Road, I crashed into the back of the Car and landed on top of it. The driver who was sitting in the Car jumped out to see what had happened, I just said, it's alright and jumped back on my Bike and continued on and into Adam's Shop. As I was waiting to be served I felt something wet on my Foot,(I was in my bare Feet as I always was in Summertime), there was a large Pool of Blood on the Floor from two cuts below my right Knee. I still have the Scars today to help me remember it. When I got home my Mouth was sore, I looked in the Mirror and three of my front Teeth were damaged, there was no question in those days of fillings or anything like that so my three front Teeth continued to deteriorate until I was eighteen and working for Paddy Flanagan in Dublin, I had three front Teeth removed and got Dentures when I was only eighteen years old.

As if it were not bad enough for me to have accidents it seems I was determined to inflict suffering on others on a regular basis, like when I knocked Bridget down and jumped on her Stomach, or another day I hit her on the Head with a Hatchet, or when I stuck a Fork through Ned's Foot, or the day when Ned, Pat and I were hurling out behind the House, I was very awkward and hit Pat in the mouth with my Hurley splitting his lip. I was discussing these events with Mom and she told me that one day I put a Frog on the Chair she was about to sit down on, just by chance she put her Hand down to pull the Chair and put it on the Frog getting a terrible fright, I don't remember this but it sounded like good fun. One day we were going through the fields to collect firewood in the Ass and cart, Bridget and I were at the back of the cart with our feet dangling, the Wheel of the Cart hit a bump and Bridget fell out and tumbled head over heels, as I recall it, she ended up in hospital with a broken arm. Bridget was much brighter that me in school and often helped me with homework, her hair was black and shiny and came down to her shoulders.

I spent every summer in my bare feet; I think it was just that I liked to go in my bare feet because I don't recall any of my Brothers or Sisters doing the same thing. It was fun but a Summer would never go by without me hitting one of my big Toes on the ground and knocking a chunk of Skin off that would take quite a while to heal and made it painful to wear Shoes or Socks.

Making Butter We had a Cow which produced a Calf every year and for most of the year gave us Milk for the family with enough left over for making butter. Mom would collect the cream from the milk each day until there was enough to half fill the Churn; we took turns turning the handle until the cream had become lumps of butter. Mom made lovely shapes of the butter with two wooden Boards, I think they were called Patters, what was left over was Butter Milk and Mom used it for making bread if we had not drank it all first. Mom also made lovely Bread Pudding which we all loved and would eat as much as we could get, Country Butter and Buttermilk were two things I missed the most when I left home.

Chapter 5

Our cousins the Daly's

Our nearest cousins were the Daly's who had a large Farm and so were considered well off, Aunt Bride was Dad's Sister and was married to Matt Daly, a lot of my time was spent working on Daly's Farm when I was old enough to help, Pat also worked a lot for Daly's, I don't think we were paid very often but I just loved working with the animals and machinery. I loved Uncle Matt and have very fond memories of time spent with him; he was bald with a shiny Head and had two very large Horses for doing the farm work. When he was ploughing the large Field in front of our House I would go out to him and he would let me walk in between the Handles of the Plough which was pulled by two Horses and I would hold on to the Handles thinking I was in control, He would say to me, "you're a great little Ploughman". I believed him and was very proud of myself, or course I was not aware at the time that once the Horses started moving and the Blade of the Plough entered the Ground it would remain there until it was lifted out by the Ploughman at the other end of the Field. We often had to ask Aunt Bride for some Milk if we had none at home during the few months each when the cow was dry, another source of Milk was Tommy Malone who had some dairy cows and each day on his way home from milking the Cows he would fill a Can which we had left on a Wall at the cross roads and would collect later on and pay Tommy at the end of the Week.

My Cousin Ned Daly decided to become a Butcher and built a Slaughter House on their Farm. He opened a Butchers Shop in Allenwood at the back of Keogh's Garage, later he moved to a bigger Shop at Allenwood Cross facing Carroll's Public House. He slaughtered his own Pigs, Sheep and Cattle in his new Slaughterhouse. I was often present when he killed the Animals and while I found it fascinating I was not frightened by the process, probably because Ned explained everything to me without making a big deal about it. One day I was beating a Bullock with Stick to get it into the Slaughterhouse, Ned told me to stop as the Stick would leave marks and damage the Meat. When killing the Cattle he would bring them into the Slaughterhouse and attach a large Ring to the animal's Nose, there was a Rope attached to the Ring and the Rope was pulled through another Ring which was fixed into the concrete Floor. This was used to pull the animals Head to the Ground and hold it there while Ned got a special Gun which was called a Humane Killer, he held the Gun against the animal's Forehead and fired, the bolt from the gun went straight into the animal's Brain whereupon he instantly fell to his Knees and rolled over dead.

On some occasions Ned used a Hammer about the same size of a Sledge Hammer, one side of the Hammer was pointed and Ned would swing the Hammer and drive the point into the centre of the animal's Forehead and it went into the animal's Brain killing him instantly. A Chain was then attached to the animal's legs and it was hoisted into the air upside down, then a very sharp Knife was used to cut the Throat and allow the Blood to flow into a Container on the Floor. He then had the job of skinning and removing the innards. To kill a Pig he used a long sharp Knife which he drove into the Pig's Throat and down into the Heart, the Pig was then shaved rather than skinned, that's why you have the rind on a Rasher. I don't recall how the Sheep was killed but I think it was similar to the Pig. Ned had a great sense of hummer but could also be very crude with his language, one day he said to me, by Jesus Jim you're a great little worker, and you're just like a Horse only you can't Shite trotting. Another day when James Kenna and I were helping Ned to pick Potatoes it was a freezing cold Day and Ned said, I bet you there will be more snotty noses than standing Pricks today.

Later Ned Daly and His Brother Patsy started growing vegetables and began a Vegetable round in Killana and Allenwood. I went with him to help and we called to the Houses where we would have to weigh the Potatoes, Onions, Cabbages, Carrots and other Vegetables they grew in the Bog Field, Daly's had a Car or Van as long as I can remember and we often had to call on them for help when we needed transport in an emergency. One time Marie's Finger was caught in a Door as it was closing and was almost severed, I had to go down and ask Ned Daly to bring Marie to the Doctor in Carbury. Dad would sometimes take Drills in Uncle Matt's Field for growing Potatoes and Turnips to save having to get our own Field ploughed and tilled and then to have Drills opened and closed again when the Potatoes were sown, we also had Drills in Teddy Mullaly's Field one year.

Carbury Boxing Club: I was about fifteen when a boxing club was started and I was among the first to join up, I loved boxing and trained very hard at it. Dutch Brereton, a former boxer from Edenderry was our trainer and came out two nights each week along with his brother Joe who was already an experienced boxer with Edenderry boxing club. This new club was well received in the parish and there were lots of willing helpers. Larly Adams built a boxing Ring which was easily dismantled when not in use and put into storage.

It was a good ring and was owned by the club, the extra benefit from this new form of training was that I became fit for playing football and could run much faster, my boxing career only lasted a year but I has some success in that time winning the County Kildare Championship and the Leinster Championship where I knocked out two of my opponents in one evening. The National Championships were held in the National Stadium where I got to the final but lost to John O'Rourke who went on to become one of Ireland's leading boxers for many years.

I fought against him again at a tournament in Prosperous and it ended up in a draw, which was my last fight, it was the end of my boxing as I ended up in hospital with pleurisy soon after that. Perhaps the best fight seen at any of the tournament's we had was between my Brother Pat and "Red" Pat Kenny who had been in Edenderry Boxing for a number of years and was very fit and very muscular like you expect a boxer to be. Pat was also very fit from playing football and working on farms but no one expected him to have much of a chance against Pat Kenny. In amateur boxing it's not often you see a fight were two boxers hammer away at each other nonstop for three full rounds simply because they are never strong enough to keep going, but in this case they did just that and nearly brought the house down with applause, my Brother Pat won that fight and went on to fight in the National Championships where he might have won were it not for the fact that he was disqualified for hitting his opponent while he was on the rebound from bouncing off the ropes. Our trainer Dutch Brereton told Pat he could have a great future in boxing and wanted him to keep it up but pat was more interested in Gaelic Football and he never boxed again.

Our ass: When we were young a Donkey was always referred to as "The Ass", and Dad bought our Ass from Tommy Cummins (no relation) for £6, Pat and I went to collect him in Parsonstown where Tommy Cummins lived. We took him home and put him in Uncle John's field beside our house, within an hour he broke out and went missing, we went back to where we had bought him and sure enough he had gone right back to his first home, that was the first of many times he went missing. It was a constant challenge trying to keep him where he should be. Having said that he was a great worker and served us well for many years doing anything we asked of him.

Bringing home the turf: We had our own peat Bog and each year Dad would cut the Turf, each of us had to help as we became old enough, Girls included, the cutting took place in April/May with Dad cutting and Ned, Pat and I catching and wheeling it out on wheelbarrows and spreading it over the flat area where it was left to dry. after a few weeks we all came back to the bog, boys and girls this time and made the turf into small heaps to allow it to dry some more, we would light a fire to boil our Billy can and make tea as it was too far to go home for lunch, it was during the Summer holidays that we brought the turf home and made it into a large clamp, for this we used our Ass and Cart but we were also allowed to use Uncle John's Ass and Cart, we brought two loads before lunch and two loads after lunch each day for about a week until we had all the home.

When building the large Clamp of Turf at home we had to build the outside Sods like a Wall and sloping in all the way to the top so that the Rain Water ran off and the Turf on the inside remained dry. Later on when Ned had gone to London to work Pat was strong enough to do the cutting while John and I did the catching and wheeling, one day when Brendan was very young he was in the Bog with us, he slipped into a Ditch full of Water, it was above his Waist and he might have drowned but luckily we were close by and pulled him out before he slipped in any further. Our Ass was almost like a pet and when the day's work was done he would come and stand outside the Door until someone brought him a few slices of Bread, then he would head off to the River to have a drink of Water. One year we had a loan of Pender's pony for bringing home the Turf and when the work was done we took him down to the River to let him have a drink but he would not take a drink from the river, we were very worried about this but had to leave him alone, perhaps he had a drink later because he was still alive the next day.

Chapter 6

My early working Life

I left School at age thirteen to start working and help Mon and Dad support the five children who were younger than me. My first job was working on the Bog futting Turf for Bord Na Mona during summer months and working for farmers like Dick Cully picking potatoes and feeding the pigs and calves and helping Dick castrate a young Bull Calf. I worked for Dempsey's bringing in Hay and snagging Turnips, I worked for Jimmy Fitzsimons and also for Padraig Bourke, Padraig taught me how to drive a Tractor. My Sister Maura also worked there; my younger sister Marie also worked there after Maura had left.

In 1959 Mom had a big operation on her Back and had 3 Ribs removed because there was a Growth on them, even though the Growth was non malignant it was considered better to remove It, because of that Mom was always a bit twisted in her upper body and had to wear a large Corset for support. She was in hospital from May until July and during that time Dad and Maura managed the household, the after affects of the Second World War was still being felt and there was a shortage of many items then and one such item was Butter, we had a Ration Book and were allowed one pound of Butter a week. Because of the shortage Dad decided it would be a good idea to save up the Butter, in those days there was no such thing as a fridge so the butter was kept in a Press and being summer time the Butter did not keep very well and when Mom came home a lot of Butter had to be thrown out,

The Pioneers, when I received my confirmation I was invited to become a member of the Pioneer Total Abstinence Association, this is an organisation within the Catholic Church which tries to limit the damage done by Alcohol by asking young people to take a pledge to abstain from all alcohol until they are mature enough to make sensible judgements on the matter themselves, I took the pledge and never felt the need to drink alcohol and I still have no desire to drink alcohol, 2 of my brothers and one Sister are also non drinkers, Cigarettes were always in our house because Both Mom and Dad smoked and some of our Family followed their example but I never started so I never had the problem of trying to get off them.

Working in O'Brien's: I was about fifteen when I got a job as a Yard Man in John O'Brien's Public House, Guinness and Smithwicks were bottled on site and that was my job, but first the Bottles had to be washed by hand using an Electric Brush, one bottle at a time, sometimes I would spend the whole day washing Bottles. Guinness and Smithwicks came in a huge wooden Barrel called a Hogshead and it was a full day's work to bottle one of them. Leo Feely was the manager and had moved to Carbury from Westmeath to take on the job, Bridgie Judge from Ticknevin and Maureen Moore worked in the Shop which was attached to the Pub. While I was there John O'Brien started a new business supplying Grass Seed to local farmers, filling and weighing the Sacks of Grass Seed became part of my job and also serving in the Bar from time to time.

The first time I had to pull a Pint of Guinness was when Leo the manager had stepped out for a few minutes, Dan Connolly was the customer and he was a very difficult and cantankerous character with a set of teeth that would make Shane McGowan look good, I handed the Pint to Dan and said that's 1s and 3d (one shilling and three pence) and could not understand why Dan kept staring at me making ugly faces and making no attempt to pay me, he said, you expect me to drink that fu*   * *ng thing, as it was my first Pint I had no idea there was supposed to be a white Head on it, the Glass was full to the brim but all black, no sign of a white Head anywhere to be seen. Dan told me what he thought of my Pint and what I could do with it. Another day Dan was in the Bar with Uncle John and some other Men, the front of my Shirt was open and one of the men said I had Hair on my Chest just like my Uncle John, Dan said, "your Uncle John might have Hair on his Chest but he has f**k all on his Head", Uncle John's Head was as shiny as could be just like Dad's other brothers Tom and Jim.

I became good friends with the Manager Leo Feely and even more so with Maureen Moore. She was going out with my cousin Patsy Daly and when they had a row they would use me as a go between to get back together again, they later married and had four or five children. Patsy died from a Heart attack in 2010. I was at his wake and Maureen and I had a long chat about old times that night. Maureen reminded me of the day I was coming down the Stairs carrying a Box for her; I slipped on the Step and bounced on my Backside all the way to the bottom. Maureen thought it was hilarious but it took a long time for the left Cheek of my Bottom to regain its normal shape.

A short spell working in Dublin: I had been in O'Brien's for about a year when one day Pat Smith (who is now Pat's close friend in New York) came in and said he knew of a Pub owner in Dublin that was looking for an apprentice and would I be interested in going for it, I went home and discussed it with Mom and Dad and decided to go for it. I left home for Dublin a week later on a Sunday evening; I got the Dublin Bus where I was met at Store Street Bus Station by Joe O'Keefe who was the owner of the Pub I was going to work in. He had arranged lodgings for me in a House in North King Street at one pound ten shillings a week. Next morning I got my first lesson about life away from Home when at Breakfast I asked the landlady for more Tea, she said, oh, you only get one Cup of Tea at each Meal,

A crowded Pub in Dublin is very different to O'Brien's and I had to move a lot faster, unfortunately Maths was not my best subject in School and I often had difficulty when I would have to serve five or six different Drinks to one Customer and all different prices. Sometimes I would disappear round a corner and make up the Bill on my fingers, I did not like the job, I did not like the Lodgings and it was not a happy time for me. I had only one set of clothes and one day the boss Joe O'Keefe took me to a drapery shop and bought me a new shirt, jacket and pants so that I could be dressed better in front of the customers.

My illness:
After six weeks on the job I went home for the weekend and was feeling unwell so Mom got the Doctor for me and when he examined me he thought I had Pleurisy and sent me to Naas Hospital where they confirmed it was Pleurisy. If Pleurisy is not looked after in time it could

develop into Tuberculosis which could be much more serious, they kept me in Naas for two weeks and then sent me by Ambulance to Firmount Sanatorium near Clane where I was in for four more weeks. It was in Firmount I developed my love of reading because they had a Library and it was the first time I had seen or heard of an Encyclopaedia, I was fascinated by this Book that had the answer to everything in its Pages. I saw it as a way to further educate myself while not going to School, by the time I was going home I had put on a lot of weight from eating so much with no work of any sort, however my appetite was small compared to Bill Fulton from Allenwood, whatever Meals were left over were brought to Bill and he would keep eating as long as the Food kept coming. Most of the patients had TB and were in for Months rather than Weeks.

In Dublin the publican Joe O'Keefe had spent twenty pounds on my new clothes and it was to be stopped at a pound a week from my wages but I never went back to work in the Bar in Dublin and was glad to be away from it. I always intended to pay back the money and one day when I was in Dublin working for Paddy Flanagan I decided to call and talk to Mr O'Keefe only to find that the pub was no longer trading and the shopkeeper next door told me Joe O'Keefe had died a year ago so that was the end of that.

Working for Dempsey's:

Pat spent most of his teenage years working for Lou Dempsey in Kilkeaskin but then his job moved to Cadamstown where Tom Dempsey was Farm Manager on a large Farm which was owned by Brendan Kelly who was a brother of Dermott Kelly the Car dealer form Kilcock. I never met Brendan Kelly but I believe he was paralysed and confined to a Wheel Chair; he lived in a large House beside the Bridge in Leixlip. When the Farm needed extra help Pat arranged for me to go and work both in Kilkeaskin and Cadamstown. Tom Dempsey is long since dead but Lou is over eighty years old and stilling working his Farm in Kilkeaskin, the last time I talked to Lou he reminded me of the year I had been working for him snagging Turnips, it was a freezing cold Morning and when it was tea break time I had a Pitchfork in my Hand and I stuck in the Ground as I started walking towards the House, unfortunately I did not pay much attention to what I was doing and the Fork went through Lou Dempsey's wellington Boot and then through between his big toe and the next toe. When Lou yelled out I pulled the fork back out of his foot, Lou could laugh about it now but he said to me that if it had not been so cold that morning he would have killed me.

I was best man for Ned at his wedding to Mary M'Connan in London

My first passport photo in 1968

Dad on left and pat on right when they both in their early 20s

Chapter 7

My brother Ned, **Saturday 30-06-90, phone call from my Sister Maura, who is at home with Dolores since last Thursday, Ned, is in hospital, he has cancer of the lymph gland, he's been in for two weeks and has lost a lot of weight, and he is also anemic and looks very poorly. There is a good chance that he can be treated by chemotherapy; the Dr says that where he has it is about the best place to treat Cancer of this kind.**

Ned was the oldest in our family but not by much, Ned was born in 1940, Pat 1941, Maura 1943, Jim 1944, Bridget 1945, Marie and John (Twins) 1946, that's seven Babies in six years, Mom and Dad took a break for a few years and then went on to have three more children, Brendan, Kathleen and Dolores. Ned was the first to go out into the World and started doing things like having girlfriends which the rest of us were amazed at, especially when he began asking Mom for money to take a girl to the pictures in Edenderry. While Ned may have been working at the time it was normal then to hand up your wages to Mom and if you needed some Money you asked for it and hoped there would be some to spare. Ned was about seventeen when he went to work in London, I don't know if he had anyone to go to or if he went and just found his way around. I do remember when he came home again dressed as a Teddy boy with drainpipe Trousers, (tight on the legs) winkle picker Shoes (long pointed toes) and sleek black Hair with a DA style (Duck's Arse) at the back. This style was established but not necessarily accepted in the big cities of England and Ireland but certainly not in a small rural place like Carbury.

I think it's fair to say Ned was Carbury's first Teddy Boy and he did not care what people thought of him, Ned got married in London and I was proud to act as his best Man when he married Mary McConnon from Castleblaney in County Monahan, Ned was a small Man but he had no fear of other Men no matter how big they were, he would take them on in a fight and would usually win the fight. It appears that when you lived among the Irish building workers in London back then it was very easy to get into a fight and you needed to be able to look after yourself when necessary.

Ned did well at School and was often said to have been the most intelligent of the ten Children, like the rest of us he left School at fourteen and began his working life immediately. The exception to this rule of course was Brendan who is now an electrical Contractor, Kathleen is a School Teacher and Dolores who runs a Dry Cleaning Business, they all went on to further education. Ned was only 49 years old when he died from Cancer and is buried in Urmston near Manchester where his Widow Mary and his Children Bridget, and Siobhan still live with their children. His Son Gary is married and living in North Wales.

Working for Paddy Flanagan: March 1961, my Cousin Patsy Daly contacted me to say Paddy Flanagan had been talking to him and wanted to know if I would be interested in working for him as a helper on his Truck. I knew very little about Paddy except that he was a cousin of my Father and lived in Dublin and that my Brother Pat was going out with his Daughter Marie. It was the idea of going to work on a Truck that appealed to me and I agreed to the job offer right away. Paddy came down the next Sunday and collected me and took me back with him to Dublin. They lived at Nephin Road, Cabra, just off the Navan Road.

They had arranged lodgings for me with Mrs Gibbons who lived across the Road so I did not have far to go to work. Paddy parked his Truck in the entrance to the local secondary School which was directly across from his House. Mrs Gibbons was from County Mayo and was rather bad tempered. She had two sons, Paddy who was about ten and Tommy who was about twelve. Her husband was away working in England and that might explain why she always seemed to be in bad form because she had to look after her two sons and three lodgers on her own. The job was the same almost every Day, Paddy had a Contract with Spicers Bakeries in Navan, Kells and Trim in county Meath to draw all their Flower requirements form Flower Mills in Dublin and this involved us collecting a load of flour in 10 stone bags, (loading with Pallets and

Forklifts had not yet become the way to load a truck) so each Day we had to load 110 x 10 Stone Bags of Flour(64kg)or (140pounds) by hand and off load it by Hand at one of the Bakeries in County Meath, At Spicer's bakery in Trim the bags had to be carried up a stairs as there was no hoist to pull them up, The store man there was named Jack and he complained nonstop as he and I carried every 2nd bag of flour up the stairs on our shoulders. We then travelled on to the Brick Works in Kingscourt in County Cavan and loaded 4000 building Bricks by hand, most days we would be given 2 or 3 men to help us load the bricks, we then drove 50 miles back to Dublin and delivered them to a building site, sometimes we would be late getting back to Dublin but the Load always had to be delivered that evening because the Truck had to be empty for another load of flour the next Morning. The work was hard but I liked it because it made me strong, in the Brickworks I became known as the Lad with the big Arms as I could lift up to 18 bricks from the ground on to the truck in one go.

Paddy's son Liam was about eleven and Jim was fifteen, Noreen was around my age, almost eighteen and was doing her leaving cert that summer. I had been with Paddy Flanagan three and a half years when Paddy broke his Ankle and could neither Drive the Truck nor help with the loading or off loading so my Brother John came to work with me on the Truck. My wages at the time were about £12, there was no overtime pay even though I worked about 10 hours a Day. I don't remember being unhappy about it but John could not accept it and was quite unhappy, he was always trying to get me to ask Paddy for more Money but I was reluctant to do it.

Then one Friday evening we arrived back from Cavan with a load of Bricks at about 6pm and the Bricks still had to be delivered to a building site in Ballsbridge. John refused to come with me so I dropped him at Dorset Street where he was lodging. I went on and delivered the Bricks on my own and got home about 9pm. I said nothing to Paddy but he found out about it by accident when he was talking to the Foreman from the building Site, Paddy came to me demanding an explanation and he was furious when I told him what had happened, the outcome of it all was that Paddy started to pay us overtime. The row was the first one I had had with Paddy and it made me think of looking for other work which I did as soon as Paddy was well enough to drive the Truck again. Paddy had difficulty getting someone to take my place because although I was only 21 years old I was able to drive his truck and do all the work and when Paddy was injured I took over and ran the job with very little help from him.

Apart from my parents there are a few people who I believe had some influence in how I lived my life and Paddy Flanagan would have been one of them, Although he took Life serious Paddy had a great sense of humour and loved to tell stories about other people he knew, he thought me how to drive a Truck when I was only 17 before I could drive a car, he was a very careful driver and told me to treat everything and everyone with respect, he said, neither Man or Machine will benefit from abuse, but he could also be quick to tell people what he thought of them if he thought it necessary, one day we were driving down Manor Street in Dublin where the Cattle, Sheep and Pig Markets took place each week, on Market days you were certain to be delayed as animals were unloaded from Trucks on the side of the Street and then herded along the Street to holding Pens where they were kept until it was their turn to be shown for sale, one Man was driving a large herd of pigs along the Street but the pigs had stopped and the Man in charge was making no effort to move them or to help us get past. Paddy put his Hand out the Window and started banging his hand on the Door of the Truck hoping the noise would get the Pigs moving, the man in charge of the Pigs got annoyed and said who do you think you are in your big Truck, Paddy said, will you move those animals, I don't know whether you or the Pigs are the dirtiest, the Man waved his stick threatening to hit Paddy but eventually moved his Pigs and we got going again,

One very sad period for Paddy was when his Wife Lena had a stroke on the Morning his Daughter Marie who is married to my Brother Pat was due home on holiday from New York where they live, the first I knew of it was when Paddy's Son Liam came to our house at 7.30 am to say his Mother had had a Stroke and was in Blanchardstown Hospital and would I go along with his Father to meet Pat and Marie at the Airport. In all the years I had known Paddy it was the first time I had seen him not to be in Control of a situation, we met Pat and Marie at the Airport and the first question from Marie was, where is Mammy, Paddy said she is not well and did not feel like coming to the Airport, Marie was clearly not happy with this answer but Paddy avoided telling her what had really happened and it was only when we arrived at the House and Marie's Sister Noreen came out in tears to meet her that the truth came out, Lena survived for about 2 weeks but never regained consciousness. Paddy lived to age 90 and drove his Car right up to his 90th Birthday, when his Driving Licence expired Liam was very concerned that his father was going to try and renew his licence and went to the Family Doctor to express his concern and ask the Doctor not to give him a medical clearance for the new license, the Doctor said he did not have much discretion in the matter because there was a very specific set of tests which had to be passed for a licence and if Paddy passed them all the Doctor could not refuse to issue the certificate. As it turned out there was no problem because Paddy decided without consulting anyone that he would not renew his Driving Licence. I am happy to list Paddy not just as a friend but as one man who helped steer me in the right direction during the time I worked for him and in later years as we always kept in touch,

Paddy passed on the Haulage Business to his Son Liam who expanded and grew the Business but later wound it up in favour of other Business interests, Liam developed Throat Cancer and died in 2011, I had known Liam for 50 years and had become good friends, we would consult each other on business matters and would meet with him and his Wife Blánaid once or twice a year for a meal and I miss him a lot. I am still good friends with Noreen who is married to mike Duggan and living in Sligo and also with Jim Flanagan who lives with his Wife Ann in Florida.

Brendan Nolan, while lodging with Mrs Gibbons I met Brendan Nolan and his Brother Martin, Brendan was a Carpenter and Martin was an apprentice Carpenter, they told me about their younger Brother Finbarr who was 13 years old and was the seventh brother in a family of 7 Boys. Because their Father had also been the seventh son of a family of seven Boys it was believed that a seventh Son of a seventh Son was born with the ability to cure all types of illness just by laying hands on the person who was sick. They told me Finbarr had already cured a lot of sick people; the first was when he was only 5 years old. As Finbarr got older he became world famous as a Faith Healer and drew great crowds at his healing sessions, when I was living in Australia many years later I read a full page article in the Australian Newspaper about Finbarr and how he never charged for laying hands on sick people but because people believed they might be cured they would often leave donations and he later got into trouble with the Revenue Commissioners over what should be classified as income, if the News Papers were to be believed he should have made millions from donations but I don't know what was the outcome of his discussions with the Revenue Commissioners.

At the height of Finbarr's popularity his brother Brendan worked as his manager booking Venues and Coaches to take People from all parts of the Country to where Finbarr would be holding his Healing sessions, the real irony of this Story is that while Brendan was organising healing session for thousands of other people he took ill himself with Multiple Sclerosis. I had lost contact with Brendan and Martin and it was just by chance I found out about his illness through my Secretary Lily Murphy when I was running the PMPA Oil Company, for some reason I told Lily about knowing the Nolan's and she said, I live next Door to Brendan Nolan but he is very ill at present, through Lily I arranged to visit Brendan at his Home in Santry in North Dublin, my Wife Pat came with me and when I saw Brendan for the first time in 20 years I received a terrible shock, he was in a Wheelchair and when I extended my hand to shake hands his Wife Geraldine said Brendan is paralysed, having talked to him for a few minutes I produced some old photographs of Him and I together, he said, I can't see them Jim, my sight is almost gone. He was 42 years old but looks older. Brendan is lucky to have a wonderful Wife, who devotes her life to looking after him, it must be a 24 Hour 7 Day a week job to look after someone in Brendan's condition.

Brendan died about 6 months after our visit to him; I was at the Funeral and met the whole family including Finbarr who I had not met before, Lily Murphy and her Husband Alf travelled with me to the Graveyard, Lily's Husband Alf later suffered from Alzheimer's and died in 1995. Lily and I still keep in touch at Christmas each year, if I don't call her she will call me for a chat and just to say hello. I was with Brendan and Martin Nolan when President Kennedy came to Ireland; we were staying with Sheila and George Cartwright in a house just off Dorset St and we watched his arrival at Dublin Airport on the Television and then we walked out on to Dorset Street where we watched him pass by, he was standing up in an open topped Car and was wearing a Blue Suit as he headed into Dublin City. Six Months later Brendan, Martin and I were sitting in our Room when George our Landlord came up and said, it's on the News that President Kennedy has been shot, it was a few Hours before it was confirmed that he had Died from the Bullet Wounds to his Head in Dallas Texas.

Driving for CIE

I was only out of work for about two weeks when I applied for a Driving Job in C.I.E which is the state Transport Company and having done a Driving Test got a job driving Trucks. I was based at their Broadstone Depot which is now one of their main Bus depots. I worked for 3 years in C.I.E before leaving for Australia. In C.I.E I got a wide experience of different makes of Trucks and I learned to work drawbar Trailers and Articulated Trucks with every type of Load you could think of.

As a junior driver I got all the rubbish work and the worst of the Trucks to do it with, some of the Trucks were very old at the time. In those years Trucks seemed to be built only for the work they had to do and there was very little consideration given to driver comfort or to his welfare. Some days you would be a physical wreck at the end of your day from being bounced around in a Truck that you thought was about to disintegrate beneath you. In those days the Roads were very bad compared to today and I suppose that was why so many of the Trucks were falling apart.

It was while working in C.I.E that I made some friends which are still very dear to me today, like Tommy Kelly who started as a driver around the same time as me, like Packie Fitzpatrick who I met through some other fellows I stayed in digs with. While living at home and working with Paddy Flanagan my life had been somewhat sheltered but in C.I.E that was all changed.

There were men there who were quite happy to steal from their employer so long as they got away with it. It seemed to me that most Men who were married saw nothing wrong about going out with other Women when they got a chance to do so but if there was any suggestion that the Wife was unfaithful she would be beaten up by the Husband, still some of those stories had a funny side to them, like one driver who heard about a Wife swapping party and wanted to go to it but he knew his Wife would not agree so he went down to the Quays and picked up a Prostitute and brought her as his Wife and swapped her for some other fellows Wife for the night. Then there was Molly from Arklow, now Molly was an old prostitute who lived in a cottage on the main Dublin to Arklow Road. She and her daughter Margaret entertained Lorry drivers for years until the Neighbours complained so much that the Gardai had "no parking" Signs erected on both sides of the road for ¼ of a mile in every direction to prevent Trucks stopping or parking there. This looked stupid because her house was actually in a lay by which should have been available for trucks to stop for a break, on the other side of the road straight across from Molly's house there was a cemetery and that also had no parking signs at the entrance.

Now why any self respecting Driver would go near Molly was beyond my comprehension, although I only ever saw her from my truck while passing. She looked about seventy and full of Wrinkles, I believe she had no Teeth left at this stage. One driver who I knew well called there so often he was eventually christened "Molly", he died young, I knew another driver who travelled that road a lot but would never go near Molly, One day he had a new Helper with him who had never heard of Molly and so knew nothing about her. He stopped his Truck outside Molly's house and told the Helper the "the Lady in this House always gives us boiling Water to make Tea for our Tea break, go in and ask her for some", well the poor helper did as he was told and asked Molly for boiling Water, Molly said "you want what", The helper again asked her for boiling Water to make Tea. Molly asked him", are you sure that's all you want", the Helper said "yes what else would I want", at this Molly lifted up the front of her skirt and said "this", she had no pants on. The helper ran back to the truck while the driver almost fell out of the truck he was laughing so much.

Chapter 8

Enter Pat Boileau

One Saturday evening I had arranged to go to a dance in Bray with Tommy Kelly and his girlfriend Kay Cooper. I was living in Donnybrook with the Birrane family (Packie Fitzpatrick was also living there at the time). Tommy called to collect me as we were going in his Car to Bray, when I came out to him he said, me and Kay thought it was not right that you should be on your own so we brought along a nice girl for you, now remember you are supposed to know all about this arrangement so don't act surprised. In the back of the car was a lovely Girl who was introduced as Pat Boileau who worked with Kay Cooper in Roche's Stores and lived in Ballyfermot. We got on very well that night and I remember one time when we were dancing thinking to myself, this is a lovely Girl, the sort I would like to marry, I fell in love with Pat Boileau that night and am still in love with her 45 years later.

For whatever reason I did not ask Pat for another date, I think it was because I did not expect her to say yes and I did not want to be turned down. About two weeks later Tommy Kelly said to me, Pat wants to know if you will you take her out again, at the same time Kay Cooper was saying to Pat, Jim wants to know will you go out with him again. It was only on our second date that I realised Pat had red Hair; it came as a shock to me. I think what happened on the first night was that we were in the dark in the Car and in the Dancehall there was every colour of light so I just thought her Hair was a dark colour. At this time I had just bought my first Car, a Ford Anglia Deluxe and I used to collect Pat from work each Saturday evening and take her home where her Mom would get us Tea before we went out for the evening.

Going to Australia

Around this time I became good friends with Packie Fitzpatrick and we began talking about immigrating to Canada but gave up on Canada when we were told that we must have £300 each on arrival to support ourselves. I was delivering a truck load of steel on the South Circular Road in Dublin and when everyone stopped work for Lunch I walked to the nearest Phone Box and rang the Australian Embassy and asked about immigrating to Australia. They sent me Forms to fill in and when I told Packie what I had done he did likewise. That was late 1967, we were soon called for interview and in a few weeks we were accepted. I waited until after Christmas to tell Pat. She was quite upset at the news; we had been going steady for about a year and were very happy together. I stayed for the wedding of Pats Sister Yvonne to Gay Fagan in early May 1967. The night before leaving I stayed in Pat's House in Ballyfermot sleeping on the Couch having said goodbye to my Family earlier that day.

In today's world it seems extraordinary that such a scheme should have existed but the Australian Government operated what they called the assisted passage scheme to help cope with a labour shortage. They brought men and women from all over Europe both skilled, semi skilled and unskilled, Ireland and Britain was the main target, due to the English language and historical connections. We had to contribute £12 towards the fare. Our fare was paid from Dublin Airport to London, overnight hotel in London we then flew via Middle East and Hong Kong to Sydney. The plane was a Boeing 707 which was the largest Passenger Plane in the World at that time, we had three or four stops and at each Airport I sent a Card home to Mom and to Pat. On arrival in Sydney we were taken to a large Hostel at Villawood (like an army barracks) and given a room with two single beds. It was dark when we arrived and were given the Key to our Hut, but we could not find a Light Switch and had to open the Door to get in enough Light to find our Beds. Next morning we found the Light Switch, it was a pull String from the Light Bulb. The same hostel was in the news last year (2011), it is currently in use as a holding Centre for Refugees who are claiming political asylum, and there had been riots by the Refugees who had set the place on fire, they were resisting being sent home to the Country they had run away from.

We got a few days work in the Barracks moving Furniture and that type of thing but we were anxious to get some real work so we went to a Dance in the Sydney Irish Club where we met lots of other Irish people. One of the best known Irish Men in Sydney was Seamus Gill from Kilcock who had been there for ten years and was a building contractor. Seamus was an extraordinary character who had a wife called Francis from Belfast, it turned out Frances was not his wife at all, his real wife had gone back to live in Ireland. She was from Donadea near Kilcock, they had gone to Australia when Seamus was only twenty one and his wife was twenty, they already had one child. They had four more children in Australia (all boys) the Wife could not cope with life in Australia and went back to Ireland with the children. One by one the children were sent to Kilashee boarding school at Naas, (now the Kilashee Hotel) and Seamus paid for their Board and Education while running his Construction Business in Sydney. Seamus and his new partner Frances and stayed together for over thirty years.

In 2002 Seamus made a trip home to Ireland with his new Partner, a Pilipino Lady called Carol who is expecting his Baby, she is thirty eight and Seamus is sixty eight. He is recovering from a stroke he had early in 2002, he also survived a stabbing attack about ten years ago when robbers broke into his Office, he was critical for over a week before he came good again. Over the years he made and lost several fortunes but is still quite wealthy today.

We stayed in Sydney looking for work for two weeks, having been a Truck Driver at home my instinct was to look for the same type of work in Sydney. To do that I first had to get an Australian Driving Licence which only required an oral Test. It was a one hour trip to Liverpool outside Sydney to do the Test which I passed but as I had forgotten my Irish licence they would not issue the new licence, they said bring back the Irish Licence and we will give it without having to do the Test again. I never got back there because we had heard about work in Mount Isa Mines in Queensland. They had an office in Sydney where we applied for and got jobs as Miners.

Mount Isa

Our problem now was how to get to Mount Isa, almost 2000 miles away, I had left home with £80 and had £20 left, and Packie left home with £60 and had £10 left. We went to the Immigration office and told them we had got work in Mount Isa and because it was our first real job in Australia they paid our Air Fare to Mount Isa. A staff member of Mount Isa Mines met us at the airport in Mount Isa in a Mini Bus and took us to a Motel for the night, next day we went to the Mine Office where we were formally started and given accommodation which was basic but clean and comfortable, as good as we were accustomed to. There was a large canteen where we got three meals a day and a packed lunch when going to work in the mine. There were about 1500 men in the Barracks from all over the World. A large part of the population in Mount Isa were Irish including some married couples who had been there for many years and some of them had their own Houses and young Families. There was an Irish Club which was one of the main Centres of entertainment with a Bar and Dancehall.

Our new life was very different from what we had been used to at home, most Irishmen were trained for working underground in the Mines as they had a reputation for being good workers. We were selected for Mining School which lasts for two weeks and included the use of various types of drilling Machines and also the use of many types of Explosives as each Crew of two Men had to do their own drilling and blasting, safety training played a big part but even so there was a high level of serious accidents and some fatal accidents each year. The most serious accidents were where Explosives went off prematurely due to carelessness or Miners taking shortcuts because they had to blast at the end of their shift and were running out of time.

The other cause of serious accidents were when miners went into a rock face after blasting without checking for loose rocks in the ceiling, when drilling started the rocks would vibrate loose and if you were directly under it you were in trouble. I had one narrow escape while drilling when from some unknown reason I stopped and looked up, a huge rock was about to drop, I jumped clear just in time but my Drill was wrecked when the Rock landed right where I had been standing. I still have no idea why I stopped and looked up when I did. One other day a sharp Rock fell and hit my right Arm, although it was not a large Rock it was very sharp and I still have a scar on my right Arm from it.

While I was in Mining School I met Brian Byrnes an Australian from Coffs Harbour about fifty miles north of Sidney. Brian was the same age as me, twenty four; we became good friends and remain good friends right up to the present day. Brian and his wife Rhonda visited Ireland in 2001 and stayed with us, in the 3 weeks they were in Ireland there was only 2 days that it did not rain. Through Brian we met many others who also became good friends. Bill White whom Brian had known for many years and his wife Wendy, they had three kids, Bruce, Kelly and Kerryanne. Some years after we left Australia Bill and Wendy separated, later Bill had a Leg amputated, he said it was a result of smoking, one Christmas we received a letter from Bill but instead of a card he included a picture of his artificial Leg on a Chair. That was typical of his sense of hummer.

Bill introduced us to his sister Margaret Goodwin and her husband Morry who was a Mining Instructor. They had three Children, Robert, Ronnie and Janet. We became good friends and when we started our family we named our first child Brian after Brian Byrnes. Our son Brian only lived three days (I will come back to that later). Our other children were named Robert, Ronnie and Jenny. Margaret Goodwin used to call her little girl Jen which I took to be Jenny but it was Janet so we named our three children after the Goodwin's. It may seem a strange thing to do but we found that Morry and Margaret were very good living people and their children were very well behaved, we had to find a name for our number five which we called Philip.

It was while we lived in Mount Isa that Pat acquired the name Puddin. I don't remember why or when I started calling her that name but it has remained with her to the extent I never refer to her as Pat except when she is introduced to a stranger and then it's to avoid causing her embarrassment.

Even after I started work in the Mines I still longed to get back to Truck driving especially when I see the Road Trains passing through Mount Isa which is the main Route from Sydney and Brisbane on the East Coast to Darwin in the far North and Alice Spring in the "Red Centre" it's called red centre due to the red colour of its Soil and Rocks. Australian Road Trains are something to behold. A tractor unit pulling 3 X 50 foot Trailers with a gross weight of more than 100 tons and travelling at 60 miles (100 km) per hour.

Another reason why so many Road Trains visit Mount Isa is that the Railway Tracks which link the East coast over six hundred miles away ends in Mount Isa and so all transport from there to Darwin and Alice Springs and all of the Northern Territory has to be served by Road Trains, Darwin is 1000 miles away and so is Alice Springs with almost nothing in between except occasional Truck stops and a few very small Towns which are used to service the huge Cattle Stations, some of which are over a million acres. There was a local transport company called Wrights Haulage which had a fleet of Road Trains and specialised in Cattle haulage, I went to see them one day about a driving job (even though I still did not have an Australian driving licence). The boss was not there and I was told to call back again. I never did call back because around that time I suggested to Pat that she would like it in Mount Isa and should consider coming to me. Well Pat needed no encouragement and immediately told her Mom and Dad that she wanted to go to be with me in Australia.

Pat's Mom was horrified at the idea of her nineteen year old daughter going to the other end of the world, in those days when someone left home and went to Australia they very often never came home again, Pat's Mom thought she might never see her daughter again, she tried every way she could to talk Pat around and change her mind but Pat had her mind made up, she wanted to be with Jim and nothing or nobody would make her change her mind. Pat's Mom came up with a great idea and said to Pat, come with me to see the parish priest and tell him what you want to do, if he gives you his blessing to go then I won't try to stop you any more (Of course she knew that the parish priest who was quite old would not agree to Pat going to Australia at such a young age). Pat agreed to go with her Mom and see the Parish Priest who turned out to be a new young Parish Priest and not the older man Pat's Mom expected to see. When Pat's Mom told him what Pat wanted to do he said "I think it's a wonderful idea". Mother Boileau was speechless but what could she say, she agreed, provided Pat agreed to come Home again in two years. Pat agreed but never told me about the 2 years part of it.

When Pat arrived I had arranged accommodation for her in a single Girl's Hostel where she stayed until we got married. Pat had a variety of jobs in Mount Isa over the next two years. Her first job was as a Bar Maid in the Mount Isa Hotel which could be best described as resembling a wild west Saloon in an old cowboy movie. The most regular customers seemed to be Aborigines who drank a lot. Pat had great difficulty with the accents of those Black Fellas as they were called locally. She stayed in that job for about two days, she then worked in a large Store called Coles Stores and after that with Mount Isa Mines in the Canteen which served management and office staff, she stayed in this job for quite some time but had great difficulty with the manager "Mrs Green" who for whatever reason took a dislike to Pat and made life very hard for her.

My friend Packie Fitzpatrick was also sent to work underground and had a very well paid contract, some types of mining produced much more ore than other types and therefore paid better wages. But to get into those contracts one had to be considered a "top gun miner" and Packie very soon fitted into that group. I made it to the same contract after about six months and remained there until we moved to Sidney in 1970.

Up to the time Pat came to Australia we had never really discussed marriage and I don't remember having any great discussions about it in Mount Isa either. Puddin has a better memory on this matter and claims my proposal to her came one day as we were passing a jewellery shop when I said to her something like, "Why don't we go in and get a ring ". We got married on Easter Monday 7th April 1969, Pat was 20 years old and I turned 25 two days before our Wedding Day. While Mount Isa was very remote it was still a pretty decent sized town, population 21,000, it had a Cinema and a Drive in Cinema, lots of Pubs and one decent Hotel as well as a few smaller Hotels. The flying Doctor had a Base there. In fact Mount Isa was the first flying Doctor base in Australia. If you go north from Mount Isa the next town Cammoweal is 170 miles away, it consists of a petrol station, a shop, a pub and four or five houses. The shop has a sign which says "you're in the sticks now so don't expect city prices". If you head east from Mt Isa the next small Town is Cloncurry 137 miles and it is another Mining Town. Townsville which is at the centre of the Great Barrier Reef is the nearest city and is 600 miles to the east.

A visit to Julia Creek

We have many good memories of Mount Isa, one of the more unusual is the time we had a visit from our Parish Priest Father Ryan who had married us and we knew quite well, he told us he had to stand in for the bishop at a Deb's Ball where he would be the guest of honour, as it was in Julia Creek which was over 300 miles away, He did not fancy making the journey on his own and asked if we would like to travel with him, we said of course we would and when we mentioned it to some more of our Irish friends they said they would also like to come. In the end so many wanted to come that we hired a coach and about thirty five of us went with Fr Ryan to assist him at his task of being guest of honour.

It was a night to remember for all the wrong reasons, our group included one John O'Donoghue who was from County Mayo; John was big and the more he had to drink the more likely he was to get into trouble. About 11pm the local Police Sergeant came to the hall where we were enjoying ourselves, he was looking for someone in charge of the Irish group, Berni Pendergast and I went with him to the Police Station where John O'Donoghue was locked in a Cell. The Sergeant on duty told us that John had attacked and beaten up some Aborigines, he had also been very abusive to the Policeman who had been called to the Scene. It took two Policemen to arrest him and put Handcuffs on him. When they took him to the Station there was no empty Cell so they put him in with an Aborigine who was arrested for being drunk and disorderly. It seems John did not like Aborigines because he attacked his cell mate with a steel cup which was in the cell, the police had to take out the Aborigine for his own safety but kept John locked up.

The Sergeant asked us to talk to John and try to get him to calm down so we went to see him; the cell block was a small steel building out in the back garden away from the main building. As we approached we could hear John shouting and roaring even though there was no one there. We talked to John for about ten minutes but we could get no good of him at all so we gave up and went back to see the sergeant who told us that John would appear in Court the next morning on assault charges. We told the Sergeant our coach would be leaving for Mount Isa in about an hour and would it not be better to let him go with us. The Sergeant said the only way he could free him was if he paid a $20 fine to avoid going to Court. We tried to talk to John to get him to pay the fine but he just wanted to kill everyone. We told the Sergeant we would pay the fine and the Sergeant agreed but would not free John until our Coach was parked outside the Station and so we rounded up all our gang and then drove to the Police Station and parked outside. Two policemen marched out with John, still in handcuffs which were only removed as he was stepping on to the Bus.

Hatches Creek Mine

Another unusual experience was when one night we went to visit Ray and Evelyn McRory who were from Belfast. Ray had a large Truck and had a Contract hauling Ore to the Railway in Mount Isa from another mine called "Mary Kathleen" which was only about 100 miles away. Ray said that he was going on a trip to the Northern Territory with a load of Steel and other supplies and asked me if I would like to go with him and of course I said yes, Ray did not say how far it was to Hatches Creek Mine but that he would be leaving about midnight Friday Night. It was about 2am before our load was ready and the Truck checked out and filled with Diesel, we drove all through the night and stopped at a Truck Stop for Breakfast at 7.30 am, we took off again and took turns driving and sleeping until we reached a junction called "3 Ways ", this is where the road from Mount Isa joins with the Darwin to Alice Springs road which runs in a North/South direction, it was 3.30 Saturday afternoon and we had already travelled about 500 miles from Mount Isa. We had Dinner here and filled up with Diesel, Ray had never been to Hatches Creek Mine before but he knew that it was somewhere off the road to Alice Springs.

We drove about two hours to Tennant Creek, another town built around Mines of Gold, Copper and Silver but it's also a centre of supplies for the large Cattle Stations in that part of the Country. We stopped here for Tea and Sandwiches and asked the Café owner for directions to Hatches Creek. He said "it's simple" just head out the Alice Springs road for about ninety miles and you should see a "Tree" on the right hand side of the road, turn left here and it's another ninety miles of dirt Track through the Bush. We thought he was joking about the Tree but he was spot on, around ninety miles later the tree was standing all on its own in a countryside that was barren except for "Spinifex" which is a very rough Grass that grows in large tufts and can survive the worst drought but can be eaten by Cattle.

It was almost dark when we got to this point, we did not like the idea of ninety miles over dirt Roads in the dark but we did not want to sleep in the Truck so we kept going. For most of the journey the Road was reasonable but there were spots where recent rains had left part of the Road flooded, a Dirt Road is bad enough when its dry but when its wet you dare not stop as you might not get moving again, When we saw a Flood on the Road ahead Ray would put his Boot down and hit it with as much speed as possible hoping that the Truck's own momentum would take us through and out the other side without going into a skid and losing control, it worked every time. The other scary moments were going over mountains and round hairpin Bends on a Track only wide enough for one Truck, you prayed that you did not meet other Trucks and we never met anyone or anything until we arrived at the Mine at 9.30 pm Saturday night, twenty two and a half hours after we left Home in Mount Isa.

Hatches Creek Mine had thirty six Miners, a Manager and four Women staff who did Office and Canteen work, when we arrived they had just finished watching a Film in the Canteen which doubled as a Cinema and a Bar at certain hours which was determined by the Manager who was an eccentric English Man and who ran the place like a military Barracks, but he did allow for some flexibility in the rules. For example fights were only allowed on Saturday Evenings and then there had to be a referee which of course was the Manager himself. This rule was not so daft as it might seem, while allowing the hotheads to have a fight it also created a cooling off period as they waited for Saturday to come and in most cases the fight never took place but we were assured that there had been some nasty fights.

Hatches Creek is a small mine but a very important one as it produces a rare Metal called Wolfram, the main component of which is Tungsten, on its own Wolfram is not much use but when mixed with other Metals it forms one of the hardest metals available in the world. Some Miners had gone on holidays so there were spare Beds which they gave to us; they also gave us an evening Meal and Breakfast next Morning. It was a lonely existence living at Hatches Creek but one of their benefits was a free flight to the nearest town which was Mount Isa every two weeks, there is a landing strip where small Planes can land and take off. When our Load was delivered we had another Meal before departing for home. We arrived back in Mount Isa at midnight Sunday night, forty eight hours and about 1450 miles later. On the journey we passed "Devils Marbles", huge round Rocks up to 100 feet in diameter, There are about thirty of them, we also passed hundreds of huge Ant Hills up to thirty feet tall (10 metres) and looking like Chimneys standing alone, they can be just as deep underground and each one has many millions of Ants inside.

our first date, 1967, l to r Kay Cooper Tommy Kelly
Marie Moore Jimmy Canavan Pat and Me

Chapter 9

Our wedding, we were married in Mt Isa but our wedding was very modest by today's standards, there was forty five Guests form seven different Countries, Packie Fitzpatrick was my Best Man and Margaret Bishop an Australian was Bridesmaid for Pat. Bill White took the place of Pat's Father and gave Pat away, he also read out a lovely Letter he had received from Pat's Dad. This was a complete surprise to Pat and it was very emotional for her. Although I had been in Australia for 12 months and Pat had been there for 8 months our only contact with home was by letter but on this special day we arranged with both our families that we would ring them, my mom and dad travelled to Pats family home and we rang them after the wedding, it was great talking to them after such a long period. We postponed our honeymoon because my brother Pat was supposed to be coming to Sydney later that year with the New York Gaelic Football team so we planned to take our holidays then and meet him, that trip never took place because Pat's tour was cancelled. Many of the guests at our wedding were of a different religion to us and some were of no religion at all but we soon learned that it does not take religion to make a person good or decent; some of our Australian friends like the Goodwins don't practice any religion that I know of but we thought so much of them we named our children after their children.

The Rodeo

Every year in August the Rodeo takes place in Mount Isa, it's said to be the biggest Rodeo in Australia and is a very big event in that part of Australia, everyone comes from the Cattle Stations in Queensland and the Northern Territory, a lot of Aborigines who work as Stockmen on Cattle Stations would arrive and they would have their whole

Family with them, at rodeo time they all bundle into a pickup Truck and head for "The Isa" as its usually referred to. They would stay for about a week in Tents close to the Rodeo grounds, they appear to drink nonstop and constantly fight with each other, and they provide as much entertainment with their fighting as the Rodeo itself.

Part of the entertainment each year is provided by top Country and Western Singers. In the 1960's the number one was Slim Dusty who had a hit Worldwide with "The Pub with no beer". Around that time Chad Morgan came on tour to Mount Isa, Brian Byrnes had introduced me to his music and I had bought some of his LP's, we went to his concert and it was an extraordinary experience listening to his unique style of singing and referring to his buck teeth. He said his teeth were so prominent he was the only man who could eat an apple through a tennis racquet. Over the years the Chad Morgan Song "The Fatal Wedding" became my party piece and provided quite a lot of entertainment to a lot of People.

As a Footnote to this Paragraph when we returned to Australia for our Thirtieth Wedding Anniversary in 1999 I wanted to see if Chad Morgan music was available on CD so one day we went shopping with Brian Byrnes and his wife Rhonda, we had a lot of laughs at Rhonda who said she would not be seen dead asking for Chad Morgan music so she went round the music shops hoping to find it on the shelves but with no success. In the end she got up enough courage to ask the shop assistant and she actually got some of what I wanted, we got separated from them and Rhonda thought we were lost so she had our names called over the PA system, next day we played the Chad Morgan CD on our way to Canberra and had a lot of laughs at some Songs we had not heard before, particularly "The Trashing Machine".

Water in Mount Isa is very precious; the sole source of supply is the "Leichardt River" which is named after a German explorer Ludwig Leichardt. To provide Water for the Town the size of Mount Isa and its huge mine it was necessary to dam the River and so created Lake Mondarra which not only provided Water for the Town and the Mines but also became a great recreational facility with Lawns, Palm Trees, Swimming and Boating areas. In recent times they have introduced a large Flock of Peacocks who are quite tame and hang around the picnic areas where they are fed by Visitors.

In the dry Season which can last from three to six months the River Bed is completely dry and people use it as a Horse riding route, but when the rains come the river goes into flood and because the land is so flat and so hard the River forms Lakes over thirty miles wide which can last for Days or Weeks and many Roads are impassable, at times like this travellers try to make it to a Truck Stop where they can shelter until the roads are open again. At one such Truck Stop on the Road from Mount Isa to Darwin a crowd of about 30 motorists were stranded for a week because the road was flooded for miles in both directions. Food was running out so the owner of the Restaurant killed his 2 Dogs and fed them to the customers as Kangaroo Meat, no one complained and it only became public knowledge when the owner of the Truck Stop was interviewed by a News Paper reporter asking how he coped during the Floods.

Miners Wages *includes bonus for the Lead Poison you were almost certain to get if you stay long enough,* pay in Mount Isa Mines was good, before I left home in 1968 my pay as a Lorry Driver was £14 a week. In Mount Isa the basic pay was $104 (about £55) and most weeks with bonus and overtime the pay could be double that, of course this was for a job that was quite dangerous with a fairly high risk of accidents but the agreement with the Union was that because you were paid this bonus every week you could not claim compensation if you got Lead poisoning. It was a job that most people stayed no more that about five years, saved up as much as they could and then moved on. When we went back in 1999 on our Thirtieth Wedding Anniversary we were surprised to find so many of our old Friends still there, the friends we left were all in their 20s but now they were all either bald or fat or grey haired and like ourselves have Grandchildren, but most of them had left the Mine and made good in other jobs, my friend and workmate Ben Gillic from Kells is now general manager of the Irish Club which has become a huge venture and made large amounts of money. About 1990 the mining company changed their operation by putting all mining work out to outside contractors and let go all their own miners, with no more miners they did not have to provide accommodation for them so they closed down the Barracks and Canteen and let go all the Staff that worked there.

Of course the contracting companies who got the work had to employ Miners and they had to provide Accommodation as no one would come to work in a place like Mount Isa unless they knew they had somewhere to live, Ben Gillic and the other directors of the Irish Club did a deal with the Mining Company whereby the Irish club bought up all the portacabin type houses which were air conditioned and in good condition and relocated them on spare land beside the Irish club, they can now rent those Houses to the new Companies for their Miners, their Business plan for this project showed that if they could keep the Nine Hundred rooms even 60% full they would make money but they have almost 100% occupancy. They provide the miners with three Meals a Day. When we were there in 1999 the Irish Club was half way through a $10 Million expansion so the future looks good for them.

Another Irishman who did well is John Heatherington from Galway, he left the Mine and set up a Construction Company working for the Mine but he is now building Roads and Bridges throughout Queensland. They put on a Bar B Q. for us and had some Irish and Australian Friends over to join us. One Australian friend who is not doing so good is Barry McKay who was my shift boss for a while, when I told Barry we were getting married and he was invited to the Wedding he told me that he and his wife Beverly or Bev as he called her were leaving to work in another Mine at Cobar in New South Wales, he asked if we would like to mind his house until they were sure about the move, so we started our married life with a lovely house on its own ground with lovely gardens. Unfortunately they were not there for the wedding. We later lost contact with Barry and Bev and were surprised when Morry Goodwin told us that they had come back and were now retired and living in Mount Isa. When I rang him 30 years later and told them we were back in Mount Isa Barry was very excited, we had some good times with them and keep in touch by phone, Barry gave us some bad news at Christmas 2001 when he told me he had prostate cancer. He has been fighting it with herbal remedies and is still keeping well but he can't get rid of it completely, we must wait and see how he gets on. Fast forward to 2003 Barry's Daughter Megan rang saying that Barry had passed away last night; I rang Ben Gillic in Mt Isa and had him leave some flowers on Barry's Grave on our behalf, we still make contact with Bev and Megan each Christmas.

Packie Fitzpatrick I met Packie while living in Donnybrook in Dublin, he was in the same Lodging House and we quickly became good friends, we were both non drinkers and had similar interests so it was natural that when one of us thought about going abroad that both of us would think about it, Packie came from a farming background and had been through Agricultural College but when I met him he was driving Bulldozers in Dublin. We left for Australia together and worked in the same jobs in Mount Isa Mines and later in Sydney, Packie was my Best Man when I got married in Mount Isa although we missed out on his Wedding because we had left Australia and returned home to Ireland before he got married in Sydney to his girlfriend Hilda Mulvihill from County Roscommon, they later came home and Packie took over the Family Farm when his Father became ill and when the Father died the Farm became their permanent Family home, Packie suffered from High Blood Pressure and when his supply of Medication ran out he was carless about getting a new supply, his Wife Hilda was unaware that the tablets were all gone until Packie complained of severe Head Aches and by the time a new supply of Tablets arrived Packie had suffered a Brain Haemorrhage, Pat and I were on a weekend break in Cork when I was contacted by Packie's Daughter Fiona with the bad news, we went straight to Beaumont Hospital where Packie was still alive and spoke to us but from that moment he went downhill and died soon after that, we were with him when the life support Machine was turned off and so were his wife Hilda and his children Brendan Fiona, Colleen and Cathal, Packie's neighbour and friend John Beglan was also there when Packie passed away, we are still close friends with Hilda and her children and see them on a regular basis. We recently attended the wedding of Hilda's youngest Son Cathal to a lovely young Woman Grainne Kennedy from Anascaul in County Kerry.

Moving to Sydney

We decided to leave Mount Isa in September 1970, our friend Packie had left and gone to Sydney some months before and so had Brian Byrnes, Packie was working for Seamus Gill converting older Houses into Apartments. Brian Byrnes had bought a Truck and started his own haulage business. We decided to travel to Sydney by Bus to see some of the Country. Our Bus departed at 7.30am Saturday morning and arrived in Sydney at 3.30 Monday afternoon. We had been on the go for 80 hours, had changed drivers five times and had a four hour break in Brisbane, apart from that we only stopped for meals and to refuel. The Road from Mount Isa to the East Coast has a tarmac surface all the way today but in 1970 about three hundred miles of it was rough Dirt Road, it was very hot but we could not open Windows because of the Dust from the Tyres of the Bus and from Cars and Trucks we met on the Road. We would drive for hours through open Country with no Fences, lots of Skeletons of Cattle that had died from drought which occurs about every four years. At one time an Emu ran alongside our Bus for about a mile before giving up the race. Because we travelled right through the Night Saturday and Sunday we saw less of the Country than we expected to.

Packie met us in Sydney and took us to one of Seamus Gills Houses where he and some other Irish lads were living. We stayed there for a few weeks until one of Seamus Gills apartments was ready and we moved in and rented it from Seamus until we left Sydney the following Christmas. I worked for Seamus for a while and then I got a job with another Irish contractor John O'Brien who was clearing a huge site for a new Power Station; because of my experience with Explosives they gave me a job of blasting Rock on the Site when I was not using a Jack Hammer.

Back home again

Christmas 1970, we came home for a Holiday but when Puddin got talking to her Mom she changed her mind about going back, she was expecting our first Child (Brian) which was due in April 1971. I had to go back to Sydney to collect what belongings we had and pack them into boxes for sending home, then get them to a shipping agent to ship them to Ireland. We had a TV set on hire purchase and I arranged for Packie and the other Irish lads to put it up for a raffle at a dance in the Irish club and from the proceeds he would pay the balance due on it. I then went back to Mount Isa and got my old job back again but only stayed about two months as I wanted to be home for the birth of our first child in April. I made enough to pay the shipping company and pay my fare home. While there I sold some Shares I had bought in ABC bank, their value had gone down but I got $250 clear. I had also invested $1200 in a mining company called Westmoreland but from the day I bought the shares they fell in value and I lost my $1200 investment. I still had £600 clear when I got home and with that we built a one bedroom wooden House in Yvonne and Gay's back Garden in Diswellstown.

When I came home our baby Brian was due in a few weeks, I set about getting a job as soon as possible, my brother John got me a job as a labourer with PJ Walls a big Contractor who was building a new Runway at Dublin Airport to take Boeing 747 (Jumbo Jets) which were already coming into Dublin Airport. Most days there would be a jumbo parked on the apron beside where we were working and one day when it was raining we took shelter under the jumbo so I sat on the wheel of a Jumbo Jet long before I travelled as a passenger in one of them. We were staying with Pat's Sister Yvonne and her Husband Gay and Gay loaned me his Honda motor bike which I used to travel from Diswellstown to the Airport. It was in April and the weather was still quite cold, I was not dressed for a Motor Bike and I would be freezing from the cold at each end of my journey.

Our wedding day, 7-4-1969

Mt Isa 1970

Pat in her school uniform

Chapter 10

Our first Child Brian James, April 1971

I was still working at the airport when Pat went in to have Brian, it was the middle of the night when she decided to go and we had to get her to St James Hospital. Gay used an old white van which he used to make deliveries as a courier; there was only one passenger seat so Gay put an armchair for Pat in the back of the van while I sat on a spare wheel. The entrance door to the hospital was locked at night and we had to ring a bell for admission, Pat gave her name and the nurse said alright Mr Cummins we will look after her from here and I was not allowed past the front Door, compare that with today where the Husband is expected to stay with his Wife right through the birth of the Baby.

Next morning I had to find a Telephone on my way to work and rang the Hospital to be told we had a Baby Boy and Mother and Child were both well, I was very happy to tell my workmates that I was a Dad although I had not yet seen my Son. That evening I came home and got changed into clean clothes and went on my 50cc Honda to see Puddin and Baby, when I got to the ward and asked to see Patricia Cummins the Staff Nurse told me that all was not well with the Baby but the Mother is fine, I can't remember much of what I was told but it was to the effect that the Baby had multiple abnormalities and might not live long.

I went in to see Pat and she said "Jim they have not let me see the Baby and I'm worried that there is something wrong with him", he was taken from me at birth and put into an Incubator, after a while I asked if I could see the Baby and I went with the Nurse but Puddin stayed in her bed. At first sight there seemed to be very little wrong with Brian, that's because most of his problems were inside his little Body, his Heart, Liver,

Kidneys had not developed properly, his Feet had no Bones in them, he had a beautiful little Face and I think he would have looked like Bobby or Jenny. I went back to Pat and tried to keep her spirits up without giving her too much hope. It was the second day when Pat came with me to see Brian, he was still in the Incubator so we never got to hold him or touch him and he died when only three days old. I was at work and used the public Phone at the Airport to ring the Hospital and was told he had died during the Night, I asked the Nurse on the phone not to tell Pat until I got in to see her. When I broke the news to her and we both cried our eyes out.

The Hospital staff told us it was normal in cases like this that they would look after the burial and he would go to the little Angels Plot, we were so distraught we agreed to this but also because we were told it would be necessary to have a Post Mortem to determine the cause of Death and that could take a Week or more. We were promised that we would be given the results of the post mortem but never got anything and because we were trying to get our life back together we dropped it. We still visit his Grave at what is called the little angels plot in Glasnevin Cemetery and had a Plaque erected in his memory.

Motor Bike Accident

Two weeks after baby Brian died we had been visiting Pats Mom and were going Home to Castleknock, it was dark and the shortest route was across The Phoenix Park, we were travelling on Gay Fagan's Motor Bike and had just turned from the main Road heading to Whites Gate Exit when we were struck from behind by a Car, when I picked myself up off the Ground Pat was lying flat out in the middle of the Road, there was no movement except for a few feeble kicks from one foot which reminded me of the last movement of a cow that had been killed in the Slaughter House, I thought she was dead, I looked round for someone to ask for help, the Car which had struck us was stopped about 200 Yards down the Road and the Driver was standing by his car looking back at us, I called to him asking for help but he got into his car and drove away at high speed, we were on a side Road in the Park which had no traffic on it at 11.30 PM so I had to leave Pat lying in the middle of the Road and run out on to the Main Road to stop traffic and ask for help, in those days there was no such thing as a Mobile Phone so someone had to drive to Castleknock for a Public Telephone to ring for an Ambulance, Pat was still unconscious when the Ambulance arrived and I travelled with her in the Ambulance to St James's Hospital where she regained consciousness'. Pat's first reaction when she came round was to feel her tummy and say "where's my Baby" I said the Baby's OK, I did not think it was the right time to tell her that her Baby had died 2 weeks earlier. Soon after that her Memory came back and she gave me a thump and said "why did you lie to me", I know now the Baby is Dead, it was a difficult situation but a great relief that she was coming back to normal. Pat was kept in Hospital overnight for observation but I now had the difficult task of telling her family, it was well after midnight so I got a Taxi to her Parents House and knocked on the door, they were all in bed, her Mother looked out the upstairs window and said, Jim, what's wrong, I blurted out, Pat's had an accident and Mrs, Boileau came down and opened the Door in a hysterical condition thinking Pat was Dead, it took a long time to calm her down and convince her that Pat was OK and would be out of Hospital Tomorrow.

I wanted to get back to driving trucks so I contacted Jim Sheridan who I had worked with as a driver in C.I.E before I went to Australia. Jim had now built himself a good haulage business called "Shertrans" with four or five trucks; he gave me some part time work driving but did not have full time work.

Around that time we moved in with Pat's Granny and her Son Tommy, we had the use of one Bedroom and the Kitchen. Granny had grown up in hard times when she never knew where the next Meal was coming from and she lived her life as if she were still in poverty. Tommy worked as a Night Watchman on Building Sites and probably had some Money saved up because he never spent any and this is probably why Granny was so worried about her Food, she used to worry that we were eating her Food, Pat would put Money in the Gas Meter to be sure we paid for what we were using but Granny never saw her putting it in and thought we had not put it in at all.

Our new 10 Year old Car is stolen.

It was when we were living with Granny and Tommy in Cole Park Road in Ballyfermot that we bought a car which was an old Ford Cortina for £180 from Hayden's Garage in Hill St Dublin, it had a front Wing pushed in so that when you opened or closed the driver's Door it made a loud creaking noise. The first Night we had it Home we had just got undressed for Bed when I heard a loud creaking noise, I looked out the window and saw some Men pushing our Car down the road. This car was our lifeline and the thought of it being stolen drove me crazy. I ran around the Bedroom in circles looking for my Jeans, Pat picked it up and gave it to me, we both ran downstairs and down the Road after our new Car which was about ten years old.

As I approached them with Pat hot on my heels they spotted us, they were in the Car trying to start it. One Fellow got out the passenger side and ran off but the Guy that was in the driver's side was slower to get out. As I approached him I made a flying leap and landed on top of him, he went down like a Sack of Potatoes. Having told him how we would kill him and strangle him and break his neck if he tried to escape, I bundled him into the back of the car. I held him by the Hair with my left Hand as I drove the Car having to steer and change Gears with my right Hand. Pat was holding him back with both her Hands and me telling him how I would kill him if he moved.

We made it to the Garda Station and handed him over to the Gardai. Next day about six men came to Granny's House looking for me and said that their Brother was not trying to steal our Car but had found it in the middle of the Road and was trying to find out who owned it. They said I should not give any more details to the Gardai so that he would be let go without being charged. Next day I told the Gardai about this visit, the Gardai said they were a nasty bunch and were used to intimidating people in this way. Eventually he went to Court and on my evidence he was fined £20 which would have been a week's pay in 1971.

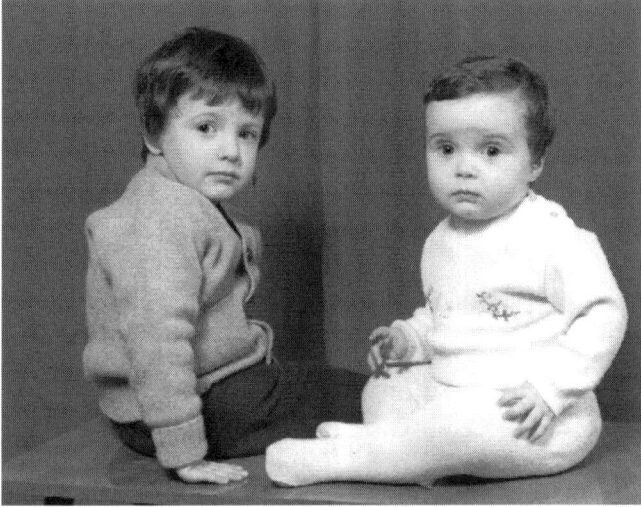

Rob two, Jenny one year old

Ronnie showing great determination at one year old

Phil aged two

Chapter 11

Looking for Work

Over the next twelve months I had several Truck driving jobs, with General Electric, delivering electrical goods from their factory in Dunleer County Louth and their Warehouse in Benburb Street to all parts Ireland, with Molloy and Sherry collecting Timber and Containers from Dublin Docks to Factories and Timber Merchants, Shertrans Haulage doing Dublin and Country deliveries, a few years later Jim Sheridan who owned the business suffered badly from depression, his business suffered and eventually went into liquidation. One of the more memorable jobs was with a Company called Irish Forwarding Agents which included a lot of Cross Channel Haulage collecting Meat from Factories around Ireland and delivering it to Glasgow or to the Meat Market in London, we had no children at this time and Pat came with me on some of the runs, one such trip that comes to mind was on a Ferry from Dublin Port to Liverpool, my fare was paid for with the Truck but we were short of Money for Pat's fare so I put her into the Bunk and covered her up with blankets saying you can come out when we are on the Ferry. I drove the Truck on to the Ferry and stopped where the Dock worker told me to stop, what I had forgotten was that the Truck would have to be chained to the floor of the Ferry and the Chains were under the Bunk in which Pat was now lying. A dock worker came and asked me for the Chains so that he could secure the Truck, I told him "it's ok I will do it" but he said no it's my job to make sure each Truck is secure so I had to try to lift the Bunk with Pat in it to pull the Chains out. Pat said what are you doing, I said I have to get the chains out, the worker waiting for the Chains thought I was talking to him and came over closer and said, "what's that" Pat kept asking what was happening and I told her to shut up and keep quiet, the Dock Worker heard this and thought I had told him to shut up and said to me "what did you just say" I managed to get the Chains out and told the worker I was sorry for the delay, he was not impressed with me so I left him to do his job in peace, when all was quite Pat came out and I gave her my Berth on the ferry which was included in my Fare, I then had to sneak back down and sleep in the Truck for the 10 hour journey to Liverpool.

Continental Oil Company, (JET)

Early 1972, I was still looking for a full time job, I went down to the Docks and called into every one of the Oil Companies on Alexandra Road looking for a driving job, in Jet Oil Company Harry Donnelly gave me an application Form and told me to come back next week, when I came back he and the Terminal Manager Denis Cousins interviewed me and told me to ring him later. After doing a driving test I got the job and started on 23rd March 1972. My time in Jet was very memorable and I suppose it laid the Foundation for the rest of my working Life. Jet, which was owned by an American Company "Continental Oil Company" and traded in Ireland as CONOCO using the brand name "Jet" for their Petrol and Diesel.

My experience of driving with Paddy Flanagan from age seventeen to twenty one and then three years driving in C.I.E gave me experience of driving almost every make and type of Truck with two, three and four Axels and Articulated Trucks with every type of Trailer and every type of Load from live Cattle to dead Cattle in carcase form to bulk Cement Tankers and Oil Tankers. I had also spent some time on cross channel haulage. So I was quite capable of driving any Truck they had in Jet. However I had to work a three months probation period during which I had a few minor accidents and made some mistakes and at the end of my probation I was told I was being let go.

I came home devastated and told Puddin I had lost my job, this was early 1972 when Puddin was expecting Bobby and we had no place to live but we were staying with Yvonne and Gay in their cottage in Diswellstown. I went into work the next day and talked to the Union shop steward about me being let go, he came with me to see Mr Cousins the terminal manager and the transport manager Pat Hughes. They agreed to give me another chance and I never looked back from there, in fact the irony of the meeting I just mentioned above is that three and a half years later Pat Hughes was demoted from the job of Transport Manager because of consistent absence due to bad health. I applied for his job and was appointed Transport Manager when I was aged thirty one. I was put in charge of about thirty Drivers and Trucks, a Workshop with four Mechanics and a Foreman Mechanic. After about two years in that job things took another unexpected turn when Denis Cousins the Terminal Manager who had employed me and then sacked me and then gave me another chance was himself removed from the Job for incompetence.

I was offered the job of terminal manager with overall responsibility for Drivers, Mechanics, and Yardmen who loaded the Trucks; my responsibilities included shipping, transport, terminal stocks and administration. It had been a very steep learning curve for a few years and it was really only beginning for me. I had left school at age thirteen and was able to read and write but that was the extent of my education, my ability at Maths was very limited. Many people including friends and family often asked me," how did you do it" I can only say, things just seemed to work out for me, with a lot of help from a lot of people.

At the time I started as a driver in Jet Oil the Company and the Unions had agreed a new Productivity Agreement which provided for increased wages in return for fixed times for drivers on each run, but as always seems to happen with these agreements some things were things in dispute as to what had really been agreed. One of those items was a new pension scheme for all manual workers. The Shop Steward was very frustrated because he could not get agreement on the outstanding issues so he quit as Shop Steward.

The Union Branch Secretary arranged a meeting of all workers and I was appointed Shop Steward. I had only been working in Jet for one year and had no idea of how to do the job I had been elected to. The first thing I did was to request a meeting with Management and the Union and proposed that we hold a joint meeting of Jet workers from Dublin along with workers from the other Terminals at Cork and Arklow. We all met in a hotel in Urlingford and took a vote on what we had negotiated with the company, our proposals were accepted unanimously and that was the biggest single problem out of the way.

Eamonn Brandon who was operations manager in Jet at the time was delighted at the news and that was probably the beginning of what turned out to be a long relationship based on respect for each other. Over the next three months we worked out all the outstanding issues and I continued as Shop Steward until I got my first promotion.

Problems with Trucks can usually be sorted out once you have the money and a good plan, not so with people, some people go on a power trip such as happened with Peter who was one of the oldest and most senior drivers in Jet, he had also been Shop Steward for many years before I started and it was he who quit as Shop Steward because he could not resolve the pension problem and other outstanding issues with management. Other drivers said Peter expected everyone at the meeting to refuse to accept his resignation and ask him to carry on with a free hand to just blame management for everything, but that did not happen, no one asked him to carry on, instead someone proposed a new meeting to elect a new Shop Steward, at that meeting there was a lot of debate about outstanding problems. Three names were proposed but eventually the other two men said they would vote for me and so it was a one horse race and I was elected shopsteward.

I was completely unprepared for the new task but had to learn fast as I had to meet the management team the next morning and tell them I was the new Shop Steward as of today. During my time as Shop Steward I had almost as many problems with the former Shop Steward as I had with management, Peter would complain about things that had not been a problem before and demand that I arrange a meeting to discuss it, then one day he went to the Routing Clarke and told him he was having problems with his Back and would not be able to continue doing the long distance work which he did most days but he said that he should be able to do local deliveries ok. When Peter was on long distance work he was on one of the biggest and best Trucks in the Fleet; he thought that he would be left to local deliveries but also keep the best Truck in the Fleet. Instead the routing Clerk asked me would I go on long distance work driving what used to be called "Peter's truck"; of course I agreed not knowing that this was going to upset Peter even more.

This situation continued until the Transport Manager's job was advertised, I applied for the job and got it so I had to stand down as

Shop Steward as I was now on the management's side of the table, the Shop Steward's job was up for grabs again and guess who got it "Peter" who had previously been Shop Steward. Peter was now in an ideal position to get back at me for whatever it was he thought I had done to him and he did everything he could to make life difficult for me.

My first Promotion

When the job of Transport Manager was advertised in Jet I had no intention of applying for it until the Operations Manager Eamon Brandon asked me why I had not applied, I told him I did not have the education or experience necessary for doing the job. Eamon said to me, well you have a lot of experience at driving and you know a lot about Trucks, you also have a large Vocabulary and are very articulate, you have shown as Shop Steward that you can lead people and solve problems so I think you should apply, you would be in with as good a chance as the other people who have applied, I was now aged thirty one and had been working from age thirteen, my formal education still only amounted to being able to read and write, my ability at Maths would not have been great. None of the jobs I had done as a labourer or lorry driver or as a Miner in Australia prepared me for organising and supervising a large group of Men, most of them were older than me and had more experience of driving and particularly in the Oil business. However having listened to my Boss saying why he thought I should put my name forward I decided to have ago as my driving job still be there and I would be no worse off if I did not get the Job. I applied and was appointed to the position of Transport Manager on 15 November 1976 with a starting salary of £4700 and a Company Car.

Because the previous Transport Manager had been absent so often for several years due to illness the job was in a mess. Our fleet of Trucks was in bits, breakdowns were a regular occurrence, there was no Service Plan in place, and Tyre blow outs were frequent because remoulds were used on all our Trailers to keep down costs and tyres were not correctly inflated. Tyres are a big cost factor in a fleet of Trucks, there were over two hundred Tyres and they need a lot of looking after.

I needed to become an expert on Tyres so I got to know Bill Molten the Dunlop Sales Manager and got him to invite me to every Seminar and

Workshop that was on in any part of Ireland. I learned that underinflated tyres wear out very quickly, the correct pressure for truck tyres was 120 psi and for every 1lb of pressure it is underinflated the life of that tyre is reduced by 1%, and most tyres were running at about half the required pressure. I introduced a regime where every Driver had to check and pump his Truck Tyres once a week, this brought about some improvement but because Drivers would often have to change Trucks or would be out sick or on holidays I had to try something else so I engaged Hanover Tyres to send in a Mobile Unit every Saturday or Sunday to spend the day checking Tyre pressures and pumping Tyres to correct pressures, but also checking for damage or wear or if a Tyre needed to be changed he would change it and the Trucks were all ready for Monday Morning and there would be a report for me on everything he had done. The next thing I did was stop using Remould Tyres altogether and started using a premium tyre which was much more expensive but which had a very good grip and lasted a long time. Blow outs became a thing of the past; drivers were more productive because Tyre changes took place while they were at home or on another Truck.

A bigger problem was the general condition of the Truck's, I knew it would take forever if I left it to our own Garage Staff to bring everything to the standard I was looking for so I made arrangements with Tom Hendron of Summerhill Engineering and Mick Murphy of Murphy's Truck Centre to get priority on our Trucks on condition that there would be a constant flow of work until I was happy with the Fleet. It took about eighteen months and Eamonn Brandon said I spent a fortune but our Trucks were not breaking down any more and deliveries were being done when they should be done.

Even though the trucks were being serviced on time and rarely broke down they were all very old and expensive to keep moving so I talked to Eamonn Brandon about it, he agreed that we should replace almost all of our Trucks, he said, what exactly are you talking about.

I said we need seven new Tractor Units, Seven new Trailers, Three new 3 Axel Trucks and Four new 2 Axel Trucks. Eamon said that would cost a fortune but he wanted the new Trucks as much as I did (this was in 1976). Continental Oil Company is an American company (Conoco) and all Money for Trucks or new Buildings had to be approved from the USA.

Our Managing Director in Ireland Delmar Williams was an American from Florida and Eamonn Brandon prepared a presentation and had to convince Delmar Williams, which he did and then Delmar had to convince his boss in the USA to give us the money. We got everything we asked for but it was spread over two Years rather than one, we were happy enough with this.

I had been driving Trucks for about fourteen years and by now had gained some experience in looking after them but the only thing I had bought was a second hand Car for a few hundred Pounds so I had to find out about what Trucks we should buy and from whom, in those years there was a very small selection of Trucks available and they were mostly British Trucks. Leyland, AEC, ERF, Foden. Volvo and Scania were being introduced to Ireland but were unproven and were a lot more expensive; it would be a big risk to start buying them, so we stuck with Leyland and Bedford's and Ford's, as they were being built to order in the UK. I made occasional trips there to check their progress.

When the first of our Seven Trailers arrived there was a problem with Dip Tubes which were in the wrong position in each compartment and so were illegal under Irish law. Fortunately we had specified in our order that each trailer must comply fully with all Irish laws. Eamon Brandon deliberately put this in because of my lack of experience in this area so it was up to the Tank manufacturer to get it right and they paid for the modifications to each Trailer. I then had to get each new Truck painted and have the Jet and Conoco Logo's painted on to each of them, after two years we had new fleet of gleaming Trucks and we were the envy of drivers in other oil companies and we heard stories about Shop Stewards in other oil companies complaining to their boss about "why can't we have a fleet like they have in Jet.

My Second Promotion

When I started work as a driver Paddy Hughes was in charge of transport and Denis Cousins was Terminal Manager, I had taken over the transport job from Paddy Hughes and now after only 14 Months the position of Terminal Manager was advertised, Denis Cousins had been at loggerheads with Eamon Brandon about how the Terminal should be managed and he had been moved to head office where he was given odd jobs to do but retained his full salary, he later joined the Union and eventually negotiated a severance package and left Conoco.

November 12th 1976 I got my second promotion in just 14 months when I was appointed Terminal Manager, starting salary £6400 and a company car, it was a Ford Cortina. Another Driver Bill Flynn took over the position I had just left and proved to be very capable in that role, he was now reporting to me so I had overall responsibility for transport as well as shipping and Terminal Management and administration, my Boss was still Eamon Brandon who said to me, I'm putting all my Eggs in one basket in giving you so much responsibility, don't let me down. Peter was still Shop Steward and became even more difficult as time went on.

The worst incident was one Monday morning I came in to find there had been a problem over the weekend while a Ship was pumping off five thousand tonnes of Petrol, I don't remember what it was that went wrong but Peter as Shop Steward came in with George O'Toole the yardman who was on duty when this incident occurred to talk to me about it (I was terminal manager at this stage), I pointed out what happened had clearly been human error but that if the proper procedures had been followed it would not have happened. Peter launched a verbal attack on me saying who did I think I was I to tell him what was right or wrong, he said I would be nothing and would not even have a job here if it were not for him, he was referring to the time I was on probation and was being let go when he came in with me as shop steward and management agreed to give me a second chance.

The abuse was so bad and went on so long that I had to end the meeting and tell Peter to leave. I rang my boss Eamonn Brandon and told him what had happened. Eamon rang John Harmon the Branch Secretary at the Union and a meeting was arranged for later that day. John Harmon came along to represent Peter and Eamonn came along with me. At the meeting Peter was apologetic but kept trying to bring up other issues where he was blaming the Company but which had nothing at all to do with what had gone wrong at the weekend or his behaviour towards me.

John Harmon was a wonderful talker who could talk nonstop for a half an hour and in the end you realised he said nothing but it still seemed very reasonable. Eamonn Brandon is also a wonderful talker but he is also very pragmatic and knows when he is in a difficult situation. In those years all driving and shipping work was done by direct labour unlike now where all that work is contracted out and the contractors have to sort out problems such as this. In most Oil Companies the workers were led by a very militant shop steward who is willing to call a stoppage without notice and call all the workers to a meeting which could go on for a half hour or a half day. Peter was like that although he was not the worst of them. Eamonn knew that there was no question of sacking Peter or there would be an all out strike and what's more Peter and his mates would go to the shop stewards in all the other oil companies and ask for their support with a good chance that they would get it, this could result with all movements of Oil and Petrol out of Dublin Port being stopped.

Even if we had suspended Peter there was a strong chance of unofficial action by militant workers who would stop work in support of Peter and the rest of them dare not pass the Picket or they would become an outcast and be called a Scab and a Black Leg. So Eamonn and John waffled on for about two hours until I said, look here, it seems that you have lost sight of what we are here about and I am being cast as bad a Peter, I turned to Eamonn and said to him if you are prepared to tolerate this behaviour from Peter then you don't need me and I walked out of the meeting and went straight home rather than back to the office. I told Pat what had happened and of course she was very supportive and told me that whatever I decided to do she would support my decision. Next day I rang Eamon Brandon and asked if I could come to see him in his office and talk about what had happened, Eamon said sure but he wanted to bring the Managing Director Delmar Williams along and suggested we meet for lunch in the Elm Park Golf Club. It was the first time I had a formal meeting with the MD and I knew very little about him except that he was from Florida in the USA.

At the meeting with the Union Eamon said that Peter had apologised after I left the meeting and offered to apologise to me as well although he was still trying to find a way to blame the Company for what had happened during the Ship discharge. My response was that such an apology from Peter would not be sincere and so would mean nothing to me, my choice was either get on with the job or quit and walk away, I was not going to let Peter drive me out of a good job that I was happy in so I would stay and do my best. Eamon and Mr. Williams were delighted and said there was a good future in store as long as I stayed in Conoco.

My time in Conoco (Continental Oil Company) prepared me well for the future; they sent me on various management courses on how to manage People, make more efficient use of resources and public speaking, the first time I was asked to make a presentation was at a management meeting and I was not prepared for it, although I knew everything about what was being discussed I was dumbstruck and could not speak a word, My Boss Eamon Brandon came to my rescue on that occasion and later sent me on a Dale Carnegie course to help me to speak in public. One of the things I learned on those courses is that if you want to change something which is not right you must first accept it as it is, then study the situation and try to find a way to change it to the way you think it should be, this will require you to know your topic inside out and then to try by discussion to get other people to see the logic in doing it your way. Logic may not always be enough if it's going to cost the other person money.

Chapter 12

New Job

In April 1980 an ad appeared in the Sunday Press looking for a CEO Designate in PMPA Oil Company, this was a new Oil Company being set up by PMPA Insurance Company and the person who gets the job will be responsible for setting up and running of the business. While I had a good job in Conoco who traded as "Jet" I found it frustrating in having to tolerate the restrictive practices which were still rampant in all Oil Companies and the difficulties of dealing with any breach of working conditions, unofficial stoppages were completely against the productivity agreement but the Union Representative while agreeing that it should not happen would never condemn the action or instruct the workers to return to work and I still to this day see Union Officials being hypocritical in the way they will sometimes agree that the action of workers who take unofficial action is wrong but they look for some way to blame the employer for causing the workers to stop work, it's still commonplace although all out strikes are not so common.

I applied for the job in PMPA and heard nothing for several months so I thought the job was gone but then a letter came asking me to ring and arrange a time and date for an interview. The interview took place on a Saturday Morning in Wolfe Tone House, the Head Office of PMPA and which is now the Head Quarters of AXA Insurance in Ireland. Three people interviewed me that morning, Seamus O'Mordha Managing Director of PMPA, Sam Synnot Financial Controller PMPA and Eamon Keating who was Project Manager in PMPA. It was August before I heard from them again asking me to come in for another interview, this time it was just Eamon Keating and Seamus O'Mordha (Seamus was the son of Joe Moore Chairman and founder of PMPA). They told me that the job on offer had changed somewhat and it was now referred to as Operations Manager, they said I was the most suitable candidate but that because of my limited experience in financial matters I would not be responsible for that part of the Business, this would be retained by the financial controller Sam Synnot himself. This suited me and they offered me the job, starting salary £11,000 and a company Car, a 2 Litre Vauxhall Carlton, and an Expense Account.

When I gave in my notice to Eamon Brandon he said I was making a mistake because PMPA could never offer me as good a future as I would have in Conoco and that further Promotions would almost certainly come in the future. I told him I was very grateful for all that he had thought me and the opportunities he had given me but that I now had a chance to start a new Business from scratch and without the restrictions that existing Oil Companies have to endure, He wished me well and we parted as friends. Eamon would be one of a small number of people who I believe had a positive influence on me and I would often look back with gratitude and remember when Eamon encouraged me and made me believe that I could do things that I never would have thought Possible. In my early days in management I considered going to night school with a view to doing the Leaving Cert and particularly to improve my ability in Maths, when I discussed this with Eamon he said, when a young Man or Woman does their leaving Cert and gets an Office job what's the first thing they are given for doing the job, it's a Calculator, and you know how to use the Calculator, there is a lot more to the job than numbers and you have experience which is the most important thing.

PMPA, <u>Private Motorists Protection Association</u> In 1982 PMPA Insurance Company had 404,000 Policy Holders and 2,720 Employees throughout the 26 Counties, It was formed in the 1951 to try and get better value Insurance for Irish motorists, up to then the insurance market was dominated by British Insurance Companies and there was very few to choose from. Joe Moore was a retired School Teacher and was over 60 Years old when he became Chairman and he ruled it until it was placed in Administration in October 1983, his Son Seamus O'Mordha was Joint Managing Director along with Michael Dore, another son Joseph Moore Junior was Manager of the Claims Department in the Insurance Company. It was set up initially to provide cheaper Insurance for the Irish motorist but they gradually expanded into many other areas of business, not all of them looking after the Private Motorist. They opened an investment Bank called the **Private Motorist Protection Society, PMPS.** The **Ireland Benefit Building Society, IBBS.** They became owners of News papers like **Leinster Express** and the **Sunday Journal,** there was an In House News Paper called the **Private Motorist** the editor of which was Dermot O'Looney, it was a source of advertising for all the other Companies in the group as well as the Insurance Company, when the **PMPA Oil Company** was Launched there were Pictures of Me beside one of the new Oil Tankers along with a feature article about me and the New Oil Company, they set up a **Vehicle Recovery Service Called VRS,** they opened **35 Garages throughout Ireland,** a **Stationary company,** *called* Broadberrys an **Office Machines Company,** **a Driving School** which included Trucks and Buses, **a Coach Tour Company** which had the largest fleet of Touring Coaches in Ireland apart from CIE, a **Wholesale Car Accessories' Company.** They bought McCairns Motors which had distribution rights in Ireland for Vauxhall Cars and Bedford Trucks; they had great plans for the expansion of **McCairns Motors** and in 1979 they purchased a 10.5 acre Site at the Red Cow on the Naas Road for £600,000 where they Built a huge state of the art Building that was to be the new Distribution Centre for Vauxhall Cars and Bedford Trucks in Ireland. Unfortunately when they had just finished the new Building Vauxhall decided to cease selling their Cars in Ireland altogether and they were left with the new building on their hands having spend about £1,000,000 to build it. They used another part of the Site as an Oil Depot which is where I came into the Picture. They owned 49% of Ola an Oil Company based in Drogheda and when they failed to gain full control they decided to set up their own Oil Company which was the new Company that I would run for them. They also had a share in Campus Oil. They invested heavily in Oil Exploration which included Gaelic Oil 8.4%, Eglinton Oil 1.3% Bula Resources 5%

PMPA Oil Company

September 1980, I became the first employee of PMPA Oil Company and was given Office space in Ossary Road on Dublin's North Strand where the PMPA Garage Division had their Head Office, I was able to call upon Garage Division staff for secretarial and book-keeping services until I had time to recruit my own staff. The first management meeting was attended by myself, Seamus O'Mordha, Eamon Keating and Sam Synnot the three PMPA senior executives who had interviewed me for the job. They told me that my first task was to go to Carrickmacross in County Monahan where they had Purchased an Oil Storage Depot which had a small Petrol Station attached, the longer term plan was that the Oil Depot would become a part of our Oil Distribution Network but in the short term they wanted to get the Petrol Station reopened as soon as possible and my job was to go up to Carrickmacross where I knew nobody and find a suitable person to run the Petrol Station.

Next day I set off for Carrickmacross with no plan other than to go and look at the premises and take it from there, on my way I stopped to give a lift to a young woman and as we had quite a journey ahead of we had lots of time to talk, I was impressed by her and by the time we reached our destination I had offered her a job running our petrol station and she had accepted it, her Name was Ann Holland and she became the second employee of PMPA Oil Company, she was a loyal and dedicated employee and remained so until the Station was closed in 1984. At our next Management meeting the first thing up for discussion was how had did I get on in Carrickmacross; I said I had employed a young Woman to manage the Station and it would be opened next week. They said oh that's great, how did you recruit her; I said I had picked up a hitch hiker on my way to Carrickmacross and offered her the job and she had accepted it. They all stared at me and then at each other and asked if I was joking, I assured them I was not, Eamon Keating said, well it was a difficult task you were given and we will have to accept your judgement and hope it works out ok, fortunately for me it did work out ok.

Seamus O'Mordha had already purchased a Tractor Unit and Trailer for delivering Petrol to PMPA Garages while the other Oil Companies were on strike and had borrowed a driver from the PMPA Coach Company to drive the Oil Truck, unfortunately this driver had little or no experience of driving Articulated trucks and he crashed into a railway level crossing in Kells and wrote off the trailer. Eamon Keating who was Projects Manager in PMPA had developed a terrific communications system by 2 Way Radio connecting Head Office with all the Garages and the Vehicle Recovery Service, from the very start I had 2 way Radios fitted into all our Oil Tankers and a radio base in our office, I did not want our Drivers having a say in whether they would agree to operate them,

They also had a car telephone installed for a few senior Executives and I was one of them, it was a far cry from what we call a Mobile Phone today, you had to press a button and hold it while you were speaking, when you had the Button pressed to speak the Person at the other end could hear you but if they wanted to interrupt you as people often do you could not hear them until you released the button, this often caused confusion because the other person would not understand that you could not hear them and would think you were ignoring them. To make a phone call using this system you had to press a red button which put you through to a Company called Skyline, you had to give them the number you wanted to call and they connected the 2 numbers.

The intention for the new Company was that it should be developed in 2 directions at once; Heating Oil was to be a big part of the business and there was a readymade market for Petrol because PMPA Garage division owned 35 Garages / Petrol Stations spread throughout the 26 counties, some of them were under contract to other Oil Companies so we could not supply them until their existing contract expired, my leaving Conoco and starting with PMPA coincided with an all out strike in all the Dublin based Oil Companies which resulted in a lot of PMPA Garages running out of Petrol and Diesel. Seamus O'Mordha had already imported a shipment of Petrol and Diesel through Morris Oil in Fiddown County Kilkenny, their Terminal is on the River Suir about 10 Miles up River from Waterford City. He had also purchased a 10 acre Site from the Plant hire firm W H Bridges beside the Red Cow Pub on the Naas Road with the intention of locating the PMPA Oil Company's Dublin Depot there, there was already a large Oil storage Tank on the site which had been used by W H Bridges to supply their Cranes and Machinery and it was hoped this would qualify the site for Planning Permission to use it as an Oil Depot. The next employee I took on was Bobby Barr as my assistant, he had worked for a Company called Tanker Services and knew all about Oil Tankers and the type of equipment that should be fitted to new Trucks. Michael Hayden was employed as a Sales Rep and his job was to go round the country and sign up owners of Petrol Stations to convert to selling the Primo brand of Petrol, the word Primo was made up of the first 3 letters of the word Private and the first 2 letters of the word Motorist, PRI-MO. Michael would later become my business partner and has remained so for almost 30 years, we would later adopt the word Primo as our own Company Name, "Primo Oil Company Ltd"

PMPA Oil Company traded successfully and was profitable, however some other Companies in the group were not profitable such as the Garages which we were supplying with Petrol and Diesel and because we all had the same Financial Controller the garages were given extended credit on their Petrol and Diesel bills to help them with their financial problems, as well as that the Leinster Express News Paper in the Midlands which was also owned by PMPA was short of funds and it was given a loan of over £300,000 from our Company funds.

17th October 1983, big plans ahead Meeting in Wolfe Tone House attended by Seamus O'Mordha, Jim Cummins and Eamon Keating, Seamus produced details of a scheme he wanted introduced almost immediately, with every Motor Insurance Policy issued there would be vouchers which gave the Car owner reduced Prices for Petrol and Diesel at all Primo Outlets. If the increase in sales lived up to what Seamus expected the effect would be to increase our sales by 800%, I explained to Seamus that I would not be able to deliver this with my existing fleet and number of Drivers, Seamus said, what will you need to be able to cope with it, I said for a start I would need 4 additional Articulated Trucks which I can buy second hand quickly in the UK, it would take a Month to recruit and train new Drivers. Seamus said OK, do it. I contacted Donal McCarthy in Cork who I knew had good contacts for used Oil Tankers in the UK, we flew over to Birmingham where I selected 4 good used Tanker Trailers, the Plan was that they would be ready for shipping in a week, Donal would import them and have them calibrated and ready for the Road. I would have to make another trip to find and buy used Tractor Units but this trip never took place because of momentous events which were about to unfold.

Collapse of PMPA Insurance Company,

19 October 1983. I went to lunch in the PMPA Garage Canteen in Long Mile Road where I met Frank Curran who was Manager of Vehicle Recovery Services, another subsidiary of PMPA Insurance Company, Frank said, it's on the news that the Government have gone into an emergency meeting because a Major Insurance Company is in serious trouble, there is speculation about whether it could be PMPA. That afternoon rumours were all pointing to PMPA and so I rang John Doherty who was Group Personnel Manager in Wolfe Tone House and asked him if he knew what was going on, John said, well Jim it looks as if PMPA could be the Company in question but of course they are denying any possibility that PMPA could be in financial trouble.

Thursday 20ᵗʰ October 11.50am my brother John rang me to know what was going to happen to PMPA, he was concerned about £400 he had in shares in PMPA and what would happen to them.

12oc Kevin Kelly of accountancy firm Coopers and Lybrand, accompanied by John Mahon and Niall O'Donnell and a string of other staff walked into PMPA Head Office Wolfe Tone House and asked to be shown to Joe Moore's office, he told Joe Moore that by an order of the High Court he had been appointed Administrator of PMPA Insurance Company and that he Joe Moore and his Son Seamus O'Mordha and Michael Dore were all being sent home on leave of absence and that they should take their personal belongings and leave immediately.

12.10 am, because of Johns concern about his shares in PMPA I rang Seamus O'Mordha on his direct line as I would normally do, not knowing that Kevin Kelly had arrived and at that very moment was in Seamus O'Mordha's office waiting for Seamus to leave, Seamus answered the phone and told me there was no truth in the claim made by the government that PMPA was insolvent but he could not say what would happen to the value of PMPA Shares as trading in them had been suspended on the Stock Exchange. When Seamus was leaving Kevin Kelly asked him if there was any large Cheque's about to be paid, Seamus said that a cheque had been signed for Gulf Oil for £320,000 from PMPA Oil Company for a cargo of Oil we had already received a week ago. Kevin Kelly stopped payment of this Cheque and in response Gulf Oil stopped the next Shipment to PMPA Oil Company which was about to be loaded in Milford Haven Oil Refinery.

4.30 PM, Visitors to the PMPA Oil Depot, Jim Quigley and Frank Glynn arrived and asked to see me, the handed me a document saying that Kevin Kelly had been appointed Administrator of PMPA Insurance Company and it was expected he would be appointed Receiver and Manager of the PMPA Oil Company and all other Companies within the PMPA group. They explained that their intention was not to close down the Oil Company but to help in any way they could to keep it going. Eamon Keating, Project Manager and Con O'Brien our Accountant were with me and we spent the next few hours explaining the running of the Oil Company and our supply arrangements with Morris Oil and Campus Oil who not only supplied us with petrol and diesel but also had their Dublin Based Distributors collect their supplies from our Depot.

Friday 21st October, all PMPA Oil Co. Staff are at work as usual, we continued making deliveries but were concerned that Customers would take deliveries and then refuse to pay if they had lost money in PMPS (Private Motorist Provident Society) which was an Investment Bank owned by PMPA Insurance Company and whose future was very uncertain, or they may have bought shares in PMPA Insurance Company and were almost certain to lose everything they had invested. Our 2 Sales Rep's Michael Hayden and John Dean were taken off Petrol promotions while there was such uncertainty about the future.

Stories were coming in about panic reactions by Car suppliers to the PMPA collapse, Datsun (now called Nissan) staff raided several PMPA Garages which were Datsun Dealers and confiscated 25 unsold new Cars, Smiths Distributors did the same thing and took all unsold new Renault Cars, suppliers were refusing to supply goods to Companies in the PMPA Group because no one could guarantee payment for anything. The problem was that at this stage Kevin Kelly had been appointed Administrator to PMPA Insurance Company, the Court Order made no reference to companies which were owned by PMPA Insurance Company but which were operated as separate Limited Companies, even though his Managers had moved in and taken control of all the other companies Kevin Kelly was saying that his brief was to protect PMPA Insurance Company and try to bring it to a Profit making situation. There was total confusion as to what should happen to other Companies in the group.

Gulf Oil in Milford Haven Oil Refinery refused to load a Shipment of Oil due for PMPA Oil Company because Kevin Kelly had stopped a cheque due to them for £320,000. Andrew Rhodes from Gulf Oil arranged to come to Dublin and meet John Mahon who was 2ND in command for Kevin Kelly but Andrew got no guarantee that their money would ever be paid, and in the end they had to settle for 29p in the £.

Tuesday 25ᵗʰ October 1983

We had used up all our stocks of Gas Oil and Diesel held for us in Morris Oil and were drawing from Campus in New Ross on the basis that Campus distributors in Dublin could draw what they needed from our Depot at the Red Cow on the Naas Road but this arrangement went sour when 2 of our Oil Tankers went to the Campus Terminal in New Ross to collect 2 loads of Diesel, our Drivers Larry Mitchell and Joe Bonnie were told we were not getting any more Oil until the PMPA account was settled, no one had told the Campus loader about this and he had loaded Joe Bonnie's truck with diesel and Joe left with his load, when the Terminal Manager heard about this he lost the Head and called our other Driver Larry Mitchell to his Office and while Larry was talking to the Manager one of the Yard Men went out and took the Keys from Larry's Truck and locked the Door, the Manager then told Larry his Truck was being confiscated until the PMPA account was settled, but Larry was too smart for them, he ran out to the Truck where he managed to reach his Arm in through the Fly Window to where he had a spare key taped to the Sun Visor, he then unlocked his Truck, jumped in and drove out the gate and away to freedom. Larry later started his own Oil Business called Dunboyne Oil Company, Larry is now deceased.

Later that day we were informed that PMPA Oil Company was in Receivership under the control of Kevin Kelly and next day John Mahon, Jim Quigley and Frank Flynn arrived in my office and presented me with a copy of the Court Order, they assured me that they did not want to disrupt the running of the Company and they wanted to keep it going until they had made a proper assessment of its chance of survival into the future. Although PMPA Oil Company had been trading profitably it was deemed to be insolvent due to the fact the Garages within the PMPA Group that we had been supplying with Petrol and Diesel were all losing money and had been given extended credit to the Tune of over £600,000 and another Company in the Group Leinster Express News Paper had been loaned more than £300,000 from our Cash Flow so we were owed almost £1,000,000 by Companies within our own group and at the time the Receiver was appointed all those Companies were insolvent and could not pay us with the knock on effect that we could not pay Gulf Oil what we owed them and so that made our Company insolvent as well.

Jim Cummins

I negotiated a deal with Gerry McNamara who was Managing Director of Campus Oil for them to import Petrol and Diesel on our behalf but this would require the Receiver to guarantee payment of over £300,000 which he was not prepared to do so I had to find an Oil Company that would sell us Petrol and Diesel by the Truck load, Paddy Holden Former Dublin Footballer who was then Sales Director of Tedcastles Oil Products (TOP) offered to supply us at a price and with credit that satisfied the Receiver, that gave us breathing space and time to think about what to do next.

November 9, 1983. I sent a letter to the Receiver stating my interest in Buying PMPA Oil Company should a decision be made to sell the Business, I had no money and no idea where I would get the sort of funds needed to buy and run a substantial business but I wanted to avoid a situation where it was sold without me knowing anything about it.

November 12 1983. **Meeting in Aylesbury**

A meeting was held at our home in Aylesbury to consider what if anything we could do to protect our own interests, six people attended, a Director of PMPA, and a senior Manager in PMPA, Con O'Brien an Accountant in PMPA, my assistant Bobby Barr and one of our Sales Rep's Michael Hayden. Everyone wanted to be part of a Company that would hopefully take over and continue to run the business but it was soon agreed that a business of this size could not support 6 families and the meeting centred on the role each person could play, the outcome of the meeting and subsequent meeting's was that only 3 of us would be owners of the new **Primo Oil Company** which had already been registered in the Company's Office and which we hoped would continue and hold on to the business which was already established. The 3 Director/Shareholders of the new Company were to be, Jim Cummins, Michael Hayden and our accountant Con O'Brien.

November 18 1983, **meeting Kevin Kelly**

Kevin Kelly as Administrator of PMPA Insurance Company called a meeting of Managers of all Companies which were subsidiaries of PMPA Insurance Company. It was the first time I had met Kevin Kelly and it was not a pleasant experience, he came across as a ruthless operator who already had his mind made up and he was here to tell us what was to happen, he was not interested in what anyone thought of his plan and would only tolerate anyone asking a question if it was to have clarification on some part of his plan. Of 31 Garages owned by PMPA 17 were to close immediately with the loss of 234 jobs, a total 348 people would lose jobs immediately and he made it clear that this was only an interim measure, his duty was to protect the interests of PMPA Insurance Company and any other business that could not be sold would be closed, none of the remaining business would be allowed to borrow money or to buy anything on credit without his prior approval. Of the 348 staff being let go, 2 were from our company and were sales staff. As time went on he closed dozens of Companies within the PMPA group and did away with over 1500 jobs, at the same time the Government imposed a Levy on all Insurance Policies to compensate for losses incurred by PMPA Insurance that was supposed to be temporary but it continued so long that most People forgot why it was imposed in the first place. When Kevin Kelly was finished speaking he left the room without saying goodbye or thank you to anyone, although there was heating on in the room there was a distinct chill, it was like being at a wake. The reason given for the collapse of PMPA Insurance Company was that they had not made adequate provision for future claims in their Cash reserves, I never heard any commentator say that the collapse was caused by other Companies within the Group although with so many of them losing money it must have had an adverse affect on cash flows in general. Kevin Kelly died in 2011

We opened a Bank Account for our new **Primo Oil Company** in Bank of Ireland and got approval to borrow €100,000 but on condition that we show proof of a supply agreement with one of the major Oil Companies, We had already got such an agreement with Tedcastles. I continued to run the business for the Receiver while trying to put together a deal where we could take it over Lock Stock and Barrel. **January1984,** the receiver wants to put the Business and assets of PMPA oil Company on the Market and I have to give him a full list of the assets and an estimated value on the Trucks, storage Tanks and Offices which were Portable buildings The receiver was looking for £190,000 for the business and assets but not the site, he later revised this figure to £150,000, and anyone who took over the business would have to move to another Site.

January 19th **1984** PMPA Oil Company was advertised for sale in the National News Papers and within a few days I had people calling to inspect Trucks Tanks and Buildings, most of them were from other Oil Companies and they either knew me or knew of me, I let them know of my interest in buying the Business myself and that if I was successful I would be selling some of the Trucks as we would not need them all because our business of supplying PMPA garages would be gone, The Garages were also up for sale and if they could not be sold they would be closed.

April 5th 1984, my 40th Birthday, we made a formal bid of £100,000 for the Business, other People offered to buy Trucks or Tanks but no one was offering to buy the lot in one go. Anyone who has ever been involved in a business collapse will know that Receivers tend to move slowly, we have been allowed to keep the business going because we have a positive cash flow and don't have to borrow or go into overdraft in the Bank,

June 6th **1984**, we have a new problem, Con O'Brien who is our accountant and is one of the 3 Shareholders in the new Primo Oil Company hoping to buy out PMPA Oil Company loses his nerve, he is concerned that the deal we have agreed with Tedcastles for future supplies does not give us enough profit margin, I tell him it's make up your mind time and he says I'm pulling out of the deal, Michael Hayden and I were happy to let him go and got him to sign a letter of resignation. We told John Rehill of Tedcastles that Con O'Brien had pulled out and now it was just me and Michael Hayden going forward as Primo Oil Company, John expressed concern at the fact that Con who was our Accountant had lost confidence, he said if your accountant has lost confidence maybe we should also have a rethink, next day John rang me to say "our deal is dismantled". I had to ring Kevin Lynn who was looking after PMPA Oil Company as well as the Garages as part of Kevin Kelly's team; I told Kevin that our offer for the business still stands but that because TOP had pulled out as our supplier I would need more time to secure a new supplier. Kevin agreed to give me more time but said he could not wait indefinitely.

June 25th **1984,** All PMPA Oil Company staff including me was made redundant, I would be kept on as a casual employee along with enough office staff and drivers to keep the business ticking over, but it could be closed down at the discretion of the Receiver and at short notice. We had negotiations with several Oil Companies but kept coming back to TOP as our best option for Supplies and eventually agreed a new deal with them and told Kevin Lynn our offer still stands.

September 28 1984. Kevin Lynn rang and asked me to meet him at PMPA Office in Long Mile Road. He told me he had talked to Kevin Kelly and that our offer for the Business is accepted. We set the 12th October as changeover day but now we had a new problem, getting insurance cover for our Trucks to carry Petroleum Products, when PMPA Insurance Company owned our business they were happy to provide insurance cover but it was not the type of cover they went after in the Market Place and the Premium they quoted to us was prohibitive, no other Insurance Company would even give us a quote due to the PMPA connection so we had to change the closing date from 12th October to the 19th October, we still had not succeeded in getting Insurance Cover and the 19th had to be cancelled. I discussed our Insurance problem with Kevin Lynn who contacted Niall O'Donnell who is 2nd in command at PMPA Insurance Company who in turn contacted Gus Hatch the new CEO, next day we got word that the premiums being charged to us had been reduced to a level we could afford.

October 22nd New problem Phone call from john Rehill in TOP, their drivers see us as new competition and will refuse to deliver to us unless they are paid £2,000 per Man, they also want TOP to employ 1 additional Driver, 1 new Loader, 2 new Mechanics and build a new Canteen, John said they were not prepared to give in to those demands and so once again they are pulling out of our deal. Next day I had to go to Kevin Lynn again and tell him what had happened and ask him for more time to get a new supplier, I think it was at this point Mick Hayden in desperation went and signed on the Dole, Kevin Lynn was upset but agreed to give me 2 more weeks, but only if we agree to pay a £10,000 deposit, I agreed and set about looking for a new supplier. Morris Oil came to our rescue but would only give us one week's credit and we would have to collect it from their terminal in Fiddown near Waterford which was a 7 hour round trip for each load. A new date of Friday November 28th was set for the closing of the sale and Kevin Lynn said, "this is it Jim", PMPA Oil Company will close on 28 November whether the deal goes through or not. One day before closing Date, one of the Solicitors involved had to postpone the meeting until the following Monday at 4pm. All that weekend, Friday Night, Saturday Night, Sunday Night I never slept one minute and went in to the Oil Depot Monday Morning not knowing what we should do, there were some deliveries due that day but we rang customers and put them off until the following day. PMPA Oil Company was no longer trading but Primo Oil could not make deliveries because we did not yet own the business, so we took orders for delivery the following day hoping that everything would be ok, Clodagh Morgan who was the last Office Person to work for PMPA Oil Company was staying on with us and she took care of the Office while Michael Hayden and I went off to sign on the dotted line.

Me with new oil tanker for PMPA Oil Company 1981

Pat and Me beside a typical road train in the oil depot which was managed by our friend Tony Harris

Chapter 13

Change from PMPA to Primo Oil

Finally on 30 November 1984 everything went ok and the Business changed from PMPA oil Company Ltd to Primo Oil Company Ltd, Clodagh waited for us until we got back with the good news but **she** also had news for us, one of our customers had been on and they were insisting we must deliver Oil to them that evening so I put on my Overalls and loaded up some heating Oil and drove to the Customer in Sandymount and made the delivery, as the docket was being signed I asked why could they not wait until Tomorrow, I was told the Man of the House had died and was being waked in the House so they needed to have the Heat turned on, that was the 1st delivery from Primo Oil Company on 30 November 1984.

Because TOP had let us down twice we appealed to them for help and they very generously gave us a short term loan of £30,000 to help us with our immediate Cash Flow requirements, we committed ourselves to paying this Money back in 21 Days so we had to be very careful to only buy what Oil and Petrol we need for a week and to make sure we got paid for everything on time, because we had lost most of PMPA Garage Business we needed a lot less Trucks and we had buyers lined up for the surplus Trucks. We arranged for Morris Oil to do our remaining Petrol deliveries for us on a commission basis and so we only had the Dublin Heating and Diesel business to worry about. We paid back the £30,000 we had borrowed from TOP within the agreed period of 21 days and Michael Hayden and I worked 7 days a week right through the first Winter Heating Season to keep down Staff numbers and to maintain a good service to our Customers. In March 1985 TOP had sorted out their IR problems with their Drivers and proposed a new

Supply Agreement to us which had better credit terms and they would deliver all our Oil so we could sell another Truck and help our cash flow even more. We resumed getting supplies from TOP in April 1985 and continued to buy from them for the next 15 years.

Family Reunion 1984 Sometime in 1983 I had the idea of getting all the Family together for a reunion, although we had always remained close as a Family we were scattered around the world, Pat was in New York with his Family and Maura and her Husband PJ and Bridget and her Husband Seamus were bringing up their families in Manchester, Ned was also living with his Wife Mary and their children in Manchester but he spent a lot of time working in the Middle East where he supervised the building of Gas and Oil Pipelines through the Deserts of Saudi Arabia and Jordan so we never had all the Families together at one time, at that time I was Operations Manager in PMPA Oil Company and had a very good Secretary called Lily Murphy who typed letters for me to each member of the family asking them could they make it in August 1984, Dad was not alive then but Mom was and her Sister Aunt Kate came with her Husband Jim Connolly, Paddy Flanagan was alive then and was invited as a friend of the Family, all our Families were young then and the total gathering only came to 46, none of our children were old enough to have Boy Friend's or Girl Friends, we booked out a large a Bed and Breakfast Guest House in Prosperous and moved in for the weekend.

25 years later in 2009 we had another reunion and the Family had grown to 106, unfortunately only 96 could make it this time, we took over a batch of Houses in the Avon RI Leisure Resort at Blessington County Wicklow for the August weekend. This time our Family was very different from the first Reunion, some who were young children at the first reunion have already been married and are already separated, some are still married and some others are living with partners and have Children with them. One Family member who is Gay came along with his partner; we are planning another Reunion for 2014 so I shall have to get working on that soon.

Christmas 1982

Pats mom and dad came to stay for Christmas and that's when the sickness began, Pat's mom already had the flu when she arrived, 2 days later we got the Dr for her, next day I came down with the flu and Dr Jordan came to treat me. That night Robert and Ronnie got sick and next day Jenny got sick.

The only people still standing in the house is Pat, her dad and Philip, they had to write a spread sheet for all the medication to ensure no one overdosed, it cost us a fortune and Dr Jordan said he was coming so often he might move in until it was all over.

Our first Property, Greenhills Road

We only had a 2 year Lease from PMPA on our Oil Depot site and so we had to set about finding a new Site as quickly as possible, Michael came up with the idea that we should look for a Site that is suitable for an Oil Depot but one that would also suit a Petrol Station. One day an Auctioneer called Bill Riordan called to our office to collect keys for a property next door to ours, it was owned by PMPA and we had agreed to hold the keys and hand them over when potential buyers came to view the property, Michael asked Bill if he knew of a site that would suit our needs, Bill thought about it and said, "let me think about it and come back to you". Within a few days he was back with a drawing of A proposed Petrol Station on Greenhills Road in Tallaght with space for an Oil Depot at the rear, it was a 2 Acre Site but we only needed 1 ¼ Acres for both our properties, eventually a price of £120,000 was agreed subject to us getting planning permission for the Oil Depot and the Petrol Station, Bill Riordan suggested an Architect Called Paul O'Connell to prepare Drawings and apply for Planning Permission, Paul would also act as a contact between us and the seller of the Property who was not to be identified, but if any advice or guidance was needed with the Planning process it would be provided by Liam Lawlor the Local TD and County Councillor who lived in Lucan, Because of this offer we came to the conclusion that Liam Lawlor was also the seller of the property but that as a politician he wanted to remain anonymous. The deal became very complicated because when contracts were issued it transpired that the Property was still owned by John Sisk the building contractor although it was being sold to us by a Company called Hawkwind which was registered in the Isle of Man. John Sisk had intended to build his new Head Office on this site but gave up that idea because of demands for compensation by staff for moving to this site.

Planning Permission for our project was refused by Dublin County Council on the grounds that there was an Industrial Estate opposite our site which had Planning Permission to open an Entrance / Exit on to Greenhills Road although they had never opened it in the 10 years that the Estate had been built. I went to see Liam Lawlor at his Home in Lucan and he said we will have to go for a Section 4 Motion. This is where a Motion is put at a Council Meeting and each member of the Council can speak for or against the Motion, if the Motion is passed then the County Manager must sign the Order and the Permission is granted, that was before County Dublin was split into the 3 separate Councils which we now have, **Fingal,** for North Dublin, **Dún Laoghaire Rathdown** for the South and the new Council for the area to include Tallaght where our new property was located became **South Dublin County.**

In 1989 all of County Dublin was controlled by Dublin County Council and I think it had 85 members; my aim was to get enough support from the 85 members to have the Motion passed and to achieve this I wrote to each Councillor explaining my Case and followed up with Phone calls asking for their support. The Motion was proposed by local Councillor Chris Flood who made a very strong case in our favour, we had cross Party support, Alan Shatter was scathing in his criticism of the Council's handling of the application, Nora Owen spoke in favour, Pat Rabbit and the late Mervyn Taylor of the Labour party were present but did not speak, as there was no opposition the Motion was passed without a vote and we got our Planning Permission. During this and other planning applications I learned a lot about planning laws in Ireland and it stood to me because each new planning application brought new battles with the planning department or with other objectors.

Getting Planning Permission had been difficult but was nothing compared to the problems we had in concluding the purchase of the property, after a delay of 8 months with nothing happening we were told that there was a problem over the Title, when John Sisk had purchased the Property from the Catholic Church Priory in Tallaght in 1942 some papers had not been properly completed and until that was sorted the sale could not proceed, although there was 3 different sets of Solicitors involved none of them were doing anything to sort it out so I contacted the Parish Priest in the Priory and arranged a meeting with myself and our Architect Paul O'Connell, we explained our problem to the Parish

Priest and asked him to sign the papers necessary to allow the sale go through. The Priest had great sympathy for us but explained that when it came to property matters he could sign nothing without first calling a conference of all the Priests in the Priory and getting their approval to sign the Papers. He did this and 2 weeks later we were handed back our papers duly signed, it took a total of 2 years to conclude the purchase of our first Property and we opened our first Petrol Station on August Weekend 1989. We were then asked if we would like to purchase the remaining ¾ of an acre of the site which we did for £42,000 in 1990, we had no plans for it at the time but we later built a large Car Showrooms and Repair Shop which we leased to Stuarts Garages who are Main Dealers for Land Rover and Range Rover.

The Square Property

We were always on the lookout for suitable sites for new Petrol Stations but we knew we could never hope to out bid any of the major Oil Companies for good Sites so we had to keep looking out for something that the other Oil companies would not know about which was very unlikely or the other possibility was that we might be prepared to take a chance where the Big Guys might walk away. In 1990 South Dublin County Council advertised a 1 ½ Site at The Square shopping Centre in Tallaght, it was designated Motor Related Business which would include a Petrol Station and had an asking price of £500,000 which was completely out of our range even though the Area would suit us perfectly. We were in with Alan Nolan of Dublin Corporation discussing a site in Ballymount Industrial Estate which might have been suitable as a new location for our Oil Depot, when Mick Hayden asked him what had happened to the Site they had for sale at the Square, Alan said they had a deal done on it but they were not 100% sure if it would go ahead, Michael said if you hear of anything that might suit us please give us a call and he left his Business Card.

It was many months later Michael had a call from Alan Kavanagh who had a Business with his Brother Paraic selling and installing hot and cold Power Washing Machines for use in garages or any place that needed Steam Cleaning Equipment. Alan said he had been given Michaels name in Dublin Corporation by Alan Nolan who was selling the site at The Square and was told that we were looking for a Site suitable for a Petrol

Station, Michael said, that's right, do you know of any suitable Sites. Alan went on to explain that he and his Brother Paraic had done a deal for the Site at The Square and they intended to set up a super Car Washing operation there, the site of 1 ½ acres was more than they needed so they had done a deal with Texaco where Texaco would take half the site for a Petrol Station and that would cut their cost in half and make it affordable for them to build their Car Washing Centre. His problem was that while Texaco in Dublin were keen to proceed with the project, the Contracts for such Property purchases had to be approved in London before it could go ahead and while London had approved it in Principal they still had not given the final approval that would allow the Contract to be signed. The problem Alan Kavanagh now had was that the County Council wanted a 10% deposit in 3 weeks time and he was not prepared to go ahead without Texaco taking their share of the cost. Michael asked Alan what was the price of the site. Alan said £300,000, so they want a £30,000 deposit and its non refundable, we are not prepared to take that chance but we thought you might be interested in trying to buy it at that price.

We were surprised to hear that the site was being sold for £300,000 when the asking price had been £500,000. It transpired that no Oil Company had made a bid for the Site because they considered it a big risk to have a Petrol Station located where it was largely dependent on Traffic from a Shopping Centre, even a large one like The Square which at that time was probably the largest Shopping Centre in Ireland. We had no such Concerns and asked for a meeting with Alan Nolan In Dublin Corporation who was charged with selling the Property for Dublin County Council. When we met Alan Nolan he was not aware of our contacts with Alan and Paraic Kavanagh and said the Property was on the market for £500,000, after a while Mick said, look Alan we know what price it was being sold at and it's nowhere near £500,000, Alan was surprised and said, what do you know about the price. Mick said "the price agreed was £300,000 and that's what we are willing to pay for it and we are willing to pay a 10% deposit right now, that bit about the deposit was a bluff because Mick had not checked our cash flow and he was making it up as he went along. As it turned out Alan said he could not accept our offer without going back to the County Manager but he agreed to take our offer and see what the response was. Following a lot of meetings with the Deputy County Manager Tom Doherty and his Senior Officials about what we would be allowed to put on the Site our offer of £300,000 was accepted.

We only needed a ½ acre site for our Petrol Station which left one acre for other Motor related Business, we were not speculators and wanted to stick to what we knew best so we talked to our Financial Advisor Anthuan Xavier of Accountancy Firm Simpson Xavier, Anthuan said he knew someone who may be interested in developing the rest of the site, the other person agreed to take one acre of the sight and develop it as a Motor Centre and the price was divided proportionately with them paying £200,000 and we paying £100,000 for our Petrol Station Site which we considered was a bargain. When we built and opened our new Petrol Station on November 30th 1992 we heard on the Grape Vine that the other Oil Companies were kicking themselves for letting this one slip through the Net, it proved to be the most profitable and valuable of our Petrol Stations,

Taylors Lane Petrol Station

My partner Mick Hayden was like a Blood Hound and was always sniffing around for new Properties, one day he showed me a notice in the paper of a site for sale at Auction on Taylors Lane in Rathfarnham, County Dublin. Once again we contacted our adviser Anthuan Xavier who said, this property is in liquation, he knew the Liquidator and suggested contacting him to see if it could be sold without going to Auction, we agreed to this approach and a few days later Anthuan rang to say that maybe it could be sold before Auction but to clear the debt on the site it would have to sell for at least £115,000, we had a short meeting between ourselves and rang Anthuan back and told him to offer the liquidator £120,000. In our research about the site we learned that it had already been sold twice but the sale had fallen through each time because the title was faulty, many years before it had come into the possession of a man who continued to use it until he died without ever having established legal ownership of the property, it was then taken over by a Car Dealer who ran a Business Called Ascot Garages for about 12 years before going into Liquidation owing a lot of Money to Bank of Ireland. The Liquidator having failed twice to sell the Property because of problems with the Title was not going to make the same mistake again so he got as full a history of the Site as he could get and then went to the High Court and asked the Judge to accept that everything possible had been done to establish all the facts and to confirm that the title was now in order in so far as it was possible, The Judge gave his approval and the site was now up for Sale once again.

Tedcastles were still our suppliers and we contacted their Retail Manager Oliver Lupton to get his opinion on the suitability of the site for a Petrol Station, the response was that it was too small, it was only I/3 of an acre, and there was problems with the Title, we were told that other Oil Companies had looked at the Site and walked away from it for the same reason. Our Financial Advisor got back to us saying that our offer of £120,000 could not be accepted as the Bank insisted that it must be seen that the best possible price had been obtained and the way to do that was at a Public Auction. We were very disappointed at this news because we expected some other Oil Companies to bid for it in spite of what we had been told about the Site being too small. We also knew that Edward Meade who ran a large Builders Providers Business next door was very keen to get it because it would fit perfectly in with his Business, all he would have to do is knock the Wall dividing the 2 Properties and it would increase his Yard by 25% and make it into a perfect square. Although I was satisfied that the Site was large enough for a Petrol Forecourt along with a Car Wash I wanted to be sure so I set up a mock Forecourt at our Greenhills Road property and then had our Artic driver Pat Brady drive our 38,000 litre Tanker in and out from every angle because I knew that if we could manoeuvre this Tanker in and out then we would have no problems with Car or Van movements, it worked a treat and that was another problem that we could cross off the list.

The day of the Auction came and because neither Mick nor I had any experience of buying a property at Auction we asked our Solicitor Paddy Kennedy to come along and handle the bidding on our behalf. We knew nobody in the Room except Edward Meade but there were about a dozen people there so it was entirely possible that there would be someone there on behalf of some other Oil Company. The bidding started at around £60,000 and proceeded very slowly, it reached £100,000 and Pat Kennedy still had not put up his hand until the auctioneer was about to drop his hammer and close the sale, everyone looked round to see who the new bidder was and eventually Edward Meade made another bid of £101,000 and immediately Pat Kennedy increased his bid by £1,000 and kept doing it and thereby sending out the message that he was determined to get his way. When Pat bid £111,000 Edward Meade remained still and the Auctioneer brought his

Hammer down and the property was ours, the amazing thing about this purchase was that we had already offered £120,000 and had been turned down but more importantly we were prepared to go as far as £250,000 which was the going price for a good Petrol Station Site. Later I was told by Eamon Brandon my former boss in Conoco that they had their Architect look at that site and were told it was too small for a Petrol Station.

When you lodge a Planning Application you must also display a Site Notice for 30 days where you intend to build giving details of what you intend to build and where the Application can be inspected, we put up the Site Notice and lodged our Planning application, about 3 weeks later we got a letter from the County Council to say their Inspector had been out to check our Site notice and it was not on display so we must put up a new Notice and the planning Application will only start from the day the new Site Notice goes up, some objector or vandal had torn down our Site Notice and this caused us a delay of 6 weeks. Planning Permission was granted but there is a 30 day period when interested parties can lodge an objection and there was one objection at 4.30 pm on the 30th day, it was from Paul Massey who owns a local Cost Cutters Supermarket and he claimed it would damage his business if we were allowed to go ahead with our plans. Mick and I paid a visit to Paul and asked him to withdraw his objection as ours would be a completely different business to his and should not do him any harm, and anyway we believed his grounds for objecting were certain to fail but it was costing us a lot of money. Paul said my grounds for objecting may not be good enough to stop you but they will cause you long delays and it's not my problem if it's costing you money so I'm not going to withdraw my objection. We finally received Planning Permission but the objection caused a 6 months delay and cost us a lot of money to employ a planning Consultant to handle the appeal on our behalf. We often wondered if the same objector had been responsible for tearing down our Site Notice.

Rathcoole Site

Around this time Mick heard about a Site that was for sale near where he lives in Rathcoole Village, there was controversy over the Site because previously a man who wanted to buy it had made a Planning

Application for a Petrol Station without the owner's permission and the Planning Application was turned down so now the owner was trying to sell a Site which had a failed Planning Application to its name and the owner was very unhappy about this. We managed to buy this Site for £62,000 and set about getting Planning Permission for a Petrol Station. In Rathcoole there is a very well organised group of people who see it as their duty to object to any new development in the Village, our Site had a derelict Cottage on it which was an eyesore but for their own strange reasons they would prefer to have a derelict Cottage on the main Street than a Petrol Station with a convenience Store, they said our Station would create extra traffic and cause a safety hazard close to the School. The County Council accepted their argument and refused permission for our Petrol Station so we wondered what we could do with the site, the fact that the refusal was on the grounds of safety to do with traffic ruled out any other type of shop so we thought a block of Apartments might succeed, when we were on our third set of Apartment drawings we had a call from our Property adviser Declan Stone of Jackson Stops Auctioneers who said he was in contact with Tesco who were developing small local shops around the country and they might be interested in our site in Rathcoole. We were surprised at this because of the fact that our plans had been turned down on grounds of safety but we thought if Tesco want to have a go that's up to them, we sold it to Tesco and got on with our other projects, today there is a Tesco shop where we were told our Petrol Station would cause a traffic hazard, I wonder how Tesco got around the local objectors. This was at the peak of our growth period and as well as the Rathcoole project we were in the middle of building our Station at Taylors Lane and were about to start building the Car Showrooms which we later leased to Stuarts Garages.

Building Problems

Mick Hayden deserves credit for locating all the Properties we bought and was very much involved in each building project but it fell to me to oversee the development of each Site, I worked closely with Architects, Engineers and Builders with a visit to the building Site every day if possible and a Site meeting each week which was organised and chaired by our Architect. All of our building projects had a time limit built in and a QS (Quantity Surveyor) who produced a Bill of Quantities at the start of the job and then worked closely with the Builders QS to keep costs under control, most of our job's went smoothly and on time but we had a most unusual problem during the building of our Petrol Station at the Square in Tallaght, The building on this site was 2 storey with Offices on top and a Shop below, when the Walls of the Building were almost at full height our Architect Paul Joyce rang me and said I have to meet you but not on the job, He came to my office and said Jim you won't believe this but "**your building is in the wrong place**" Paul explained that the whole building was the correct shape but it was out of place by one Metre and to make it worse it is taking up space of the Forecourt where we could not afford to lose any. All building work has stopped until we know what is to be done about it.

When you have a Site of a ½ Acre you would think the loss of one Metre won't make much difference but we were trying to make our Building as large as possible and still have enough space for our largest Petrol Tanker to drive round so that he does not have to reverse on to the road when finished offloading, in addition to that we wanted an Automatic Car Wash as well as a bay for Hand Washing Car's. We had worked out what we believed was the least amount of space needed for Cars moving in and out of the Forecourt and if we had to lose some space that would be the last place we wanted to lose it. Paul arranged a meeting with Martin Glynn the Engineer for the Builders who were Collen Construction; a very well respected Civil Engineering firm who would normally have building jobs much larger than ours but we just happened to get them when they were between jobs and so they gave us a good price to get the job. At the meeting Martin Glynn said that when his Foreman Vincent Lee was setting out the site the Drawings he had to use did not have enough detail and this was the reason for the mistake so it was not the builders fault. Paul Joyce produced a long list of drawings which had been given to the builder and signed for before work started along with a letter which said that if the drawings were not adequate he would be happy to produce any additional drawings requested by the Builder, no such request had ever been made so as far as Paul was concerned it was the builders fault but what was to be done about it. Martin Glynn said they were not accepting responsibility and were not doing any more work until **we** decided what was to be done about it. We got legal advice and it was that everything seemed to be in our favour but if we end up in court it depends on the Judge that is on duty that day and there is no guarantee that we will win. What are the options, 1? Leave the building as it is and manage as best we can. 2. Instruct the builder to knock it down and start again and see what his response is. 3. Try to negotiate with the Builder.

The job was stopped for 3 days when we asked Martin Glynn to meet and see if we can find a solution to the problem. We met Martin in Jury's hotel, Shane Mulhall who had been a financial adviser to us some years back agreed to act as mediator and listened to both sides of the argument, we let Martin have his say and when it became clear that he was sticking to his Guns we told him out straight that we were standing firmly behind our Architect and we were satisfied he had done everything that he was supposed to do. But we did not want the delay of a Court Case or of having to knock the Building and start again so we were willing to accept compensation and let the job go on. In the end we agreed to accept £25,000 off the contract price and the job got moving again.

Family reunion 1984, l to r Neds wife Mary, Ned
Momholding the Cummins, Pender family crest

Pats parents Eddie and May Boileau on holiday in
Trabolgan 1989

Mick Hayden and Me at the opening of
The Primo Diner on greenhills road

Mick and me opening our new petrol station at taylors lane

Chapter 14

Problems with South Dublin County Council

In 1995 we heard that South Dublin County Council was planning to change the Roads network leading to one side of The Square Shopping Centre and adjacent to our Petrol Station which was trading very successfully. I contacted Mr. John Henry who was head of the Roads Department and requested a meeting to discuss the proposed Changes, (he is now head of the Dublin Transportation Authority). It was to be the first of many meetings on this matter because the Road changes would divert Traffic away from our Site and we thought it was bound to damage our Business. John Henry said South Dublin County Council would give us a piece of Land which would be vacant when the Road was moved and we could extend on to this extra ground or maybe even build a second Petrol Station facing on to the new road, we employed Engineers and proposed alternative Road changes that would not have a negative effect on our business but they were rejected by the Council. Matters became more complicated when one particular County Councillor proposed that the Luas Tram Line be extended to the Old Bawn area and his Motion was passed, this was important for us because the proposed route for the Old Bawn Line was right through the piece of ground which had been offered to us and it would make it very difficult to build and operate a Petrol Station with a Tram passing your entrance and exit every 6 minutes. When the Council began to back track on some of the commitments given we proceeded to take legal action, we were advised by an excellent Senior Council called Joe Finnegan who later became a Judge in the High Court and I think he was appointed to the Supreme Court before retiring. Joe was a chain smoker and all our meetings were held in his Chambers where he would smoke nonstop all the way through a meeting which sometimes went on for hours, a Solicitor who acted for us and knew Joe well told a very interesting storey which I have no reason to disbelieve, the storey is that in his spare time Joe is a Motor Bike enthusiast and on one occasion he and a bunch of friends took their Bikes to Spain to do some touring, they stopped at a Roadside Taverna and were having a meal when another crowd of bikers pulled up and one of the other Bikers asked if he could sit at Joes table, Joe said of course and was chatting away when the other man asked him what he worked at, Joe said I'm a Barrister, a Senior Council in Ireland and the other Man said, that sounds very interesting and he wanted to know more about what it was like to be a Barrister, after a while Joe asked the other man what he worked and the man said, **I'm Juan Carlos and I'm the King of Spain.**

When it came to dealing with our problem Joe told us in a simple matter of fact sort of way that the Council had no chance of winning if this case went to Court and that when his opinion is handed to the County Council they will be told that there are only a few other Barristers in Ireland who would know as much about this type of law as Joe Finnegan and they will be advised to settle with us, Fortunately many commitments had been given in writing in response to the many Letters I wrote to many different Officials in different Departments. It took 10 years but we eventually won our Case in the High Court in front of Justice Mary Lafoy when we were awarded the Piece of Land under a Lease and compensation for damage to our Business.

Business development

While all this development and expansion was going on we still had our core business which was the Heating Oil and Diesel Oil to domestic and commercial customers in Dublin Kildare Meath and Wicklow, at one stage we were probably the largest independent Oil Company in the greater Dublin area so much so that in 1995 we had to invest £200,000 in new Trucks for our Fleet. We had an annual turnover of around €13,000,000 and were in the top 1000 Irish Companies for many years, Our Petrol Stations were all open 24 hours 7 days a week with Shops and Car Washing available round the Clock so the Business was very Labour intensive, at our peak we had 125 employees and that requires a lot of Managers because someone has to be responsible when something goes wrong, even in the middle of the Night.

Serious Incidents Mick and I were always available but were seldom called unless it was a serious matter like when my Son Robert was on night duty at the Greenhill's Station and had a Gun put to his head by a Robber, I think Robert was more excited than frightened and got over it quickly. Another night the Fire Brigade had to be called because the attendant refused to hand over The Cash and the Robber poured Petrol into the serving Hatch and set it alight, the Fire Brigade got there very quickly and the damage was minimal, apart from shock the Attendant was uninjured.

Fatal incidents

July 21 1999, about 4 am a Man came into our Station at the Square and filled 2 x 5 litre cans with Petrol; he paid for the Petrol and then drove to the Tallaght Garda Station where he walked in with the Cans of Petrol and emptied it around the Waiting Room and then took out 2 flares which he ignited and told the Garda on duty he had 2 minutes to get out, the Garda called to Sergeant Andy O'Callanan who came out with a fire extinguisher and sprayed it on the man, the flares were lit and dropped on the floor causing an explosion which slammed the door to the inside office shut trapping Sergeant O'Callanan, the man escaped but was later captured and arrested, Sergeant O'Callanan was taken to Tallaght Hospital where he was pronounced dead at 5.31 am. The man was angry following a recent confrontation with some of the local Gardai, our CCTV Camera's on our Forecourt had recorded the Man filling the 2 Cans with Petrol and paying for it and this footage became important Evidence for the Gardai when it came to the Court Case, in court the man's defence was that he only wanted to commit suicide, he was convicted of manslaughter and sentenced to 15 years in Prison. Sergeant O'Callanan was posthumously awarded the Scott Medal for bravery.

Another night there was an argument on the Forecourt at the Square between a Man and Woman in one Car and a Man in another Car, they drove off but when they had only gone about 100 yards the 2nd Car overtook the 1st Car and forced it on to the Footpath, the driver of the 2nd Car got out with a Gun, walked up to the 1st Car and shot the driver and passenger dead, once again our CCTV footage was used by the Gardai in preparing their Case.

Funny Incidents, About 1am my Phone rings, it's David Trappe one of our Night time Operators asking me to come to our Station at the Square, what happened was, a van pulled in and a young boy got out and came over to the serving hatch and asked for some Groceries, David recognised him as a Traveller boy who was barred from our Shops for stealing on many occasions and so he refused to serve him, the young boy persisted but David continued to say no. The boy went back and got in to the van and his Mother came over to the hatch and said "why won't you serve my Son", David repeated that the Boy was barred for stealing so the Woman said "will you serve me then" David said yes of course I will, you are not barred from our Shop, she asked for a Dozen Eggs and paid for them, she then stood back and smashed all 12 Eggs against the Glass of the Serving Hatch and all the egg ran down the Window and into the Tray that is used for taking in Money and passing out the Groceries making it impossible to serve any other Customer even if he could see them through the Glass covered with the Whites and the Yokes of 12 broken eggs, for security reasons he could not open the Door to come out and clean the Glass so our busy Shop was temporarily closed until I came down to assist him.

Another night David was on duty and a Traveller Man came to the Window but again David Recognised him as having been barred from the Shop and he refused to serve him, This Traveller was big and had terrified our Staff on many occasions and his wife had assaulted one of our Station Managers by punching her in the Face, the Man went to his car and came back with a Wheel Brace and began trying to smash the Glass of the Serving Hatch and demanding to be served. Even though the glass was Bullet Proof David was concerned that it would eventually give way so he pressed the Panic Button and removed the drawer with the money and ran into a back Room and locked himself in. He just sat there until everything went quiet and even then he waited for a few minutes before sticking his Head out. He went back to the Serving Hatch and looked round but could see no one until he looked down to the ground where he could see the culprit lying on the ground unconscious. Just then a Garda Squad Car arrived and although David had no idea how the man came to be on the ground the Gardai knew him as a serious trouble maker and took him away in their Car to Tallaght Hospital. What had happened was that a man on his way home from work as a Security Guard had called in to buy Petrol as the man with the Wheel Brace was trying to smash the Glass, the Security Guard told him to stop and when the man with the Wheel Brace continued the Security Man punched him so hard he fell to the ground hitting his head and lay there. As there was no one at the hatch to serve Petrol the security Man got into his car and drove off, he called in later that day and confirmed what had happened but said he did not want to be involved any further so long as everyone was ok.

Saint Bernard

In the early years of our Company Mick and I were called upon to fill many roles and one role for me was as the extra Driver when needed, Drivers get into all sort of situations and I had my share of them, some were funny and some not so funny. On one occasion I had completed a delivery of Heating Oil to an elderly Couple in Churchtown and they offered me a Cup of Tea, as I was drinking my Tea the old Lady went into the Kitchen and forgot to close the Door after her, the Dog had been locked in the Kitchen and he came Bounding up to me, It was a St Bernard and its only when you are close to a fully grown St Bernard that you realise how big they really are, from what I knew of Dogs the St Bernard is not a dangerous breed and so I was not afraid of him, he rushed up to me and jumped up putting his two front Paws on both my Shoulders and began licking my face, the old Couple thought I was frightened and they joined forces to pull him off me, I managed to finish my Tea but when I stood up to go he rushed at me from Behind forcing his huge Head in between my legs and kept going until he had me sitting on his Back, at this stage my legs were off the Ground and I lost my Balance and fell sideways on to the Couch, the dog swung round and was back up with his 2 Paws on top of me, once again the old Couple Joined forces to pull the dog off me and held him until I was out the Door and away.

Doberman

I walked up the Driveway to a House in Sutton and was met half way by 2 Doberman Dog's; they were quite friendly and trotted beside me up to the Door of the House, I rang the Bell a few times but there was no answer so I decided to leave and call back later, when I turned to walk out the Driveway the 2 Dogs were sitting in my Path and as

I approached the began snarling and stripping their Teeth, I moved sideways to walk around them but they moved to stay in front of me and continued to snarl at me, this situation was scary and was not one I had encountered before, while I don't scare easily with Dogs there was no way I was going to put those Dogs to the test by trying to walk past them. I walked back to the House and rang the Door Bell again and this time it was answered, the Lady of the house had been out in the back Garden and was not aware of my presence, when the delivery was finished the Dogs followed me out to the truck but made no attempt to stop me, it appears that when they saw me with their Master they were happy to let me go.

Bad Debt collection

Another Doggy encounter occurred one day when I was on a Bad Debt collecting mission, this customer had paid for his Oil with a Cheque that bounced and when we contacted him he promised to drop in to our Office and pay in cash but that never happened, when all else failed we came up with a plan that one of our Drivers would call to his House every single Day until he came up with the Money, they would never answer the door although we were satisfied there was someone in the House, it was my turn to call as I was doing Deliveries in that area. The Man in question had a couple of Mini Buses and had a contract for transporting one of the top Singers and his Band around the Country so we were satisfied that he could afford to pay and were determined not to let him away without paying. On this occasion I could see someone inside but they would not answer the Door no matter how many times I rang the Bell, what could I do!.

I decided to see if the side Door was open and maybe there would be someone in the Back Garden, the side door was made of steel and I could not see over it so I grabbed the Handle and pulled it towards me, when it was opened by just a few inches a Doberman lunged at me snarling like the Hound of the Baskervilles, I swear that if I had a bad heart I would have been Dead on the spot but my instincts took over and I slammed the Door shut and caught the Dogs head between the door and the Door Frame, the Dog was howling but I was afraid to let him go as he might come at me again, just then a Woman's voice said let the dog go and I will open the Door, I let go of the Door and the Woman pulled in the Dog and asked me what did I want, I said I'm' here to collect Money for Primo Oil and I won't leave until I get it, she said I don't have the Money but I will get my Husband on the Phone and you can talk to him about it, The Husband came on the phone and apologised for the delay in paying us but said he would call to our Office tomorrow with Cash, I said OK but if you don't show up I will keep coming Back until you pay us. He came in next day and paid his Bill and was told that any future Deliveries would have to be paid by cash in advance, we never heard from him again.

Charles Mitchell

One delivery I always looked forward to doing was to the late Charles Mitchell, former RTE newsreader and his Wife who lived in Dundrum, they were both the nicest gentlest people you could hope to meet, they would always give you a cup of tea and some fruit cake, and they had some Dogs which were of the same disposition as themselves, gentle and friendly.

Big Heap of Shite Pat and I had been shopping in Clondalkin with our 4 Children and when we came back to our Car it was blocked in by another Car which was double parked, we thought surely the driver won't be long so we sat back to wait, 20 minutes later a Man and woman with 2 children strolled up and got into the other Car and moved it far enough to let us get out, they never apologised or even acknowledged our presence, normally in a situation like this Pat is hopping mad and I tell her to keep Calm but this time I am at boiling point by the time the other driver came back and Pat is telling me to calm down. As I drove slowly past the other Car I wound down my Window and said to the Man who was in the driving Seat, "your nothing but a big Heap of Shite" and drove on quite satisfied with myself that I had put him in his place. I was not prepared for what happened next, as I got to the exit from the Car Park the traffic in front had stopped and so I had no choice but to stop as well, in my rear view Mirror I saw the offending motorist Get out of his Car and run up to our Car, I tried to wind up my window but the other man was too quick, as he got to our Car he was shouting, you dirty fu*   *   *r, you embarrassed me in front of my family and he began punching me through the Window, my Wife and Children were with me so I can assure you I was also embarrassed, the other Man managed to get my door opened and tried to get in at me but just in time I managed to get my foot into his Chest and my hand into his Face, we struggled in that position for some time as he continued throwing punches at me until somehow I managed to push him away and get the Car Door closed again, the traffic in front had moved on and I tore out of that Car Park like a scalded Cat, Pat could not stop laughing as I tried to find some way to explain to the children what that had been all about,

Forgetfulness as I read my notes and write my story I am amazed at how easy it is to lose touch once you move away from Home, at my Mothers Wake I was chatting to my first Cousin Jim Connolly when I said to him, Jim who is that Man Behind you, he looks familiar, Jim said that's my brother Michael, another day I was talking to a friend Tom Fox about old times when I said by the way Tom who did you get married to, Tom laughed and said, your first Cousin Mary Pender.

Chapter 15

Old Man injured on Forecourt

One day a Man who was 78 years old drove on to our Forecourt and got out of his Car and started walking towards the Shop entrance, just then a teenage Boy came flying in on his Bike and crashed into the old Man and knocked him to the Ground, the injured Man was unable to move so we called for an Ambulance to take him to Hospital where an X-Ray showed his Leg to be badly broken. Although we had not been involved in the accident we expected the injured Man would Sue for Damages and sure enough we got a Solicitors Letter accusing us of negligence and failing to exercise proper control on our Property, we had the Name and address of the15 year old Cyclist who had caused the accident but thought there would be very little use trying to make him pay for the damage which in Money terms we expected to be substantial, then someone from our Insurance Company posed the question "I wonder does the Boy's Parents have a household Insurance Policy", we inquired about this and they did have a Policy and the Bike was mentioned on the Policy document. Our Insurance Company wrote to the other Insurance Company outlining the details of the accident and asked them were they prepared to accept that the claim should be taken on board by them rather than by our Insurance Company, the extent of the claim was yet to be determined. After due time for consideration the other Insurance Company agreed to handle the Case and agreed to indemnify us against any damages that may be awarded to the injured Man, it was an unusual twist to an accident that we were sure would result in large compensation and would probably be levied against us when we went to renew our policy but this story had a better ending than we expected.

RING FINGER INJURY

When you have around 125 employees on the payroll you expect to have some on the Job Accidents, some of them we were certain were faked and were difficult to contest like a claim from one of our drivers for a back injury from lifting a heavy object, a lot of resources can go into dealing with an accident whether you believe it to be genuine or not. One accident we had no such doubt about because the damage was obvious. One of our Shop Staff members was stocking Shelves one day and was taking Boxes of goods from the Store to the Shop when the accident happened. We had an excellent General Manager Killian Tallon who was very good on safety and training of Staff. He had a Notice posted in the Store which stated clearly that Staff working in the Store must never wear Rings or other Jewellery, the Notice also stated that when removing Goods from the higher Shelves a Step Ladder must be used and there was one available in the Store and all staff had also been told verbally of those safety procedures, unfortunately the lady in question failed on two counts to follow the instructions in the Notice, she failed to remove her Ring and she failed to use a Step Ladder when removing Goods from the top Shelf, instead of using a Ladder she put her Foot on the bottom Shelf and using both Hands pulled herself up to where she could reach the Box of Goods with one Hand while holding on with the other Hand, just then her Foot slipped off the bottom Shelf and as she was falling she held on with the hand which included her Ring Finger. The ring got caught on a corner of the upright Shelf Support and stripped her Finger to the Bone.

My Office was upstairs in the same Building and I was asked to come down right away. When I came down the injured Woman was in the Canteen and all the skin on her Ring Finger was in a heap at the tip of the Finger. I immediately put her in my Car and took her to Tallaght Hospital which was only a few minutes away, at A&E she was taken in quickly and the Doctor said he would pull the skin back down along the Finger and stitch it back together again but after working on it for over an hour he decided against this course of action, instead he said "we don't have the expertise here for dealing with this injury," she will have to go to St James's Hospital in the City Centre where they will decide what to do about it. They said they would take her in an Ambulance but then said it would be at least an hour before there would be an Ambulance available to take her. I was not prepared to wait that long so

I took her in my Car again and brought her to St James's hospital where they pulled the Skin back into place and stitched it up. Within 2 days the Doctor in charge said this procedure had been a failure and said they would have to remove the top 2 Digit's of the damaged finger. Within a week the Doctor said this procedure had not worked out as planned and they would need to remove the remainder of the Finger but worse than that they would have to continue down into the hand and remove the section of bone, I think they removed it right down to where it is attached to the wrist and then pulled her 3 remaining fingers together which was intended to give better control when the hand eventually healed. The injured Woman got Compensation but never came back to Work with us. This accident caused me more distress than any other in all my years in business.

Unemployed Man Damaged Petrol Pump

A Man drove on to our forecourt one day and collided with one of the Petrol Pumps doing damage that came to about £1,300, he was very sorry for what he had done but had no Insurance and pleaded with the Manager not to report him to the Gardai, he had a Wife and 6 children and had no job so he did not know how he was going to pay for the damage, the Manager rang me for advice and I said if you are satisfied about his identity and where he lives let him go but arrange for him to come to our Head office tomorrow and I will meet him with you. Next day the Man came in along with his Wife and the first thing he wanted to do was admit his guilt and say how sorry he was for causing so much damage, both he and his Wife were very ordinary looking and seemed quite intelligent but it transpired that not only was he out of work but even though he was 28 years old he had never had a job in his life and neither had his wife ever worked outside the Home, they had both grown up in Homes where both Parents were unemployed and so there was no work ethic in the Home for them to follow. After a while we broke for Coffee and I said to our Station Manager, maybe there's a chance for us to do a good deed and get paid for our damaged Pump at the same time, so we offered the man a job working for us and suggested that we could stop a small amount from his wages each week until the damage was paid for. The Wages offered was £120 a week, his immediate response was, at present I collect £100 a week on Social Welfare so you are asking me to come and work for £20 a week and I might lose some of my other benefits as well. We said, no, we are offering you £120 a week to work 40 hours for us, this was the going rate for the job so we were not looking to take advantage of him in any way, we told him of a new scheme for long term unemployed persons where he could have a new job for some months before his dole would be reduced and then some more months before it would be stopped, but he said, will I Eventually lose my dole, I said yes of course you will but you will have wages so you won't need the Dole, he said I can't afford to lose my Dole no matter how much you pay me, that's my security for my children. I suggested it would help his self esteem to know that he was finally able to provide for his family rather than be always putting your hand out to the Social Welfare for everything you need, it made no difference. Here was a 28 year old Man who had become so accustomed to being looked after by the State that he had never developed the frame of mind that if we bring children into the world there is a responsibility on us to provide for them, as far as he was concerned it was just a matter of knowing about all the ways he could claim benefits for him and his family, the bigger tragedy is that he had no work ethic to pass on to his 6 children and they would now be in their 20s, I can't help wondering what if any contribution they have made to society or have they grown up with the same mindset as their parents. In the end we came to the conclusion that he was a hopeless case, we saw no point in taking legal action against him even though we knew we would get a judgement against him in Court, we also knew that that would be the end of it because he would still have nothing to give us and it would have cost us a lot more money so we put it down to experience.

Eye Accident., In 1982 I suffered an injury to my left Eye when I was visiting my Mother in Carbury, I took my Children for a walk in the Wood behind Mom's House and as we walked through Dense Bushes I pushed a Branch out of the way but it sprung back and hit me in the Left Eye causing great pain, the vision in that Eye was affected immediately so I took the Children and went back to Mom's House where I asked my wife Pat to drive Home, Mom's immediate reaction was to think of my older Brother Ned who had lost one Eye through an accident when he was only 3 Years old and mom was worried that the same thing was going to happen again. In the Eye and Ear hospital they said I should stay in overnight but after a few Days they said the Lens of my Eye was so badly damaged they would have to remove the Lens and when it had healed up They would give me a Contact Lens, that plan never worked because it always caused pain putting in the contact lens so I stopped using it. I continued for about 2 years with very little sight in my left Eye but then the muscles in the bad Eye had become weak and that eye had developed a life of its own and would be looking in a different direction to the right Eye so I went back to see Professor Tomkin who had carried out the first procedure on my Eye but he had died in the meantime so I saw Mr Cassidy who inserted a Glass Lens into my Left Eye and that restored my vision to about 60% of what it should be and it's still at that today.

While I was in the Eye and Ear Hospital I managed to get a Private Room and one Day there was a lot of activity in the Corridor outside my Room with 2 plain Clothes Police Men standing there with Machine Guns ready for use, I looked out the window and there were armed Soldiers in the Grounds of the Hospital, a Nurse came in to me and I asked her, what's going on, she said Eddie Gallagher is coming in for treatment to one of his Eyes, Eddie Gallagher was in the IRA and was in Prison for his part in the kidnapping and holding hostage of Dr. Tiede Herrema who was CEO of Ferenka, a Dutch owned Tyre Company based in Limerick, Gallagher and 21 Year old Marion Coyle held Dr. Herrema For 36 days which included an 18 Day siege at a House in Monasterevan, their plan was to be paid a large ransom by Ferenka. Gallagher was sentenced to 20 years and got out in 1990; Coyle was sentenced to 15 years and got out in 1985. At the time of my Eye injury I had a full Beard and my Mother used to say, will get rid of that Beard, you look just like Eddie Gallagher who also had a full Beard. Gallagher was brought in to the Room next to me in Hand cuffs, I was standing in the Corridor and as he passed he looked at me and did a double take and looked again as if he saw a likeness in me. There was some confusion at the entrance to the hospital when my neighbour came to visit me, the Guards were stopping and checking the identity of everyone as they entered, my Neighbour who came to visit me was also called Jim Cummins and he had a Beard like me and his address was the same as mine except for the House number, they held him for about 10 minutes before allowing him enter the Corridor where Eddie Gallagher and I were staying.

My Finger Accident, I was working on a Petrol Pump at our Greenhills Road Petrol Station checking the tension of the Belt which drove the Pump when it was started accidently, my index finger on the right Hand was caught between the Belt and the Pulley and top of my Finger was severed. The Manager of the Station Paddy Howe was with me and he calmly walked with me into the back Office where my Business Partner Mick Hayden was at his Desk, I showed Mick my Finger and asked him to drive me to the Hospital, we had just left in Mick's Car when I realised we had come without the top of my Finger so I used the Car Phone to ring Paddy Howe and ask him to collect the missing Finger and follow us in his Car to the Hospital, I then rang Dr Andrew Jordan who was both our Family Doctor and Company Doctor, I said Andy I have a problem, I just cut the top off my Finger and I am on my way to St James's Hospital, Andy said, well what do you want me to do. I said can you ring the Hospital and let them know I'm on my way and maybe they can put my Finger back together again, Andy said where is the other half of your Finger, I said it's following us in another Car. Andy rang the Hospital and put them on notice to expect us and when we arrived Paddy Howe arrived soon after us with part 2 of my finger, unfortunately they were not able to put it back together again and because the cut was at an angle the Doctor had to square up my Finger by cutting away some of the Bone which was protruding, he did this under local Anaesthetic and it was just like having my Nail clipped, the Nail was all gone but the Doctor said we just might be lucky and have a new Nail grow back and he was right, it did grow back, it's not a perfect Nail but it's better than none, one problem I still have with it is the cold, there is very poor circulation and when we were on our all Night climb to the Summit of Mount Kilimanjaro in –18c temperature's, it was impossible to keep it warm and it was very painful for many hours that Night.

Sale of Business

In the year 2000 Mick and I agreed to Dispose of some of our Business and following negotiations with several Oil Companies we leased our Petrol Stations to Statoil (now Topaz) but decided to keep the Heating Oil Business ourselves and continued to trade as Primo Oil, in 2006 we sold the heating oil Business to Jones Oil who continued to operate it as Primo Oil but now in 2012 it has been fully amalgamated into Jones Oil and the Name Primo Oil has finally disappeared from Public view 29 Years after we rescued it from the Ashes of PMPA.

Chapter 16

My Wife, Patricia Mary Bernadette, <u>(Maiden name Boileau)</u>

The 19 year old red Haired Beauty which I fell in love with on a blind date in 1967 and am still very much in love with 45 years later proved to be very intelligent and skilled at whatever she decided to do, Pat is the 3rd of 6 children, she has 3 Sisters, Yvonne, Phyllis now know as Kim, and Marie, she has 2 Brothers Eddie and Raymond. When she was only 21 in Australia she was making her own Clothes with a Sewing Machine I bought for her, she was also an expert knitter and created her own Designs and Patterns for the Clothes she knitted for our own Family and also for sale, she seems to know as much about Drugs and Medicine as a family Doctor and can diagnose an Illness as good as any Doctor, she is very rarely wrong with her diagnoses', people who know her would have great confidence in her opinion. Pat took up Line Dancing in the early 90s and became an expert at it, when she began to tire of Line Dancing she took up 10 Pin Bowling and became very good at that having successfully represented Ireland on many occasions and won the following Medals,

-2002, Gold in the Irish Championship All Events

-2008, Bowling Triple Crown in Guernsey

- Gold in the Ladies Singles,
- Gold in the High Game, (highest score)
- Gold in High Series, over 5 games
- Gold in the Ladies Doubles with Bernie Moriarty,
- 2010 A Bronze Medal for Ireland with Yvonne Randall in the European Championships.

Pat is an excellent Cook and really shows her best form when preparing for a large Crowd, every Christmas Day she invites all our Children and Grand Children to Dinner, she prepares every little detail to the point of perfection and produces a Banquette fit for a President, she will also do that several times during the year and even though its informal she must have everything perfect and the family love it.

Apart from having 5 Babies, (our first Child only lived 3 Days), Pat has had more than her share of medical problems

- At 3 years old she had to have a Hernia removed.
- At age 29 Pat had another Hernia removed.
- At only 32 years old she had a Hysterectomy,
- At age 37 Pat slipped on ice and fell on to her Face and broke her Jaw Bone, it had to be pinned together with Staples.
- At 42 her Ovaries were removed.
- At 43 Pat had an operation on her right Hand for Carpel Tunnel (Trapped Nerve).
- At 55, Pat had a Thyroid Operation, Half her Thyroid was removed.
- At 62, Pat had Heart problems; she has a leaky Heart Valve.
- At age 63 Carpel Tunnel Operation on Left Hand.
- Also at 63 she had her appendix removed,
- Also at age 63 Pat had Cataract Operations and had Artificial lens implanted in both Eyes.
- Also at age 63 Pat climbed Mount Kilimanjaro the World's highest free standing Mountain, Ben Nevis the highest Mountain in Great Britain, Carrantuohill the highest Mountain in Ireland and numerous other Mountains in Ireland and Great Britain.

Pat has a Chronic Back problem, when she was 33 years old she was diagnosed as having Premature Ageing on her spine which is incurable and requires regular Physiotherapy, she has Osteoarthritis in her Neck, Back and Knees and when we climbs Mountains she usually needs Pain killing Tablets to get her through the Day. Because I snore so much Pat has to take Sleeping Pills to get a night's sleep, she is fitter and stronger than she has ever been and getting fitter each time we climb another Mountain, so I wonder what she will be like at age 90 or 95, will I be able to keep up with her then!.

Pat's Family Name **Boileau** is French and was brought to Ireland by the Huguenots who came here to avoid having their heads cut off by the Guillotine. On April 13th 1685 King Louis XIV abolished a Law called "The Edict of Nantes" which had allowed for Religious Tolerance throughout France, without the protection of this law life became intolerable for the Huguenots and thousands of them fled, some with the Name Boileau came to Ireland, there are still very small numbers with that Name in Ireland, for example in the 01 Dublin Telephone Directory for 2012 there are only 3 **Boileau** entries and they are all related to Pat.

Our Children

The Birth and Death of our first Child Brian James is covered on page 60,

Robert Edward, now known as Rob was born on 21st July 1972, I was driving Oil Tankers in Jet Oil at the time and I called in to the hospital on my way home from the West of Ireland having parked my Truck on the Street outside St James's Hospital, You could not Park there now as the Luas Tramline runs along St James's Street and there is no parking allowed, when he was only a few weeks old he began what is called projectile Vomiting, that is where everything in his Stomach comes up and out like water shooting out of a Hose, the cause of the problem is a Gut in the Stomach gets into a Knot and nothing can be digested, The condition is Called Pyloric Stenosis. It requires an operation and is straight forward when it has been diagnosed but we had never heard of it and it was a very worrying time for us. Robert has 2 children Carrie and James from his Marriage to Gretta. Rob and Gretta are separated now and Rob has a New Partner Aisling who shares his passion for sports, they both compete in Triathlon's and Rob is currently training for an Iron Man Triathlon in Bolton UK which takes place on his 40th Birthday 21st July 2012, the Iron Man consists of, a 3.8km swim, a 180 km cycle and then a full Marathon which is 42km, all without stopping, Robs first Iron Man took him 12 hours 30 minutes, he keeps improving and his best time so far is 9 hours 40 minutes. His love of cycling goes back to when he was very young, when he was only 4 years old and we were Living in Clondalkin I told him to follow me on his Bike and we went for a 4 mile round trip cycle through the Traffic in Main St. Clondalkin and on up to the Green Isle Hotel on the Naas Road and back Home again, Rob was tired when we got home but was delighted to tell his Mom about his adventure. For his 12ᵀᴴ Birthday I gave him his first driving lesson and by the time he was old enough to take his driving test he was an accomplished driver and passed his driving test at age 17, the first time he went for it.

Rob spent some years working in Primo Oil but always had an ambition to do his own thing and when he was only 26 years old he told me he had spotted a need for a good Bicycle Shop in Clondalkin and wanted my opinion on his plan to open a Shop in the Mill Shopping Centre, I gave him the benefit of my experience and arranged an Architect and a Builder to make alterations and helped him get his first Cycle Shop open, I went Guarantor for him with the Bank but the need for that is long gone. He opened a second Shop in a brand new Building in Naas and kept it going for 5 years but there was never sufficient footfall in the area to provide enough customers to make it profitable and he eventually reached agreement with his Landlord and closed it to concentrate on the Shop in Clondalkin, but the Clondalkin Shop was never going to be big enough to match his ambitions and together with his new Partner Aisling they opened a large new Shop in Fonthill Retail Park near Liffy Valley Shopping Centre, this was big enough to cater for the full Triathlon sport scene and their slogan is "The Best Triathlon and Bike Shop in the Country" and I'm sure it's an apt description for it. That Shop was opened less than 12 months when Rob told me, "Dad the new Shop isn't big enough but the Unit next door is available and it's 60% larger so we are going to move into it" what do you think, while I was considering whether this was a good idea Rob and Aisling were already planning the move and within a few Weeks they had moved Shop for the second time in a year. Aisling is what's known as an Ultra Runner, she runs in races of 100km or more all over the World and is the best in Ireland at this particular sport, having competed in several Iron Man Races she has decided to concentrate on Ultra Running as that's what she enjoys most. She competed in and won a 24 hour nonstop race in July 2012. The winner needed to complete 100 Miles (161 km) inside 24 hours and Aisling had done 161 km in 21 hours and was so far ahead of the next Female competitor that even though the other Girl kept going for 24 hours she Was still nowhere near Aisling in terms of Miles/km so Aisling was still the winner. Rob is hoping to have a good enough time in the UK Iron Man in July 2012 to qualify for the World Championship which takes place in Hawaii in October 2012. Rob neither drinks nor smokes but puts all his energies into his sport and his business.

I can now confirm that Rob has qualified for the World Championship in Hawaii which takes place on 13ᵗʰ October 2012, Pat and I went to support him in the IRONMAN UK Triathlon in Bolton and our Son Phil came along with his Partner Joanna, his finishing time was 10 hours 28 minutes which is slower than his previous Personal best but then everyone's times were slower on the Day due to heat, humidity and a difficult course.

Rob's first Ironman, Niece, Sunday 22nd June 2008

When Rob told me he was going to compete in an Iron Man Triathlon I said "what's that", Rob said, you have to **swim 3.8 km (2.4 Miles)** in the Sea, **cycle 180 km (115 miles) and run a full Marathon which is 42 km** (26.2 miles), I asked him, over how many days, Rob said, you do it all in one Day without stopping and I hope to do it in about 13 hours, but he will be happy if he can finish the Race regardless of time.

I thought this is madness, why would he take on something he knows he can't win but his satisfaction will come from being able to finish in about 13 Hours. But then I think back over Rob's working life, he was never happy to be a follower, he had to be doing his own thing, when he started his own Business from nothing he soon had to open a second shop, and then he set up his own Triathlon Club. He became very competitive and soon became expert at the sport so much so that he is now seen as a specialist and is much sought after for advice on training and nutrition, his business has increased as a result, so much that he has difficulty taking time off to train for the Iron Man. When Pat heard about what Rob was planning she said we will have to go and support him so here we are in Niece and those are my notes on the event.

We had a Car hired and picked it up at the Airport, found our Hotel, contacted Rob who also had Gretta, James and Carrie with him and met up with them for Coffee. We planned to meet Rob and family for tea but Puddin was having a bad time with her legs so we stayed in and had Dinner in our Hotel and played Cards which Puddin won, went to bed at 11.30.

Woke at 9 am, Puddin not well, she slept till 10 am when we had Breakfast in a local Restaurant, had lunch in a Beech Side Cafe with a

Rottweiler asleep under my Chair, we presumed he belonged to the owners of the restaurant and tried not to disturb him. at 4 pm we went to where registration for the race was taking place, met Rob as he was checking in, he had got a lift with someone else so we took him back to his Campsite and had a meal with the whole Family, the Meal was prepared by Rob who said it was the **Last Supper before the Race.;**

Sunday 22nd June 2008, up at 5.30, saw Rob before the swim which began at 6.30 am, there are 2300 participants and Rob told me he would stay at the back as it could be dangerous at the front for anyone but the very strongest swimmers who intend to stay at the front with a chance of winning. It's difficult to describe the scene as 2300 Men and Women charge into the Sea in a confined Space at the same time and I can understand now why Rob said it could be dangerous at the front, to me it would have been dangerous anywhere unless you wait until everyone else has gone before entering the Water. There had been a warning the previous day about the presence of Jelly Fish and Rob was looking out for them, he saw a large one directly below him and put on a spurt to get away from it but he decided that he could not do that every time he saw one so he decided not to look for any more of them but to concentrate on swimming. Rob told me he should do the swim in about 1 ½ hours but he did it in 1 hour 12 minutes and came out of the water looking strong and gave a big smile when he saw us cheering him on.

The planning that goes into this event is amazing, about 4 acres have been set aside along the Quayside for Bikes which have to be checked in the day before the Race, each Bike position has a number which has to match the number on the bike and the shirt of the participant and with 2300 participants and each one having a bike valued about €5000, that means there are Bikes to the total value of about €11,500,000 parked there overnight so that alone must be a security headache for the organisers, this area is where each competitor hands in a bag which has his race number on it, this bag contains a change of clothes from swimming to cycling, then there is another area for a change from cycling gear to running gear, and again the number on the bag must match the number on the shirt front and the Bag must be hung on a hook with the same number above it. Finally there is the after race area where each competitor hands in a bag with his race number on it and this bag contains his change of clothes for when the race is over.

Rob came out of the water at 1 hour 12 minutes still looking strong and gave us a big smile and a wave when he saw us, we then ran down to the area where he changed over to his Bike and could see him through the fence and got some pictures as he started the 180 km cycle part of the race. Most of the cycle course is over high Mountains which Rob likes, he said he should do this in 6 ½ to 7 hours so we all went back to bed and set our clocks for 10 am but we were awake well before that and went back down to where the cyclists would come in.

Rob finished his 180 k cycle in 6 hours 22 minutes which was well within the time he had allowed himself, he was still looking strong although he had been on the go for 7 hours 49 minutes, he now had to start out on a full Marathon of 40 km, this was on a 10 km circuit so we got to see him each time he came in and went out again. Each 10 k was slower than the one before. We were all there to greet him on his final run in and Puddin said we will all run in with him as he comes in to the finish and we did, when the crowd saw us running with Rob they all started cheering. As we ran towards the finish line I kept thinking, I was so proud of him that nothing I say could do Justice to how I feel about Rob's great achievement. Rob still looked strong and he was smiling as we left him to run the last 100 m and cross the finish line at 12 hours 27 minutes and 43 seconds although the pained expression on his face in the Official Picture of him crossing the Finish Line shows the effects of the enormous task he had just completed.

When Rob crossed the finish line we lost sight of him so we went down to the various check in areas but could not spot him anywhere, time dragged on for over an hour and we were getting anxious as we thought he should have been out well before now, we thought he may have gone for a massage so Carrie managed to get into the massage tent but he was not there. As we waited 3 men were taken out on stretchers and put into Ambulance's and taken away, this made our concern about Rob much worse, I told Puddin, don't worry, Rob was so strong when he finished that he has to be ok. Gretta and Puddin were seriously worried so Gretta tried to get into the Tent where she thought he might be and was told only competitors are allowed in here, Gretta would not take no for an answer and eventually they agreed to let her in to look for Rob, she found him in a medical Tent connected to an intravenous drip which he had been on for over an hour and would be on it for 30 minutes more. Gretta rang us to say Rob was ok, Puddin said

I should go in to help with Rob's Bike and Bags, she went to the Woman on the gate who had some English and asked if I could go in to help our Son who was in the medical Tent, she asked the Man beside her and he said no but Puddin would not give up and was clearly showing her anger and concern, the woman on the Gate asked her to speak slowly so that she might understand her better and eventually they agreed to let me go in.

When I found Rob he was off the Drip and sitting on a bench, he wanted to stand up and get his legs moving in case they seized up again so we walked down to find his Bike, at this stage Rob was fully alert and was talking freely as we went to find Puddin, Carrie and James, it was very emotional for a few minutes when we were all together again. Rob told us that when he was on the Drip there was a young man next to him who went into convulsions and the medical staff who were looking after Rob rushed over to help him, Rob gradually came back to his normal colour, at the same time 2 more Men were brought in on stretchers and medical staff were running from one Patient to another. Rob explained later that when he stopped and sat down he found that when he tried to get up again he could not move his legs, no matter what he did his Legs would not move, that was when he was taken to the medical tent and put on the Drip, he knew we would be worried but he was helpless and unable to do anything about it.

We thought Rob would just want to go home and get into bed but he said no, let's go get something to eat so we found a nice Restaurant where we could watch the race as the Runners were still coming in and would continue up to 11.30 pm which would be 17 hours after the start at 6.30 am. For the last hour or so we watched as a group of the race staff who were volunteers came out to meet each runner and cheer them on to the finish line, it was very exciting as some people made it with only seconds to spare as a Man on the PA system counted down the last 10 seconds up to 11.30, then the clock stopped and the light at the Finish Line went out, most Runners had a Wife, a Husband, a Son a Daughter, a Boy Friend, a Girl Friend to cheer them in, some had their children run in with them. While it was exciting to watch some Runners cross the Finish Line with seconds to spare it was heartbreaking to watch some others come in a few minutes after the Clock stopped, for the competitor the difference is that those who finish inside 16 hours get a medal saying "Iron Man Niece 2008" and a Tee Shirt that says "Ironman

Finisher". Those who don't finish or finish outside the 17 hour time limit don't get a Medal, they don't get a Tee Shirt that says Iron Man Finisher, the record of the race will show that they started but where it should show their finish time it will just say DNF which means Did Not Finish. The last Runner we saw coming in was a Woman, 45 minutes after the clock stopped, it was so sad, she had given it everything she had, she had Swam, Cycled and Ran for 17 hours and 45 minutes, she would not give up until she crossed the Finish Line and the only thing she has is her Memory and the race record that says DNF beside her name.

Rob was still on a high; we are all on a high and will be for days to come, it has been an extraordinary event in our lives and one we will never forget. In the restaurant as we watched the race come to an end I told Rob that I don't think he should ever do another Iron Man as he had nothing left to prove to anyone, not even to himself. I said the risks are substantial as we saw in the medical Tent and the men on Stretchers being taken away in Ambulances, Rob told me later that as I was telling him not to do it again he was trying to work out in his mind where was the next one he could enter, he was well and truly hooked.

As Rob came in on his 10 k circuit each time we were there to cheer him on and he told us later that this was so important to him, it gave him a great lift and an increase in energy that would stay with him for several minutes and the good feeling lasted a lot longer. There were Stations along the Route where runners could get a drink and an energy bar, as the race wore on Rob decided to walk through the Stations as a way to conserve energy and it worked for him, Rob has become an expert in training and nutrition and in today's event it stood to him greatly, he is also very well known in Triathlon circles at home and this was borne out when we were walking along the Street in Niece the Day before the race, a man stopped him and said, Rob can you help me, my chain keeps coming off. The man had a set of Allen Keys and in a few minutes Rob had solved the problem and the cyclist was on his way again, I asked Rob who was that man and Rob said I don't know him he must have seen me at some of the Races at home. There were 49 Irish competitors in this race and Rob finished 9th in the placing of the Irish group, he was happy with that. In the overall result 330 people who started the Race failed to finish. Several times Puddin remarked how well Rob carried himself while running, his Posture is very impressive, and she thinks his style is very classy.

While we consider what Rob did to be amazing the story of many others is even more amazing, there was one man over 70 who finished the race well within the time allowed, there were 4 men aged over 60 who finished in a better time than Rob and then there was the Man with only one Arm who beat Rob's time, how can a man with one Arm swim 3.8 km faster than Rob, we know he did because we saw him do it, he was the only competitor with only one arm so he stood out in the crowd, and then he beat Rob at cycling and running, a normal Racing Bike has Brakes and Gear changing levers on both Handles, there is a separate Brake Lever for the front and back Wheel's, presumably he had to get his Bike modified to have all the controls on one side of the handle Bars and even then it's hard to imagine how he could have the same control as a man with 2 Hands, on a downhill stretch in the mountains cyclists can reach speeds of 60 km per hour and at that speed the slightest error can end in disaster but this man did it and finished ahead of Rob. After the Race we saw him walking around looking none the worse for what he had been through, next day I saw him with a woman and 3 young children so he seems to be a family Man, he looked about the same age as Rob, we saw the 70 year old man being taken away in an Ambulance after the Race but we don't know how bad he was, because of the language Barrier it was hard to get information about the Race, the papers were full of articles and pictures the next Day but I could not find an English Language paper so all we could do was look at the Pictures in the papers.

Because the whole event could be followed on the Iron Man Web Site Ronnie and Jenny were more up to date with rob's progress than we were. Pat in New York was following it on his Computer as was his Son Kevin at his Home outside New York. We came home on Tuesday 24th. Rob and Family stayed on until Thursday 26th but when they went to take the 10.30 pm flight they discovered the Flight went at 10.30 am, not pm. They found a hotel and decided to stay until the next available cheap flight which was 1st July so they had a few extra days' holidays, Frank was doing a good job in the shop and I had made some lodgements so everything was ok, Much later rob introduced me to another Man who had done his first Iron Man at the same event, it was Gerry Duffy from Mullingar who has since become famous for doing 32 Marathons in 32 Counties in 32 consecutive Days. Gerry went on to compete in a Decca Iron Man; this is where each competitor has to do 10 IRONMAN'S in 10 consecutive Days. This event took place in the UK, 20 Men started the Event but only 3 finished and Gerry Duffy came 1st. It was at a 50 Km race in Donadea that Rob introduced me to this amazing Man, all Gerry wanted to talk about was how strong and fit Rob was and how he would be trying hard to keep up with him or as close as possible during today's race, at the end of each lap when Gerry stopped in for a drink he would say to me, "is he far ahead of me". Rob finished his 50km in 3.57.40, Gerry Duffy finished in 4.05.40.

The storey of the Ironman Triathlon, the first Ironman took place in Hawaii in 1979 to settle an argument at a dinner table as to who was the fittest. Runners Swimmers or Cyclists; They decided to combine all 3 sports in one race which would include the Waikiki Rough water Swim of 2.4 Miles (3.8 km), the around Oahu bike race of 115 miles (180km) and the Hawaii Marathon which was 26.2 Miles (40 km), you must finish the swim in not more than two hours twenty minutes or you will not be allowed to continue, next comes the 180 Km cycle and if you are still cycling ten and a half hours after the start you will not be allowed to continue, then you have to run a full Marathon. The clock at the finish line will stop and the light goes out 17 hours after the race began and any competitor who comes in after that will have DNF meaning did not finish after their name on the race record, everyone who finishes within the specified whether man or woman is declared an Ironman. In the first Ironman in 1979 15 Men started, 12 finished and the winner was Gordon Haller, a Taxi Driver in just under 12 hours,

Kona in Hawaii is the permanent home of the Ironman World Championship and that's where our Son Rob is going in October 2012 as a competitor, his dream was to qualify for Kona and he did that in July when he came 9th out of about 500 in his age group, 40 to 44, only 8 could qualify so Rob had to wait and see if one of the other qualifiers would decide not to go and he had to wait until the Next day to find out that 2 of the 8 qualifiers were not going and he was given first choice for the spare slot and he grabbed it with great excitement, last year both Rob and Aisling missed out by just one slot each to qualify for the World Championship and for a while it looked like the same thing was going to happen in 2012 but the storey has a happy ending

Jenny Marie, Born on 22nd November 1973, that's an easy Date to remember because my Mother Died on 22 November and President

Kennedy was killed on 22 November and my little Niece Margaret Cummins died on 22nd November, what I remember about the first time I saw Jenny was that she had a great Head of Black Hair which she still has today. When she was old enough to move from her Cot to a regular Bed I warned her not to get out of Bed when she woke up but to call for me and I would come in to her, the warning worked because the next morning at 7 am she began calling "Daddy Daddy" at the top of her voice, not only did she wake me but everyone else in the House as well, From an early age Jenny had a great love of Animals and knew the Name of every Dog in Aylesbury where she grew up and through her we got to know some of the Neighbours who were dog owners. I gave Jenny her first Driving Lesson on her 12th Birthday and she soon became an excellent Driver and passed her Driving Test in London when only 18; Jenny was a typical teenager and as such was always pushing out the boundaries of what she should be allowed to do and we were typical Parents trying to hold her back as much as we could, she was taking part in a football Marathon in her school one Winter and as soon as she left for the school we went to the Kilteel Inn which is a quite Pub in the Hills near Rathcoole, about 10 pm the Bar Maid said Jim there's a phone call for you, It was Jenny's friend Roisin to say Jenny was in hospital injured, what happened was Jenny and a group of friends met at the School where the Marathon was taking place but instead of taking part in the football Marathon they hopped on a Bus and went in to the City where Jenny was struck by a Motor Bike while crossing Dame Street and suffered a Broken Leg. After doing her Leaving Cert Exam Jenny went to London to become an Au Pair for Singer Song Writer Nick Cave and his Wife Susie looking after their twin Children, she travelled to Australia with them as part of her Job, Jenny worked in Primo Oil for a few years, her last job in Primo there was as Manager of the Diner at Greenhills Road, she then went to College in London and studied to be a Nurse, we went over to London to celebrate with her on her Graduation Day. When she qualified as a Nurse she worked in Tallaght Hospital before moving to The Children's Hospital in Crumlin, her training had always been aimed at Children and that's what she loved most, later Jenny gave up Nursing to work for a Northern Ireland Company who sells Surgical Instruments in The Republic, part of her job is to attend at Theatre during surgery and witness her Instruments being used and sometimes to instruct Hospital Staff in their use. When Jenny was in London she met and fell in love with Tony, an English Man who later came to live in Ireland where they were married and had 2 beautiful Girls Abi and Lucy, Jenny and Tony have separated, Tony went back to live in London while Jenny and the Girls live close to us in Naas. Looking after 2 young children on your own is not an easy job but Jenny is an extremely competent and confident young Woman and is doing a great job with a little help from us and Ronnie and Emma who also live close to Jenny.

Ronnie Patrick, Born 16th June 1976, he was the largest at Birth, 9lb 6oz and at 6 foot 4 inches tall he is still the largest of our Children, as a Child Ronnie was easy to look after although sometimes he used his strength to get where he was not supposed to go, like wanting to go up the Stairs when there was a gate fixed at the bottom step, when he was about 2 years old he took hold of the gate and with his teeth gritted he kept pulling and lifting until it came loose. On one occasion our friends Hilda and Packie Fitzpatrick were minding our children while we stayed overnight in Northern Ireland, Hilda put Ronnie into his cot for his afternoon sleep, when she checked in on him a half hour later the base of his cot and the mattress was on the floor and Ronnie was missing, having searched the house with no sign of him Hilda was starting to Panic, she came back into the room where she had left him in the cot, she spotted his legs in the fireplace, his head and the rest of his body was up the chimney, when she managed to extract him from the chimney he was covered in soot but none the worse for his experience, we could never figure out how he managed to remove the base and mattress from the cot while still sitting on them. On his 12th Birthday I gave Ronnie his first Driving lesson, driving comes naturally to Ron and he passed his Driving Test as soon as he could do it at age 17, Ron loves all sports and is quite a good Golfer, he is a non smoker, he played Soccer but only as a pastime with his mates which is a pity because he was always a good player and would have been an asset to any team. Ronnie met and fell in love with Emma as a teenager and since then they have been like Peas in a Pod, they are married now and have two beautiful Children Sean and Niamh. After doing his Leaving Certificate he spent some years working in Primo Oil working up to Manager of our busiest Station at the Square before moving to work as a Sales Rep for the Kerry Group and later moved to the Barry Group Which is a large wholesale Company based in Cork. Ron's ambition is to start his own Business one Day and I have no doubt he will do just that.

Philip Andrew Born 21ˢᵗ September 1978 Phil had the same medical condition as Rob, the knotted Gut problem called Pyloric Stenosis which means no food can be digested and it results in Projectile Vomiting. He needed the same operation that Rob needed but it was much less of a worry this time as we understood the problem by now. Phil was always going to be different; from a very early age he displayed a degree of independence which was unusual for one so young. When he was 3 years old Pat bought him a blue Cardigan but for some reason he did not like it and would not wear it, he would never refuse to put it on but as soon as he was out of sight he would take it off and leave it on the side of the Road or wherever he was playing. One day he informed us that he was not going to drink from his Bottle anymore and threw it in the Bin. He never asked for his bottle again but his behaviour changed, he had difficulty going to sleep at night and we would often find him sitting on the Stairs looking through the Banisters long after he should be asleep, then he would come in at about 1 am and stand beside me at the bedside until I took him back and put him to Bed again. From a very early age Phil displayed an extraordinary talent for Art, with a Pencil or whatever he could find he would draw for hours, he would usually start with a Leg and then maybe an Arm but all the parts came together to form a Warrior or a Monster like something he had seen in a Comic. When he was about 12 years old he fell from a Horse and broke his Arm but he recovered with no permanent damage. Like our other Children Phil had his first driving lesson from me at age 12 but unlike the other Children he had very little interest in driving and did not pursue it until later in life when he needed to have a driving licence, he did his test and passed it in his own good time.

Phil left School early and went to find Work in London where he met a South African who was a Tattoo Artist who showed Phil some of his work, immediately Phil thought this is what I want to do and he became an Apprentice to the South African to become a Tattoo Artist. As a teenager Phil was always attracted to Punk's as a social group, they sported Mohican Style Haircuts, high in the centre and shaved at the sides, they dressed differently to other young people with Rings or Pins in their Nose's, lip's, Ear's and various other Body parts. As well as putting Tattoo's on other People he began putting Tattoo's on his own body and continues getting them now that he is in his 30s. He lives life by his own rules; most of them are made up as he goes along. Phil married Clodagh who was from Cobh in County Cork and already had a son of her own, a lovely Boy called Gary, they have 2 beautiful Boys Callan and Rian, Phil always wanted to have his own Tattoo Studio and he found a shop in Abbey Street in Dublin which he took out a Lease on and opened his own Shop in 2003. He ran this shop until work began on building the Luas Tram system when Abbey Street was closed to traffic, this had a negative effect on his business so he sold on his lease and moved House to live near Cobh in County Cork where Clodagh's Family live, he continues to run his Tattoo Business in Cork and has organised Tattoo Festivals where he brought other Tattoo Artist's from many parts of the World to participate in the Festival. He and Clodagh have separated but he plays his part in looking after his Children.

Jenny on her graduation from Thames Valley University London

Rob, Phil, Jenny and Ronnie 1992

Pat and Me with our granddaughter Carrie Cummins

Pats Dad Eddie Boileau and Jenny 1992

Family reunion 1999, l to r, front, Bridget Dolores Maura
Marie Kathleen, back l to r Pat Me John Brendan

Me and our dog Bruce pulling a cart i built for him to pull our grand children Carrie and James who are in the Cart

Our son Rob in training for the Ironman triathlon

Chapter 17

Transatlantic Yacht Race 2003

In August 2003 a Flyer came with the daily newspaper looking for people to make up a Crew for a Sailing Yacht which was taking part in a Trans Atlantic Yacht Race which is an annual event and is called the ARC, meaning Atlantic Rally for Cruisers, the Race journey is from Las Palmas in the Canary Islands to the Island of Saint Lucia in the Caribbean. The difference about this Crew is that you have to pay to become a part of it, having rang up to find out some more about it and discussed it with my wife Pat I decided to have a go as it sounded very interesting, the Boat in question was an 80 Foot Yacht built specially for racing and the Skipper described it as the equivalent of a Formula 1 Car in Motor Racing. I had no experience of Sailing, my hobby at that time was Water Skiing which I had been doing for a few years and was a member of the Golden Falls Water Ski Club near where we lived. I was told it would be very hard work with little rest and no Home comforts on the Boat. I knew that from the Water Skiing I would be strong in the Arms Legs and Shoulders but I spent some time in the Gym preparing myself and trying to improve on my strength and level of fitness. Although the Race was starting in Las Palmas our racing Yacht was moored in Dun Laoghaire outside Dublin, once I had signed up and paid up I was given the option of travelling on the Journey from Dun Laoghaire to Las Palmas which was split into 2 parts, part 1 from Dun Laoghaire to Lisbon Portugal and part 2 from Lisbon to Las Palmas, I needed more sailing experience and also to meet the other Crew members so I decided to go on the first leg of the journey as far as Lisbon, this will not be part the Race but a means of getting the Boat to where the Race will start from.

Saturday 18October 2003, Dun Laoghaire to Lisbon, Puddin dropped me out to Dun Laoghaire where I joined other crew members on board at 5.30

Skipper   Gary Keegan

The Crew:

Regular Crew,   Mark Connor, Rory Geraghty (Gunner) and James (Donk) from Australia

Guest Crew   Jimmy, Thomas (Switzerland), Wouter,(Holland), Lynn (Dublin), David (England) and Me

The Crew put finishing touches to preparations for a 6am departure tomorrow Morning, splicing Ropes, putting correct tension on Mast, and then washed down the deck with a Power Hose. at 8pm we went up town for a meal, back at 10.20, Mark gave me my first lesson in Navigation, all about tides and why we leave at 6am to get the benefit of the tide flowing with us for six hours before it turns against us off the east Coast at Wicklow. Conor and Rory suggested that I take Sea Sickness Pills for the first two days just to be safe. I was supposed to bring my own Sleeping Bag but no one had told me, there is a spare one here I can use. The Waterproof Boots I brought are only suitable for dingy sailing but there is a spare pair I can use.

Sunday Day one:

Up as 5am, breakfast not very well organised, I had two Bars Puddin had packed for me, Gary read the rules to be followed on the trip, we then had a lesson on how to dress in our Wet Gear and Life Jacket with Safety Rope which had to be clipped onto a Safety Line which ran the entire length of the Boat so you could move around with it connected. We used the Terminus Washroom for Hot Shower and shave; there is no Hot Water on the Boat so there will be no Showers until we reach Lisbon. Up on Deck Mark was hoisted up to the top of the 150 foot (46m) Mast to change Bulbs on the Lights and to check some other Fittings, about 8am we cast off. The watch rota is in two teams, one on, one off.

8am-2pm

2pm-8pm

8pm-midnight

Midnight-04.00

04.00-08.00

Four hours on, four hours off on the Night Shift. Six hours on the morning and afternoon Shift.

To start all hands are on duty but Rory and his team go below to rest at 10am, my team is, Conor as Duty Captain, Gary, Dave, James and me, we stay on duty up to 2pm at which time I am very cold, hungry and tired. Lunch is tinned Macaroni, not great but I eat it all and went to Bed.

Up again at 7.15, evening meal of Meat Balls and Pasta taken in a hurry as it was a bit late and we had to be on deck at 8pm, we are busy right away adjusting Sails to get the maximum benefit from the prevailing Wind, we are on duty until Midnight and are not kept busy all the time so the Captain on our watch suggested I put on more layers of clothes to stop the chill getting into my Bones like it did on the first shift, I go back to my bunk and put on five vests under a short sleeved shirt, even so at the end of my watch I still felt cold.

Things to get for next trip Low Alpine Thermal Tops and Bottoms, Snow-ski Gloves or Motorbike Gloves, Socks-Marine type boots, Sunglasses, cameras, Lip-Gloss that contains Suntan Lotion. We all go straight to bed and I get a few hours sleep before we are called at 3.45 am to be back on deck for 4am.

This time I am making no mistake I put on six Vests, a Short Sleeve Shirt, my good Jumper and my Fleece with Zip and Hood on it, on top of that goes my Wet Gear, Jacket and Pants which has to be worn, it consists of a Bib and Brace type Pants and heavy Jacket. At the bottom of the Leg there is a strip of Velcro which you pull tight around your Sailing Boots which are a high class Wellington that are waterproof and warm and that can also breathe.

On the Jacket the Sleeves have a double layer of Velcro, you have to roll back part of the Sleeve to tighten the inside strip of Velcro then pull down the Sleeve and tighten the outer strip of Velcro. Next is the Neck, like the Sleeve there is two layers of Velcro to be tightened, then most Sailors wear a Woolly Cap. I had my Russian type Cap and over that came the Hood of my Rain Jacket.

On top of all that clothes comes the Life Jacket which contains a Light and Torch and is self inflating if you hit the water, attached to the Life Jacked is a six foot long Safety Strap which has clips on both ends, one end hooks on to the Life Jacket and the other end to a Safety Rope which runs the entire length of the Boat so you connect to the Safety Rope and move about in safety.

With all that Clothes and Gear on you then have to work as hard as you would in a training session in the gym, it could last for ten minutes or thirty minutes and then you rest until the Skipper decides to drop a Sail and try a different one depending on Wind conditions.

On our first two days the Wind was at our Back and kept us going at a good speed but then you can be sitting for one or two hours with no activity at all and even with all that Clothes on the chill gets into your Bones, the reason for the Velcro on your Legs, Sleeves and Neck is to keep out the wet, either from Rain or from a Wave that comes over the Boat which can happen without warning. If you get wet when it's cold you will be totally miserable and you will have to go below Deck and put on dry Clothes (if you have dry clothes) and if you have time. I try my Mobile Phone on a regular basis to ring home but no Signal; we all go to Bed at the end of our watch and just get up in time again for our next watch.

The Engine and Stairs are in the centre of the Boat with the Bunks all around just hanging from the side of the Boat, three high and fully exposed; (no privacy here) unless you go the toilet or "head" as is referred to on the boat. At the start the skipper made a rule there shall be no shaving and at the end there will be a contest to see who has the best Moustache, we don't know what to do about Lynn, someone said give her a false Moustache. Not shaving has not been a problem so far as there is so little time and the Bathroom is so tiny. I am looking forward to Lisbon when we can use the Wash Room at the Port.

Dolphins alongside most days, one great display when six of them came out of the water together, second day out I nearly caused a serious Accident, I was coming down below Deck, when I was half way down the Boat rolled to one side and flung me across the Cabin only to land on Conor's right Leg, he roared out, my Leg I think it's broke, fortunately, it was only badly bruised, from then on when Conor came up on deck someone would shout, my Legs broke.

No Shower, no shave, only cold Water so washing was a very rapid affair. We are about two hours from Lisbon; at last I have a Signal to ring Puddin, all the other Guys talk about was how many Pints they would drink when they get to a pub. The regular Crew are all single Men but all have Girlfriends in various places. About three hours from Lisbon I got a Phone Signal and rang Puddin I also rang also Bob, Phil and Ron, Jennie not answering her Phone.

When we got Passport clearance we all went to the Washroom in the Port and I had a shave and a long shower after which I felt great. We stopped at a Bar for about two hours before going to a Restaurant for a Meal. After the meal we went to O'Neill's Irish Bar where I bought one round and then retired back to the Boat. I am impressed with the Skipper and Crew; they are all very experienced know all about sailing.

The middle of the Ocean on a moonlit night provides a chance to appreciate the Stars like no other time I can remember, the Sky is clear of any Cloud and our Skipper Gary Keegan seems to know every Star, and every Group of Stars, when you are just sailing along for hours you can take time to look at them in a way you never would have the time to at home. It was at times like this that I thought of Puddin and our Children and how I have been blessed with all of them.

Perhaps the nicest part of the trip was the last four of five hours into Lisbon. It was a lovely sunny day and for the first time I could shed a lot of my Clothes and we were joined by a large School of Dolphins, there must have been dozens of them because they were along both sides of the Boat as well as in front and behind, they stayed with us for about an hour and then just disappeared all at once.

While the Skipper and Crew are very professional at their job and therefore much disciplined the same does not apply when they leave the Boat and go out on the Town in Lisbon, things began to get out of hand when we were eating our Evening Meal of Fish and other Foods. Garry the Skipper and James the Australian started messing at the Table, James was already drunk from another Bar even though neither of them had huge amounts to drink.

They started throwing bits of Food at each other and then Gary started throwing bits of Fish at Rory who was at the other Table, fortunately Rory did not take the Bait and continued talking to Conor and Thomas, later Gary emptied part of a Bowl of Rice on top of Rory's Head, when we were leaving the Table it looked like it would after a children's Birthday Party.

We then went to O'Neill's Irish Pub where I asked the Waitress Shauna who was from Clonmel to get us a Table and to serve us which she did, I paid for the first round and almost immediately James (Donk) and Gary started messing and Gary threw a full Pint of beer over James, Gary passed a remark, don't start something unless you can finish it. James sat there in shock; he appeared not to know what to do while everyone else looked on speechless.

Shauna the waitress came over and had some harsh words for Gary who just grinned at her, she then got a bucket and mop and asked him to move so she could clean it up. A few minutes later I could see a male member of the bar staff hovering near our Table. I had seen enough and said to the others I would see them back at the Boat. I strolled back to the Boat and had just arrived when James and Gary arrived, James was very upset and Gary was trying to reassure him that things were not as bad as they seemed, they then left and went back to rejoin the rest of the Gang. James is aged about thirty and Garry would be about thirty five. I can only describe my evening out as most bizarre.

Friday 24th:

Woke about 9am got up about 10am, had a Shower, shave and went back to the boat, two crew members were gone but the others were fast asleep, I was quite hungry and decided to look for some place that served an Irish/English breakfast, it took about an hour but it was worth it and I came back to the boat feeling much better. I'm reading the Paper when Puddin rang and reminded me to get her Perfume and which type to get. About 2pm I went out and had a Waffle with Banana and Honey and then went to see if I could buy new Pants as I had been wearing the same pair from the time I left home. I found a Shop with nice Pants and also a nice Jacket, the Pants were about 15 inches too long and are being turned up for collection tomorrow Saturday at 11am.

The only talk about what happened last night was from Mark who said it got worse after you left, he said I'm sure you will hear all about it later. I had evening meal on my own as none of the others could decide what they wanted to do so off I went on my own, it seemed that some of the Crew were trying to avoid going out as a Crowd in case of a repeat performance, I got back to the boat about 7.30 and everyone was gone so I'm writing my notes all alone. I get a flight Home and will fly back to join them in Las Palmas on Race Day.

Las Palmas, let the Race begin, 21ˢᵗ November 2003

My Flight arrived in Las Palmas at 7pm, got a Taxi to the Port and joined rest of the crew for a Meal, then went to a Bar for about one and a half hours where all Boat Crews were getting together, 23.57 rang Puddin and I was talking to Jenny when fireworks started, wished Jenny a happy birthday, she is 30 years old tomorrow and I regret not being there to share it with her, as I was last to join the boat I got the most awkward bunk to get into.

Saturday 22ⁿᵈ November 2003, it's Jenny's Birthday, got up about 8.30 went to have a Shower in the Port Washrooms, conditions not great, no Hot Water for Showers, fortunately the Water was not that cold, there were three Washbasins but only one with a Tap that gives out Water and that one has a broken Mirror, Skipper tells us don't take Cardboard on deck as it attracts Cockroaches, if you see a Cockroach on Shore don't walk on it as it will probably have a lot of Eggs which could stick to your Shoe and if brought on board they could hatch out later, if they get on a Boat you can never get rid of them.

We had Breakfast on the boat, then some crew training after which I went to buy a couple of pairs of Shorts, I had packed the wrong ones at home; Had a Snack in Town, back to Boat for more Crew briefing, lost my phone, found it later. There is a change of Skipper from our first Trip from Dun Laoghaire, Gary is in the USA buying their second Cruiser which will be based in the Cayman Islands along with our Boat after the Race is over, Conor is our Skipper along with regular Crew, Rory, Mark, James, and Wurther has joined us as a full time crew member. There is also Dave and Thomas who were with us as far as Lisbon, new Irish Crew members are Noel and Nigel, Noel has a Shop and Petrol Station in Ratoath. The new Crew is made up of, five Germans, three Dutch, five Irish, one English man, one Swiss, one USA, one Australian, no women on this trip.

Sunday, 23rd November 2003

With 350 yachts taking part in the race there is great activity in the Las Palmas Harbour as Crews do last minute jobs getting Boats ready, large Crowds of local people came along to wave goodbye as each Boat pulled out, a local DJ had set up his music, he was playing Spanish and English language songs, we pulled out about 10.30 and sailed up and down the local Bay, the Start Line was determined by a Spanish Navy Gunboat and a line of floating Orange Markers in the Water, any Boat that crossed the Start Line before the Navy Boat sounded it's Horn would be docked three hours when they crossed the Finish Line in St Lucia, all boats had their Sails full up so they could not stand still, they had to keep moving but they wanted to be as close as possible to the Start Line when the Horn sounded, so all the Sailing Boats were crossing in front of each other and as well as that crowds of people came out in their own Boats and Jet Skis just to be there for the big occasion, there were TV crews in boats following us and filming each boat and a film Crew in a Helicopter. At exactly 12.40 the Horn sounded and we were one of the first Boats to cross the Line in sunny weather. At about 5.30pm I went below to put on warmer Clothes when I heard a shout, Whales on port side, I could not get up in time to see them.

Monday 12.30pm, Gunter is injured

We are about 24 Hours out of Port when Günter fell down Steps and dislocated his Shoulder, Conor contacted the Race Head Office on the Satellite Phone, they got a Doctor to talk to Conor, the Doctor said it's possible there is a Broken Shoulder, it's also possible that he could go into shock, they considered sending a Helicopter to airlift him from the

Boat but then decided they would not do so as his injuries were not Life threatening, they recommended we get him to a Hospital for x-ray. Conor called us together and told us that we had to turn round and go back to Grand Canaria with Günter, we would lose two or three Days in doing so but we had no choice.

Günter was very angry with himself for what was happening but for everyone else it was a big blow to moral, everyone was very quiet but we got on with the task of turning the Boat around, we had been moving at twelve to thirteen knots with the Wind behind us but when we turned the Boat we were heading right into the Wind and for most of the journey back to Grand Canaria we had to run the Engine, even with the engine running we could only make eight to nine knots of speed, it took us twenty eight hours to get back and it was a horrible journey, as we were heading into the Wind we were being hit head on by the Waves, this caused a terrible banging on the Hull of the Boat, it was worse for anyone below Deck trying to sleep as the bang each time we hit a Wave (which was every two or three minutes) was deafening and the pitching and rolling of the Boat made it almost impossible to move about.

We changed Sails several times to make up speed but it made little or no difference so we ran the engine most of the time. It was during one of the sail changes that I got sea sick, I just made it to the side of the boat in time to avoid soiling the deck, only one other crew member had got sick up to this and he did it below deck, Wurther got sick below Deck on to the Seat Covers before he managed to grab another crew members Wellington Boot and used that to finish the job. Fortunately the Boot belonged to his friend Hein who took charge and cleaned up the Mess; they took off the Seat Covers and hung them up in the Sail Room to dry. Each time we hit a wave there was a terrible bang and it felt like we had hit a Brick Wall.

When we arrived in Porto Rico in Grand Canaria there was an Ambulance waiting to take Günter to Hospital, Conor our Skipper went with him and when he came back he said Günter has not broken anything but there was so much swelling and pain they decided to put him under General Anaesthetic to relocate his Shoulder, they said he could go home tomorrow. By the time Conor got back to the Boat two German Crew members had decided to go home and not continue the journey, they had had enough hardship and left the boat to make their own way home. When I was getting seasick I asked myself "What am I doing here" I had almost made up my mind to go home when we got to Porto Rico but when I woke after a good sleep I felt much better and forgot about going home early. Remarkably, when Conor had a talk with us everyone was enthusiastic about going on, when we left Port at 10.15 on Tuesday night to start the journey all over again but everyone was upbeat and in good form.

The only weak link left now is Clouse, a sixty four year old German who is a lovely man but could best be described as a Mr McGoo the cartoon character. Everyone is worried that he will have an accident and injure himself or someone else. The next day Conor decided that he should only be allowed on Deck during Daylight hours, so our team is one Man short but everyone agrees it's the correct decision.

As we prepared to restart the race from Porto Rico James who is one of the full time Crew complained to Connor that in the last forty hours there was only one four hour rest period in which he had not been woken for a Sail change. The problem is that up to now the new crew members are still not experienced enough to manage to hoist or lower a Sail and so this means that for every Sail change the full regular Crew of five are needed even when two or three of them are off duty and asleep. The Skipper Conor tells James he has not done too badly as he Conor has not had even one four hour period without being called, however from then on Conor was inclined to carry out Sail changes without calling on Crew who were asleep and the other Crew led by Rory did likewise. This led to a lot more hard work by those on duty but less broken sleep for those who are in Bed.

Because Clouse is restricted to daylight hours on Deck he does a lot of work in the Kitchen. One day he made a Cup of Coffee for Dave the English man, Dave could not drink it and advised everyone to avoid getting Clouse to make Coffee for them. It was later discovered that he had used Sea Water for the Coffee; Dave made his own Coffee after that. The skipper tells us personal hygiene is very important as he does not want people getting sick when help could be six or seven days away. It's not easy to keep clean as both Toilets have been giving trouble on a regular basis.

We are a week at Sea now and the Toilet problem has been sorted at last. After the terrible journey back to Grand Canaria I developed a nasty cough which lasted three Days. As I began to run short of clean Socks I decided to wear my Deck Shoes without Socks but I developed a nasty Rash on my Insteps which took about three Days to clear.

Some of our Crew on the Racing Yacht,

Our Skipper Conor Kissane is from Rathfarnham, probably his finest quality is his ability to keep calm in situations which otherwise seem out of control and to still give instructions in a way that does not make things worse rather than better.

Mark Tighe is from Ashbourne and is twenty six years old but has clocked up a lot of experience for his age, Mark was on the crew of the Jeanie Johnston on her maiden voyage from Ireland to New York, he can climb up Ropes like a Monkey and would work at the very top of the Mast while the Boat is at full speed rolling from side to side and it needs to be remembered that a twenty degree movement can transfer to thirty or forty at the top of the mast.

Ruairi Herraghty from Celbridge is Graham Kerne's friend and knows my Son Ronnie back home. He is a very good all round Seaman and is second in command on the Boat. The Skipper would usually consult with him on matters of importance before making a decision.

Dr Klaus Rahe from Germany is sixty four years old; he owns a Business which is one hundred years old next year. It was started by his Grandfather in 1904. Klaus has sold the Business to his General Manager who is taking it over next year when Klaus will retire; his company has been making paper bags for all that time.

Wuther Han from Holland spent five years selling Porsche cars before deciding to take this trip; he was twenty nine the day we arrived in St Lucia.

Rory suffered a burn while handling a hot kettle and had to take some time out, this caused a change of crew, Dave came on to our watch and Wurther went on to the other watch. Everyone gets on well together, no arguments, no complaints about how hard the work is, except from

Dave the English man who slags the Skipper every now and then saying Celebrity Cruise how are you, Celebrity Cruise my Arse, it's getting to be a Catch Phrase for other Crew members. Celebrity Cruise is the name of the Yacht.

Because we expect to be at Sea for fifteen days or more the water tanks don't hold enough water to have showers when we want to. I have not shaved since we left Porto Rico four day ago. Maybe tomorrow I will get a chance to shave. (Puddin would not like it here) each day the weather is getting warmer as we head further South before picking up the trade winds heading south west towards the Caribbean sea, each day we have been able to leave off more items of Clothes and now we can do the Night watch with only our Shorts and Tee-Shirts under our heavy Rain Gear.

When I have time to think I am very conscious of the fact that all my Family are at home and I wonder if it was wrong for me to go and leave them like this. The work of changing Sails and changing course goes on as usual, when a Sail change is taking place it would seem like a mad House to someone who has not seen it before, everything is done at a frantic pace with people shouting at each other from one end of the Boat to the other, but in fact it generally runs smooth as everyone knows what their job is, apart from Günter's Shoulder and Rory burning his Hand we had no other serious injuries. I knocked a chunk of Skin off my Thumb and it's slow to heal because I am sweating so much and using tight Gloves a lot of the time.

Saturday, 29th November 2003

Wind is not strong and the sea is calm so we can do some sun bathing, we had some fun when Mark was hooked on to the end of a rope and was swung out to sea, we then let him up and down dipping him in and out of the water. We had a couple of fairly dramatic incidents, one was when the wind dropped and then picked up again rapidly, the spinnaker which is a very large head sail started flapping in the wind and before we could get it tightened enough one of the sail fixings tore off and left us with no control over the sail, fortunately the Skipper and regular crew knew their job and by telling everyone what to do we managed to get the sail back onto the boat. It's damaged but can be repaired when we reach port.

Another time when we were dropping the head Sail Nigel and I had the job of pulling it into to Deck as it came down, as it started to drop the Wind came up and filled the Sail making it almost impossible for us to hold on to it, James who was dropping the sail was shouting at us, hold on to it lads, hold on, then he was shouting at Conor who was steering the Boat saying, change course, meaning change direction to take the Wind out of the Sail, We knew that if we did not let go of the Sail we could be pulled overboard but as we had our safety harness on and attached to the Boat we were not worried about that, we managed to get the Sail on board without anyone being injured. Both incidents occurred at night, in the dark with the boat travelling at full speed. I had a Shave and feel a lot better for it, I think of Puddin and the kids all of the time, wondering if everything is okay with them.

Sunday, 30th November 2003, Problem with the main Sail Carrier which is fixed to the top of the Mast, once again Mark was hoisted to the top of the Mast while the Boat is travelling at full speed; he made a temporary repair which should last to the end of the race.

Monday, 1st December 2003, we were hoisting the Spinnaker Sail when Mark got injured, his Leg is trapped between the Rope and Forestay with a rope wrapped around his leg, we see him lying on Deck at the front of the Boat but we had to continue to hoist the sail or the Skipper could lose control of the boat. Mark's Leg is badly bruised and has some Rope Burns, he is in severe pain but it's clear nothing is broken; Mark is given painkillers and a spray to keep down the Swelling. This could have been a really serious injury as a Rope got wrapped round Marks Leg as he was falling and it was a few minutes before anyone could go to help him.

12.30 Monday 1st we were off duty but due on at 2pm. I am cleaning my teeth when there is pandemonium on the deck, Rory is shouting everybody on deck, Conor the Skipper is asleep but wakes up very quickly and we all rush up on deck. The spinnaker (a huge headsail) has wrapped part of itself around the Forestay and the rest of it is flapping wildly in the Wind. Conor takes over the Wheel and tries to control the Boat which is losing direction quickly, Conor tells James to release one of the Fixings on the Spinnaker in the hope that it will unwrap itself. James said if I do we will lose the sail, Conor, if you don't it will bring down the Rig meaning the main Mast, if this happened the Boat could probably capsize and sink. There were four or five of us trying to pull down a part of the Sail which we had managed to get hold of but it would not come away from the Forestay. James released the bottom Fixing on the Sail and it swung way out over the Sea, still connected to the top of the mast, Conor swung the Boat in such a way that the bottom part of the Sail swung in towards the Boat where a group of us was waiting to grab it which we managed to do and pull the bottom of the Sail in over the side of the Boat, we managed to hold it there while James was hoisted up the Mast to entangle the top of the Sail so that it could be lowered and as it came down we had to keep pulling like mad to stop the Wind from taking the Sail from us again, everyone sits down exhausted and I realise I have no Dentures, I had left them in the Sink where I was cleaning my Teeth, panic is over, I rush down to get them before somebody else sees them. From the time we left Porto Rico having left Günter in hospital we knew we were making good time.

When Conor asked the Race ruling Committee would we get any allowance for time lost with our medical emergency he was told to go back to the spot at sea where we were when Günter got hurt, Call in on the radio and give our position, we must fill in a full Report when we arrive at St Lucia and a decision will be made at that time so we are carrying on as if we are still in the Race. From information we have been able to get about the position of other boats it seems we were in the lead when Günter hurt himself. If the information that we have been getting lately is correct it seems we are making great progress and already have overtaken all the smaller Craft. It also appears that big Boats like our own have got into difficulty and are making poor progress, they took the shortest route and went into an area of calm weather with little or no Wind, this is what's known as being in The Doldrums, We are taking a different longer route which we hope will provide us with good Wind in the hope we can continue to close the gap with the leaders which at one time had been three to four hundred miles ahead of us.

Our first Lightening Storm was both exciting and frightening, although we managed to avoid the worst of the Storm by changing course several times, Lightening flashes every two minutes for about two hours. Radar is wonderful; it can show up a storm up to twenty five miles away so we have a chance (sometimes) to take evasive action. The Skipper told us to keep clear of all metal parts of the boat to avoid being killed if the Boat took a Lightning strike.

Tuesday, 2nd December 2003

Damage to main Sail, Rory spent about three hours up the main Mast repairing it. Mark is still restricted in what he can do due to his Leg injury yesterday. We are over half way now and had a little celebration today, two Beers for everyone "Tang for me"; we were very fortunate to have plenty of good cooks and had three good Meals every day.

Showers and Toilets are all working so we can Shave and Shower each day. I washed some Socks, some Shirts and Underwear yesterday and hung them out to dry on the Safety Wire that runs right around the Boat. I had to take them in before dark and hung them up in the Sail Room to finish drying, I put them back out on Deck this morning in the hope that they would finish drying. I could not have had enough Clothes no matter how many I brought considering we come on duty five times every two days and almost every time I would be in a lather of sweat and could do with clean Clothes every time. In reality, most times I had to wear each set of clothing four, five or six times but I hope this wash will get me through to St Lucia, we expect to arrive next Sunday all going well.

12.30 pm I am woken and told it's my turn to prepare lunch, I tell the Skipper I can't cook, I'm told get someone who can cook to help you, we had been told in the beginning that everyone will have to take their turn in the kitchen, no excuses. We are half way through making lunch when someone from above deck calls out, Jim your clothes are getting wet it's raining. I run and take them in. We call in our position each day and have been told twice that we've made the best distance of any Boat in twenty four hours but not all Boats call in each day so we can't be sure of our overall place on the Race. We are now in the Tropics so at least we don't have to wear a lot of Clothes while working, we have a water Desalinating Machine so we have a good Water supply now. This Machine takes in sea water and removes salt from it so we use flavoured sachets of Powder to make a Drink called Tang. I drink so much of it they call me Jimmy Tang. Thomas is so impressed by my muscles he calls me Arnold, Mark says I look like I would walk to a Brick Wall just to see how hard it was.

Thursday, 4ᵗʰ December 2003

For a few days we have had Flying Fish landing on the Boat, one hit the Skipper on the Shoulder while in full flight. Today is the first time I really got good views of them in full flight, they have been in front of our boat all morning, they come out of the water at fifteen to twenty miles per hour, and they are about six to ten inches long and use their flippers as wings. They fly for up to one hundred yards, sometimes skipping off the Waves to keep going. This is their way of avoiding Sharks which are hunting for them.

I keep wondering if Puddin was okay on her own each night, it's great that she feels safe at Night in our new Home, I wonder how Bob's and Phil's Shops are doing. Is Jenny still happy in her new Job, is Ron still thinking of moving from Kerry Foods. We are so far South now that the Weather is very steady, very little change in the Winds, we seem to have got away from any storms, we have had two Time changes of one hour so far and another one today as we cross into another Time Zone.

Friday, 5ᵗʰ December 2003, a Crane landed on the back of our Boat, we were about a thousand Miles from Land so he was probably tired and needed a rest, it stayed for about twenty minutes and went on its way. I thought we were finished with Storms, last night we had two very heavy Showers and finished our watch at 8am like drowned Rats. It's so hot now below deck sleeping is not easy especially when someone has to cook or is preparing food. Someone started a contest to guess when we would reach St Lucia, times predicted varied from Sunday am to late Monday. I read Puddin's card, again, it helped me to keep going. Monday, 8ᵗʰ December 2003

Man overboard drill

No, we didn't have such an emergency but our Skipper Conor prepared us well in case it should happen. He said, If you see a "Man fall overboard, shout "Man overboard" but don't take your eyes off him, keep pointing to where you last saw him and if he goes out of site keep pointing at the spot because it's possible no one else may have seen him and as the boat will keep going for several minutes before stopping and turning, with big waves no one will have a clue where to look unless you keep pointing at the spot where you last saw him. Conor said the reality is, if you go overboard in the Dark in the rough Seas there is almost no hope of you being found alive again so this is why he is so strict about always being hooked on to the Safety Rope on Deck, some Nights it is so dark that when someone comes up from below deck they have to call out their name so the Crew on Deck will know who has come up.

Thomas Meseck

On our boat we had some quite remarkable people such as Thomas Meseck from Switzerland who speaks six Languages and is an expert Navigator, he represented his country in the Olympics at Sailing. He flies Jet Planes up to about one hundred Passengers for two different Airlines as a freelance Pilot. With one Airline he does not take any payment but he has the use of their planes for his own Family use or for his Business use.

Thomas seems to be a Genius with Software and has built large Software Company which he has just sold to Microsoft; our Skipper thinks he was paid a large sum for the Business. He is still involved with his Company for one year as part of the deal, now Microsoft have asked him to come back as Chief Executive but he does not want to go back full time, he said "Jim at our time in life we don't need all those problems", we should be able to enjoy the rest of our live" he said, my problem is that whatever I am involved in I can't do it in a half hearted way, I have to give one hundred and fifty % commitment to anything I do, an example of this is that next year he intends to compete in the ARC Trans Atlantic Yacht Race but this time using his own new Yacht which is being built and should be ready by next April. I asked him why then had he gone on Celebrity Cruise this year and he said, I need to know what are the worst things that can happen, so that way can plan every little detail in advance and thereby keep the risks to a minimum. His new Yacht will be a far cry from the Boat he travelled on this year working as an ordinary Crew member doing his share of everything including cooking and washing up.

His new Yacht will cost about five Hundred Thousand Euro and could be operated by just one Person who knew enough about Sailing. The Sails will rise up at the pull of a Lever and can be adjusted by a Lever, when the Sails have to come down they will retract into the Mast at the touch of a Lever, it will have four large luxury Bedrooms with Ensuite and luxury Dining areas, apart from Thomas and his wife Ester who is also an expert sailor he will have a full time fully qualified Skipper who can operate the boat in their absence and will be his main backup on next year's ARC, along with his Wife, three Daughters and some special Guests.

Thomas has invited me and Puddin to go sailing with him and his Family on his new Boat, he asked me if I would do the ARC again and I said no thanks. Thomas is Sixty three years old and loves to talk about his Family, when I asked him about his Wife Ester he said "she is an incredible Woman, she is the best thing that has happened to me in my whole Life". He noted similarities with my Life in our attitude to Family Life, commitment to Marriage and he has known his Wife since 1968, Puddin and I met in 1967. Ester was very much involved in their Software Business and Thomas said that in many areas she was better than him.

Saturday, 6th **December 2003**, Heavy Seas, huge Waves, we have strong Winds and we are making good time, I thought I was in for an easy Day in the Sun but the Skipper got me and two others to go down to the Sail Room where we had to move a lot of Sails and lift some Floor Boards to get to the Sump for pumping out water which gets in during heavy storms, the problem with working in the Sail Room is not the hard work, it's the heat, today it's like an oven and we can't open the hatch for ventilation because of the huge Waves breaking over the Deck would flood the Hold even worse. The Sweat poured from me at a rate I never thought possible. We had just finished that job when it was time for another change of Sails so I'm on the Grinder which is a huge winch where I sweat another two litres then back down to the Sail Room to package the Sail which has just come down. Those sails are enormous, four hundred square metres each, and they have to be packed into a bag about four feet by two foot by two foot high, it takes three men about fifteen to twenty minutes to pack each Sail. We then finished our watch and Lunch was ready but I had to wait about forty five Minutes to cool down before eating anything. I had a Shave and cold Shower and now I am going to get some Sleep, its 16.20 and I am back on duty at 20.00 hours.

Sunday, 7ᵗʰ December 2003, Our last Day and we expect to arrive around Midnight Tonight, I intend to book into a Hotel for Monday and Tuesday Nights to enjoy Air Conditioning and a Bed that does not keep rolling from side to side and there will not be noise of banging and shouting both Day and Night. As the day wears on its clear we won't be in until after midnight and I'm disappointed at this as I am due on duty at Midnight and I thought if we were in before that I would not have to go back on duty and could sleep on through the Night. Of course that was silly as I had forgotten that when we do arrive we have to drop all Sails, put them in Bags and secure the main Sail on the Boom, the main Sail is never taken in, it's just folded over the Boom which is a huge horizontal Arm that is fixed to the Mast. We are called at 11.30 and I climb out of my Bunk wishing I could stay in it. I just want to get a Shower and book into a Hotel where I can call Puddin and let her know I'm okay; we have been told there is no Mobile Phone signal at St Lucia.

Arrival at St Lucia

As we approached the finish line and I get involved in the work my spirits begin to lift. We are in contact with the ARC Race Office and they talk us past various Landmarks, there is a large Boat waiting in Rodney Bay and we have to pass that to cross the Finish Line. It's a beautiful moonlit Night, very calm but of course we don't need calm, we need some Wind and as we turned into Rodney Bay we were turning against the little wind that is blowing. We have to zig zag across the Bay trying to get enough Wind in our sails to keep us moving, we call the finish line Boat and ask them have we crossed the Line yet, they say no, you will have to do another tack and pass along side us, eventually the finish Boat gave a loud blast on its horn to let us know we have crossed the Line, a big cheer goes up from everyone on board and we get a call on the Radio congratulating us and telling us that we are number Twenty Two over the finish Line at 1.45am. Number 22 out of 350 boats is not bad but our Skipper had taken this Race very seriously and had hoped for a better result, he had asked the Race committee to take account of the time we lost because of our Medical Emergency which they eventually did and restored our lost time which then left us in 3ʳᵈ place overall, a result we were all very happy with, Conor the Skipper was particularly happy, he said we had a Yacht that was built for Racing and his 4 regular Crew were very professional and the Guest

Crew Members had performed much better than he had expected so he was very pleased with the Result.

It takes us another hour to get the Sails down and the Anchor dropped, we cannot go into the Harbour as our Keel needs four and a half metres of Water and the Harbour does not have that much depth. As we crossed the Finish Line a Motorboat drove alongside us and took a lot of Pictures, as it was in the dark I don't know how they will turn out. The ARC Race Office sent out a Boat with Drinks, a Bag of Fruit, Bottles of Coca Cola and some Literature about the Island of St Lucia. Some of the Crew want to go ashore and find a Pub that's still open but they can't get a Water Taxi that time of night. Our Skipper found some Beer which had been hidden on the Boat, a small party was held and I went to Bed about 3.30am. I was wide awake again at 5.20, got up to watch the Sun rise; I got my inflatable Pillow to use as a cushion and took my Journal up on Deck to bring it up to date.

We ran out of Milk yesterday and the Skipper ran out of Cigarettes. When we got our Sails down I decided to try my Mobile Phone for a signal and was delighted to find that I had one so I rang Home thinking that it would be 9.40 PM but when Puddin answered it she said it was 5.40am. I had the Time difference wrong way round, its 7.40 now, two more Boats just crossed the Finish Line and our Crew members are waking up.

Our Skipper had to take our Passports and go to Customs before we could go ashore. It was a lovely morning so I put on my Swimmers and jumped into the Sea for a swim, as I was climbing back onto the Boat I heard my Phone ring, it was Puddin again and we had a grand chat this time as all the hustle and bustle was over. I had already rung Bob, Jenny, Phil and Ron but Puddin had already given them the news from me.

St Lucia

St Lucia is a lovely place and the people are wonderful, they are so laid back they only seem to have one speed which is first gear, if you don't like that they may just stop. At my hotel I thought I would have a Snack so I went to the Restaurant which is half in and half out of the building, I asked the waitress for a Menu and she said certainly Sir and handed over the Menu, she never came back to me so I decided to have a Coke and eat later. I got my coke at the Bar and as the Girl seemed to be new I went back to my Table to wait for my Change, about ten minutes later she consulted another Lady member of staff and came over to me and said "excuse me Sir, how much Money did you give the Waitress", I said Ten Dollars, she went back to the Girl in the Bar and they had another discussion, the second Lady came back to me again, excuse me sir, was it ten US Dollars or ten Caribbean dollars I said "US dollars" she said "Ah, that explains it", she went back to the Girl in the Bar and they had another discussion with the till open all this time, about five minutes later, she brought my Change and told me to enjoy my Drink, it was all gone by now. I wondered how they would cope in Aherns Pub on Saturday night. My Hotel is unusual in that it has no front door, just an opening about thirty feet wide with covered space for cars to drop off and pick up passengers, they get a lot of rain here from July to October but it never gets cold.

I went to Reception and asked if I could book some Tours for Tuesday, the lady at reception rang the tour company and put me on the Phone to Arran. I explained to Arran that I had only one full Day and would like to see as much as possible, he explained the various Tours and I said, "Would it be possible for me to get on two of the Tours in one Day", he said "let me ring you back", when he rang back he said "yes it's possible to get you on both provided we can pick you up at your Hotel at 7.30am", I said "no problem".

The Tour of the Rain Forest was Fifty US Dollars and the Tour of the Island was one Hundred and ten US Dollars. I set my Phone Alarm for 6.30 it went off at 2.30, I had forgotten to change the Time in my Phone which I did and went back to Bed, at 4am another Alarm went off it was the Radio Clock the last Person here must have got up at 4am and did not switch off the Alarm. I was up at 6.30 and having shaved and showered I had Tea and Scones in my room as the Dining Room did not open until 7.30.

Arran had said he would ring me at 7.20 to make sure I was up on time, when he had not rang my 7.30 I went to Reception to wait for my pickup. At 7.50 the Lady at Reception called me, Mr Cummins, there is a Phone call for you, it was Arran who said he wanted to confirm that I was going on the tour, I said, of course I am, you were supposed to have me collected at 7.30, he said, that's alright sir, your Car will be there in a few moments.

At 8.20 the lady on Reception came over and asked me what was wrong. I tell her no one came to collect me and she says I better ring them for you, I say that's okay, Can I go the bar to have a Coke as its getting quite hot at this stage, I'm half way through my coke when the lady from reception comes and says, Mr Cummins can you come with me please. I say what's wrong; Arran wants to talk to you. I say are they not going to collect me, she says he wants to talk to you on the Phone. I go to Reception and the Manageress says Mr Cummins can you come into my Office please, I follow her into the Office and she puts me onto Arran who says there is a major mix up.

It seems that because I had told them my friend Noel might be coming to stay at this hotel and if so would there be room for him on the tour and he said that there would be, they pay the driver by the number of passengers that they have and when the driver learned there was only one passenger he still wanted to be paid for two passengers. He said I would have to pay one hundred US dollars for the first tour but he could give me the second tour at forty five dollars would that be okay, I said okay, your Car will be there in a few moments.

That was 8.50 the Car eventually came at 9.20, not my intended first Driver but a very cheerful Guy who asked me what had gone wrong. I told him and he said it was too late now to get in both Tours but he had to take me to the Centre where all the Tours start from, when we arrived he said, let me go in and sort out this mess, about ten minutes later he came out and asked me to come with him to the tour company office, a lovely Girl called Sylvia assured me that I would not have to pay anything extra but as it was getting so late would it matter if my Rain Forest Tour was put off until tomorrow, as I did not have to leave for the Airport until 4pm I had time for the two and a half hour tour Wednesday morning so I was then included in today's Tour (my first tour) with nine Americans, our driver is Barnard Henry who is seventy six years old. Barnard is well able for the Mountain Roads some of which are only half built and have a constant stream of hair pin Bends. But at the start of the Tour he told us that he would not be able to talk loud enough for the people in the back to hear so he asked for someone with a loud Voice to sit in the front Seat and relay his comments back to the other Passengers. Dave from Delaware in the USA took on the job and listened very carefully to what Barnard told him but then forgot to relay it back to us until someone would ask him what Barnard had said. I have asked Barnard to take me to the Airport tomorrow, at sixty five US Dollars it's a run all the taxi drivers try to get as often as possible.

Wednesday, 10th December 2003

I go home today but first have a Tour of the Rain Forest. I rise a 6.30am and am collected at 7.30 by my Driver Augustine Paul; he is the same Driver who collected me yesterday. He greeted me by saying "Mr Cummins, do you mind if I ask what kind of business you are in". I told him what I did and asked why he wanted to know, he said I'm looking at your body structure and wondering how you keep it that way, Augustine is a real charmer, reminds me of my friend Tommy Kelly, except that he is a different Colour,

I thought I was the only one going to the Rain Forest but he already had a young Woman in the Front Seat of his Minivan, he said I just have to pick up another Man and Woman on the way, they turn out to be English and work for Cable and Wireless in St Lucia for two Weeks, they use Augustine every day to bring them to and from Work. After he dropped them he then dropped his first Woman Passenger at her place of Work and then said I just have to pick up one Lady and it won't take long. This woman had come in to a local Airport and he took her to her Mother's House way up in the Hills, all this was happening in Castries the capital of St Lucia, as we drive down the Street Augustine beeps his Horn and a Woman waves at him, it's his Sister who is a School Teacher with her Daughter, in the next Street he beeps at a Policeman who turns out to be his Brother, I said to him how many Brothers and Sisters do you have. He said I have Ten Brothers and Eleven Sisters, just one Mother and one Father, I looked at him in disbelief and he said it's true, my Dad is dead fourteen Years but my Mother is alive and looks as young as me, she lives close to the Rain Forest where we are going. I said I would love to meet her, will you take me and introduce me to her; He agreed and showed me her house close to the entrance to the Forest. He said he would take me there on the way back.

When we arrived at the Entrance to the Forest to meet my Guide Louis he was not there, there was no one there. After about ten minutes

Augustine said I will have to go and see if I can find him. About fifteen minutes later he's back, can't find Louis anywhere. Ten minutes later he says, we may go back to my Mother's House and Phone someone from there. He introduced me to his Mom and his Sisters and left me with them while he went to find Louis, the only way to describe Mrs Paul and her House is to look at the pictures I took. She is a plump but very happy Lady, she is very pleasant and so are her daughters, she proudly showed me the new House her Family are building for her, she said next time I come with my Wife we must come and visit and stay in her new House, I asked her how many of her children were still living with her, she laughed and just said "lots of them". Twenty minutes later Augustine is back and introduced me to Ti, who is to be my Guide, Ti is about Twenty Three and is Augustine's Nephew. His English is not so easy to understand and he does not know all of the Trees and Plants but he does know a lot about the forest. When walking through the Rain Forest I kept getting bad Smell's like Sewage, after a while I noticed it was only when I was close to Ti the Tour Guide that I got the bad Smell so I kept well back from him and enjoyed the Smell of the Forest instead.

We walked through the Forest for about two hours, Ti stopped and picked up a sharp stone and made a cut in the bark of a tree, a few minutes later a sticky liquid began running from the cut. Ti showed me other cuts where the liquid had dried up and gone hard, when you break of a piece of the dried Liquid and put it between your Fingers it has a nice smell and Ti tells me its Incense which is burned at certain times during religious Ceremonies in the Catholic Church. We leave the Forest and it takes twenty minutes to walk back to Mrs Paul's house but on the way Ti climbs a tree and takes down two Mangos which we eat, even though its green it's nice to eat and not bitter as I thought it would be.

We arrive in time to see Augustine's Mom open her shop which she does every afternoon. It's a wooden hut about 3 metres square (10 foot). Back at my hotel flying fish is on the menu so I try it and it's nice in batter. The people of St Lucia speak a delightful form of English, think of the song, "pass the duchy on the left hand side" and you have an idea what they sound like. There is a native language called Creole but it's not used that much.

By the standards we live by at home St Lucia would be a very poor country and it seems that most People live in what we would call Poverty.

Most Houses are very small, what we would call sheds, very old and in very bad shape, likewise the Cars are old and in bad condition, I only remember seeing three new Cars in the three days that I was there. Only the main Roads were in any sort of decent condition, on our Tours in the Hills many of the Roads are in a terrible condition with Drivers swerving from one side of Road to the other while trying to avoid Potholes.

Bananas is the main produce of the Country, even the poorest people have Bananas growing in their Gardens, they would also have Fruits such as Grapefruit, Oranges, Lemons, Mangos and other Fruit I have never heard of. I learned that there is a lot more to the Banana that just the one we know, there are several other types which all look like Bananas to me but are smaller, have other names and have to be cooked before eating.

Wednesday, 10th December 2003

Barnard arrives promptly at 4pm and my Flight departs promptly at 6.30. Should I call it a Holiday, an Adventure, an Endurance test, I think it was all of those and more. My sister Kathleen thought I was crazy going on such a trip, she said "what if you fall overboard at night, in the dark, you would never be found ". Well she may be right about not being found, that's why there was a very strict rule about wearing your Lifejacket and a Harness to stay connected to the Boat. There was one incident on our trip to Lisbon when Lynn the only woman on board fell asleep on the night watch, she was actually sliding towards the edge of the boat and could have gone over but for her Harness being hooked on to the Deck, she was able to laugh about it later but at the time she got a severe fright.

Will I ever do it again??? I don't think so

Chapter 18

Brazil Trek in aid of Barretstown, 19th May 2005

Early 2005 I see an Ad in the Sunday Paper looking for People to volunteer for a challenge by raising €5000 for Barretstown and the 2nd part of the challenge was to walk 100 km through Mountains and Jungles in Brazil, Barretstown is the Charity that was started by the Actor Paul Newman in the USA and which he called the *Hole in the Wall Gang*, in 2005 Ireland was the only other Country outside the USA to have a branch of the Charity, to get the Irish Branch started Paul Newman put in $1,000,000 of his own Money and the Irish Government which was led by Albert Reynolds gave them Barretstown Castle which had been gifted to the Irish State by billionaire Galen Weston when he departed to live in Canada. Helen O'Malley was in charge of fund raising in Barretstown and it was her who came up with the idea of trekking abroad as a way to raise Money for the Charity, Helen took her trekking seriously and had gone abroad herself and checked out the route in each Country before looking for volunteers, she then arranged an experienced Guide Robert Farley to take us out in the Wicklow Mountains to make sure we were up to the task, the following account is based on notes I took during the trip to Brazil.

Our Flight left at 5.35 to London. Our flight from London to Sao Paulo left at 10pm and took twelve hours. I slept quite a bit and felt good when we arrived in Sao Paulo at 6 am local time. At 9.30 we got a flight to Brasília which is the capital of Brazil. There we got a Coach for Alto Paraeso which took three hours up to 5pm (9pm Irish time). We stopped for Lunch on the way. I had a welcome shave and shower in the small hotel where we stayed for the night. There is one other Cummins on the trip, Lisa, who is one of Irelands top Models, she is from Finglas and joined up because she had lost a little boy at age three from Cancer. He spent some time in Barretstown before he died and Lisa wanted to give something back so she raised €5000 and came on the trip. We had an evening Meal in a local Restaurant and went to Bed at 10pm.

Sat 21st

I awoke about 5.30. Got up at 6am had Breakfast and we were ready to start walking at 8.30. Each day we have to pack everything and leave it ready for our transport crew of 6 men and one woman as we stay in a different Camp each Night. We are like an Army on the move with twenty eight Tents to be dismantled and moved by Truck to the next Campsite, they have our Tents ready when we reach our next Camp. There is also a Tent which acts as a Bar.

The Barman's name is Tattoo. He can speak good English and remembers everyone's names when he has been told it just once. The climbing is quite severe on our first day. We have been formed into two Groups of twenty one in our group and twenty two in the other Group. I am in the lead Group.

We reach a waterfall about 12 noon and have lunch and a swim. The hardest part of the Day is as we descend from the Mountain into the Valley where our Camp is set up; the descent takes about one and half hours through very dense Jungle. As we get deeper into the Valley the heat increases. The Path is strewn with loose rocks and it's very hard on the legs. When the Guide stops to tell us about a Plant or Animal the heat seems to close in on us like we were in an Oven. We have to keep moving even when we need to stop and rest. When we get to the bottom our Legs are like Jelly, we rest for fifteen minutes then walk to Camp.

Day 2 Walking

Rise at 5am, shower is lukewarm, set off at 7.30. About an hour on Dirt Road then into Jungle and up very steep Hills, three hours later we reach the first Summit. We are split into two Groups, each Group having a Guide at the front and Guide at the back. The back Guide will stay with the last Person no matter how slow they are, if it looks like someone won't be able to complete the trek there are a few points at which they can meet up with another Guide who will take them back to the Road where they can meet up with a Car. Each guide has a two way Radio and is in contact with all other Guides. There is a qualified Doctor on the trek who also has a Radio.

There is a high level of organisation and everyone has confidence in those who are looking after us. Today is the hardest day out of the six days. Twenty seven km over two Mountain Peaks, visit two Waterfalls and swim at both of them. The other Group came upon a Wolf protecting two Cubs. She snarled at them but did not attack anyone. The Brazil Wolf is like a red fox in appearance but is bigger than a German Sheppard Dog. One Woman gets a Blister and has to wait for a Doctor who is with the second group. Another Girl slips and hurts her Foot at a Waterfall. The Doctor and a Guide stay with them and they finish the trek an hour behind the rest of us.

We arrive at Camp at 6pm, eleven hours after we left this morning. Our new Camp is very basic, no Electricity, no Sink, no Mirrors, cold Showers by Candle Light. The Food is good. Our Tents are the same as last night. I thought I had Sun Block packed but too late I find that I don't have any so I had to borrow it but I still got Sunburn on my Neck. Last night was a strange one. I was so tired that as soon as I had a shower and meal I went to bed at 8.30 and fell asleep right away. I awoke in the middle of the Night and everyone was asleep. My Bladder is full and I need to go to the Toilet but I'm afraid that getting out of the Tent will wake up my Tent mate Mick Kelly. I have lost my Watch so I have no idea what time it is. I lie there thinking I will go back to sleep but no chance. The pressure gets worse.

After another hour I can't take any more. I climb over Mick's feet to reach the Zip of the tent and undo it. There are two Zips and they seem to make a lot of noise in the silence of the night but I do it and then stumble and fall on my way out. On my way back I fall into the Tent across Mick and manage to get back into my Sleeping Bag thinking I will go right back to sleep but no chance, I'm sure I woke up Mick getting back into the tent but he says nothing. Mick stretches and yawns so I'm sure he is awake now. After a while he grunts but still says nothing. I say nothing. I don't know what time I went back to sleep. The next morning my Watch had been found.

Monday 23rd

Compared too yesterday today is easy and very enjoyable. We walk two and half hours to a series of Waterfalls. There are five Waterfalls very close together. The highest one is Fifty meters (164 feet) and the ground crew have set us up for abseiling down the big fall and into the Pool below. We then have to swim across to where there are lovely flat Rocks to lie out on and watch the Waterfalls. It's so beautiful that I am sure you could wake up every day to look at it and never get tired of it. The abseiling was a wonderful experience and one I would repeat every chance I get.

It was not a good day for everyone in the group. The heat at the falls got the better of two Women who had to be taken back to camp and spend the afternoon in bed. One other Girl who suffers from MS also had to be taken back to Camp and put to Bed. The valley where those Waterfalls are located is called Dead Heat Valley and when you are in the valley you can understand why. It's surprising more people were not affected by the heat.

Tuesday 24th

Problems start early. Kelly shows us her bottom Lip which is swollen to twice its normal size. Doctor Simon says it's either a sting or a bite or maybe an allergic reaction to some of the Food. Kelly insists she is well enough to go walking but after less than an hour she was weak and had to be brought back and would be moved to the next Camp by Car. Nicky who has MS is unable to start the walk. Two other Women have Diarrhoea but Dr Simon gives them something that settles them down and allows them to go walking. Each day when I arrive back at the end of our trek I take the Drink Bobby gave me and it restores the Muscles without letting them seize up.

Up at 7am. We begin with a seven kilometre walk up the Mountain. We walk Six Km along the top and four km decent. We were told we would get signals on our mobiles on the top of the mountain but it never came. I have been out of touch from last Sunday. As we descended through the Rain Forest we came to a wooden House made of Bamboo. There was no one at Home but our Guide took us through the House as he knows the owner. It's about Twelve Foot square, two openings with no Doors or Windows. Downstairs is just one open space with seats made from logs? Some Pans and Pots in one corner for cooking, a Ladder goes upstairs to the open space of a Bedroom. When we come out of the House we are right beside a River and the owner of the House is on the Bank of the River playing Panpipes. He continues playing as we bathe our Feet in the River. We stay there about forty five minutes as he plays the Pan Pipes nonstop. The scene is like something from a dream or an ad on TV. We all gave him some money as we left and he smiled and said Abrigado (which means Thank You).

Today we were told to wear long Pants as we were going through areas of long Grass that has a lot of Ticks on the Grass and they jump on to your Leg as you pass. If you don't spot them and knock them off they will bite into your Skin and just stay there sucking your Blood and getting bigger. You have to be careful about how you remove them. If you just pull them off the Head will stay stuck in your Skin and could become infected and will be painful and difficult to remove. One day we were walking through the Hills and our Guide spotted a large Rattlesnake right in our Path. He was about two meters long and his Body was about as thick as my Arm. Later Patrick was telling other Walkers about it and he said it was as thick as his Leg. By the time he gets home it will be an Anaconda. Nicky who has MS has been in the camp all day and is not feeling well. Kelly with the big Lip is feeling much better. Her Lip is still swollen but not as bad as it was.

Our Guides are extraordinary young Men. They are as lean as our son Rob and just as strong and fit. They look like they could walk forever. They can swim like fish and when we are at Waterfalls they climb a sheer Rock Face freehand and dive from great heights into the Pools below. They all speak good English and know everything about the forests, rivers and animals and are all very conscious of how important the Environment is. They always talk about saving things rather than destroying them.

As we walked along the top of the Mountain we came to some Farmland where Workers were harvesting Soya Beans. As they passed on their Tractor they stopped to chat with our Guide Raphael who they seem to know quite well, then one of them unloads four large Water Melons which they had just pulled at the side of the Field. We had no way to slice them so one of the men hopped on the Tractor and drove to nearby Farm Buildings and came back with a Knife. We gorged ourselves until the Melons were gone. We then had some Photos taken with the Farm workers and moved on. There was also a crop of Corn on the Cob which looked ripe enough to eat.

Wednesday 25

Short walk of about five Kilometres to more extraordinary Waterfalls, in that short distance we passed five Waterfalls before settling down at one spot where two large Waterfalls from different Rivers fall into one series of pools. There are two large pools to swim in and good spots to jump or dive from. Each night after dinner we get a briefing about what to expect tomorrow and Dr. Simon gives a report on any new health problems that come up. Lots of muscular leg problems, lots of use for my Voltorol Gel and Tablets. Not many people came well prepared. Two Women and one Man suffered from falls on Rocks but nothing too serious. I lost my anti Malaria Tablets on Day two, but it's not a big worry as the Mosquitoes that spread Malaria don't come this far south, although it is a big problem up North and in the Amazon Jungle.

I slipped on Rocks at a Waterfall on Day two and my new Digital Camera got wet and misted up and did not work for two or three Days. It's still not right. As a result I will only have a small selection of Photos but there is talk of someone setting up a Website where we could send their shots and everyone could see them all. The camp we are in now for two nights is very basic; no Electricity, cold Showers and cold Water in the Taps.

We either buy Bottled Water or use Tap Water with purification Tablets and use it twenty minutes after the tablet is placed in the bottle. There are no Lights in the Camp except a Gas Light in the Dining Room which is just a big Straw Hut with no Windows, Door, Sides, Front or Back, just a Roof. A Husband and Wife team have moved with us from camp to camp providing a full body massage. They are both booked out each evening. I got two massages and fell asleep both times, cost $40. Each Day I carry out my plan to stay up with the leaders and it has resulted in a big improvement in my level of fitness. Some of the young Men and Women set a hard pace and I have to work hard to keep up or keep close but I would normally be in the first half dozen which is not bad out of twenty three in our Group.

I carry a Bag of Raisins and nibble away at them when the going gets tough, they are full of sugar and give an immediate energy boost, I work real hard trying to keep up while the young ones are singing and telling jokes and making it look easy but then I think that they were about thirty five years younger than me and I conclude that I'm doing ok, Particularly as there are fifteen or twenty behind me who are all much younger than me. After me the oldest Man and Woman are both forty eight. First Rain of the trip is very heavy during the night. We thank god the rain did not come as we were climbing or descending the Mountain. We might have been stranded for some time due to the risks.

Day 6 Walking

Today is our last Day; everyone is still in good health except Nicky who has MS. She will travel in a land rover and meet up with us for the last five Kilometres which is mostly downhill and the hope is that she can walk in with us to the tiny Village where our 105km Trek ends. Today the route has been changed from our original plan which was for 17k, it's now 22k. The change was to avoid areas infested with Ticks which would come out in millions after the rain.

We start about 8 a.m. and straight away a small group set a very hard pace. They are full of enthusiasm as it's the last day, they keep saying; just think of it, tonight we have a bed to sleep in, not many enjoyed sleeping in the tents. Imagine a tent six foot by six foot square for two adults each with rucksack's and Back Pack. In most places the Ground was very uneven and even with a Rubber Mat on the Ground it was still uncomfortable. In some Camps there was no provisions for washing Clothes and when we got in each Day our Clothes were dripping with Sweat and with no way to wash them they had to be put in a Plastic Bag but eventually I began to run short of Clothes to wear.

As soon as we got to a Camp with a Sink I had to wash some Clothes as best I could and put them to dry across the top of our Tent. I decided it would be foolish to try and keep up with the leaders at such a pace but I managed to keep them in sight most of the time. Eventually the guide who is with the lead group makes them stop and wait for the rest of us. The good thing about being with the lead group is that you get a lot more rest when you stop but today the lead group can't be held back. It reminds me of when I was young during the school holidays. We always had to draw home the Turf and when we get to the last bend before our house the Ass would start running as soon as he saw the House no matter how tired he was. The good thing is its all dirt road rather than through jungle or rocky Paths but it is still all uphill and very steep for the last three hours and then up and down a bit before the long decent.

Everyone agreed that when we got close to the Village we would wait for the rest of the group and all march in together. So for the last two kilometres it was the full pack and our five guides singing the fields of Athenry, as we approached, all the people from the village (about thirty) were out to greet us. There was a big Barretstown Banner strung across the Road which was temporarily closed. Our regular ground Crew were also there and it was a very emotional moment for everyone involved including the local villagers who had never met us before and only knew that Ireland was in Europe but nothing more than that. There are lots of Ants here and it would seem that their favourite food is my sunburned insteps. The fact that I have wiped out half of their race by now does not deter them in the least.

Helen O'Malley who is the head fundraiser for Barrettstown led us in. After we had got over the emotion and stopped congratulating and hugging each other the locals had our Food ready. The tiny Village we were in looked terribly poor. The Houses are like what you would see in Irish pictures from the time of the famine, but they were able to produce plenty of good wholesome Food for about fifty five people and everyone enjoyed it. The local company who provides the guides for those trips work with those Village People and trips like ours provide them with important income.

It was here also that we were able to buy a lovely Book of pictures taken in the part of Brazil we were in. Some of the Waterfalls are shown in the pictures and the old Lady who prepared our Food is in one of the pictures. The Book is written by Ian David who is a half owner of the company that provides our guides. I got to know him quite well. He signed my book. I also bought CD of Brazilian music and Ian is one of the musicians. In the recording, Pablo who was one of our guides also features on the CD on guitar. He and the other guides all signed my book as well. We had a one and half hour bus journey back to the small Hotel where we had started our trek from. Mobile Phone signals are very erratic here. I had got a signal here when we arrived a week ago and rang Puddin but now I can't get a signal at all so I have to use Mick Kelly's Phone to text Puddin for her to ring me on his phone and I got to talk to her very briefly. That night there is a banquet arranged for us at a local Bar/Restaurant with a very good local band singing in English and Portuguese languages. The lead singer is a brother of Tattoo, one of our guides. I bought a CD of his music and we stayed there until 2.30am and then went back to our hotel.

Friday 27th. we were called again at 4.30 for our three hour bus trip to Brasilia where we had to get a flight to Rio where we arrived at 2.30. We checked into our hotel and straight back on the bus where we were taken to the Train Station of Christ the Redeemer on a huge Rock overlooking the City. The original plan was that we would walk up to the top but we were all very happy to hear that due to time constraints we would all get the Train to the top. The Train took twenty minutes, so we can only guess at how many hours it would take to walk. I am still in trouble with my Camera and can only get two or three photos up there. This extraordinary Statue is a present from the French government and is thirty six meters tall; the views from all around the base are stunning. We go back to our Hotel and agree to meet at 9pm for dinner in the Restaurant of our own Hotel. It turned out to be a disaster. Some were given the wrong meals, some were underdone. At 11pm some were only getting their starters. It's a five star hotel and we can't understand why they can't cope with a group of our size. Some people left without their main course. I was one of a small number who was happy with what I got.

Sunday29

We leave at 4pm today and I'm planning to go to the Botanic Gardens but Owen Murray asked me will I go on a Helicopter trip. He needs four people so I say yes but that means I am rushed because we have to be checked out by 12 and we won't be back till 1.30. I also want to go for a swim on Copa Cabana Beach which is where our Hotel is., I have a half hour Swim and have a big rush to get checked out before our pick up at 10.30. In the rush I forgot my Camera but fortunately the other three people on the trip have their camera and agree to get me an extra set of Pictures. The night we arrived here I did my only shopping and got a Handbag for Puddin.

On this trip I realised that I am not the only person that snores in the group. Gary and Kath were in the tent next to me and one night as I lay awake she began snoring. It was most unusual when she produced a second layer of sound, a bit like Enya's music, layer upon layer. The youngest guide Marcella took great delight in showing me the Maps of the area we were in and he gave me one of his Maps to take home. As I do my final check out of the Hotel and our Coach is ready for the Airport, I can't find my Mobile Phone. I hope it's in with my clothes. Looking back on the last week everyone thinks it's remarkable how well everyone got on so well considering the conditions and the hardship we endured on a daily basis.

The team leader from Action Adventure Kieran had the job going around each morning and calling us at 5.30 a.m. He took great delight in this task even though he would get a chorus of, f**k off or, go away. He would respond with, thank you, thank you very much.

As we travelled through Brazil it's obvious that most of the people are very poor. In country Towns there are unusual contrast like streets lined with Houses we would call "Hovels" and in the same Street a brand new Skate Board Park and well dressed kids using it or the Hovels with a Satellite Dish on the Roof. Our guide provided a box for us to put in any Clothes or items we did not wish to take home. I gave up most of my clothes I brought out. When I explained to Pablo our guide that all our clothes were dirty and we would not have a chance to wash them he said don't worry we will get them washed.

As we drove into Rio our Guide pointed out huge slum areas. Whole Mountain sides covered in Shacks, many are of Brick but are tiny, most of those shanty towns have evolved with no official planning but still have their own tiny Shops, Bars, and Restaurants, all of which are also Shacks and from a hygiene point we would be afraid to go near them never mind go into them to eat or drink. Most of the slums are controlled by criminal gangs and are mostly no go areas for the police, when the Police do decide to go into the area to make an arrest they would go as a huge convoy with machine guns and riot gear and would expect the criminals to take them on and very often those raids result in loss of life of Police officers as well as criminal gang members. It is often said that people who live in those conditions develop immunities to the poor hygiene but it's also a fact that they have a much shorter life expectancy than people who live in better conditions.

Our Hotel in Rio is on the Copa Cabana which is a lovely Beach and is made famous in songs and films. The Beach is very wide and is four kilometres long. It is lined with permanent Goalposts for soccer and volleyball. People are using them all the time but there are so many pitches' that you can always find one to use. Our Hotel has a Rooftop Swimming Pool and Gym from which you have lovely views of the Beach from sixteen floors up. I got some nice photos from the Roof and also from the Helicopter.

Helen has kept one more surprise for us; we travelled by Bus for two hours to a coastal Port Town and got on to a motor Boat just for our group. After about one and half hours sunbathing on the Boat we anchored at a small Beach where some of us had a swim for forty five minutes. We then sailed on to a small Restaurant/bar where we had a lovely buffet meal of Fish/Meat Vegetable and Fruit. When we got back to our Hotel we only had one hour to get ready and back on the Bus again to a lovely Restaurant to eat our fill and back on the bus to a show of dancing, music and a gymnastics show that would look good in the Olympic Games.

It was one of the high lights of the trip for most of us. For Irish Men and Women the drinking was very little. Some of them ignored Dr. Simon's advice not to stay up late in the camp drinking Alcohol. They paid the price the next day in the hot Sun and losing so much sweat they were dehydrated. It really only happened one or two nights and everyone took Dr Simon more serious from then on. The amount of planning and organising that went into this trip was enormous. First you had the Barrettstown team of five people who travelled with us. Then there was the travel tour Company Action Adventure from London, Dr Simon, Ciaran, and Colo and there was the E.C.O tourism company in Brazil who provided the guides and arranged the Camp sites and Food and drinks on a daily basis.

Each evening in Camp the three teams would have a meeting and then have a briefing session with all of us about what to expect tomorrow and how to prepare for it. Ciaran, of Action Travel said we were the best prepared group he had to deal with, example Day two, 27km over two mountains and eleven hours, he expected three or four people would fail to finish but we all finished and mostly in good health. This would be thanks to Helen arranging the training weekends at Barrettstown and making sure people were properly prepared.

We are on our way home now and can reflect on the adventure which is about to end. Many of the group talked about it being an unusual experience and one that was enlightening due to meeting with and talking to such a diverse group of people. We range in age from twenty two to sixty one and come from just about every walk of life. Dave has his own glass wholesale business. Rachel is a Barrister. Derek is a bricklayer. Owen is a Car salesman. Mick has a Supermarket in Dun Laoghaire. Sharon has two Crèches in Tallaght and Blanchardstown. There are Physiotherapists and IT experts. Jacinta said she can see life from a much broader perspective. Lisa Cummins who is one of Ireland's top Models had never got over the death of her four year old son said she has found peace and believes she can face life with much more confidence due to the experience she has been through.

It was the first Trek abroad for Helen as a Barretstown fundraising Project so it's great for her that all went well and there were no accidents. On the first leg of our flight from Rio to Sao Paulo, Mary, one of the Barrettstown staff fainted. Dr. Simon looked after her on the plane and when we arrived at Sao Paulo she was back on her feet and able to walk. However she was not allowed to board the plane until a Brazilian doctor came to the airport and examined her. On the flight she is still not well so the other staff and passengers swapped around seats and somehow got her extra seats so she could lie down and sleep.

This has not been a good flight for me. The seat is hard and I can't get comfortable to have some sleep. A baby is screaming. They walk her up and down the aisle twice trying to calm her. We all have TV screens in the seat in front of us and a control panel in our arm rest but my control panel is hanging out of its socket and is not working. I can't watch a film or listen to an audio channel or even look at the map to see where I am. The light above my seat is not working so I can't read or write. It's been daylight for hours now but I could not open my window shade as the blaze of light from the sun lights up the whole plane and people are still asleep. It's only when they start to wake up I can at last read or write.

We did not see a lot of wildlife on our walks because our area was at such high altitude. The jungle only develops in patches, mostly valleys and mountain sides and that means that Animals which live up north in the Amazon could not live here in the same numbers. For example a jaguar weighs 126 kg so he eats a lot of meat but in this area he will roam over forty square kilometres and they do not share territory with other jaguars or with leopards and of course all wild animals are shy of humans and very quickly disappear if they see or hear us coming.

The most interesting Bird we saw was the Toucan. It's a very big bird but it has a huge yellow beak the size of its body. They travel in a flock of twenty or thirty but they fly in pairs very tight together while the rest of them can be scattered over a wide area. Each pair seems like they are almost touching Wing Tips and they call out caw caw like a Rook at home but only ten times louder.

As usual there are some lovely people in a group this size and there are some people that everyone will feel comfortable with regardless of age or gender. Then there are some funny ones. Georgina is a loud mouth but she is so funny you can't help liking her. Owen is like my friend Liam Flanagan for telling jokes nonstop. Patrick is a great singer and loves to sing on the Track or in the Bar. Kelly loves to sing and entertain but uses foul language. I heard her say to another girl I am getting worse at the bad language, I will have to give it up. I overheard Mary say to Kelly; after all this walking my Butt will be so hard the girls won't believe it. Most of the girls could not wait to get to Rio and to a hairdresser and its wonderful how they can look glamorous even in Clothes that have been in a Rucksack for over a week. There have been stories of two or three romances but only time will tell if they last. The Barrettstown staffs are going to arrange a reunion of the group next September which everyone is looking forward to.

One of the more unusual things we were shown by our guides was on the very top of the mountains where it is flat for miles but here and there is springs of crystal clear water. They were still flowing when we were there even though it had not rained for twenty days, It saturates the Grass as it starts to make a stream and joins with others and becomes a waterfall. The wet season which is November / December it rains and continues almost every day for two or three months. The Rivers rise by ten or fifteen feet and the Waterfalls will be much more dramatic. I would love to see them in full flow but it would probably be too dangerous to use the tracks we used if it were raining.

Brazil 2008, back to Brazil on another trek for Barretstown and still with Helen O'Malley as our Leader but this time she is leading us for her own company which she formed with Colette O'Sullivan, they do the organising that Charities would normally have to do themselves, their new Company is called **ACARA Project Management for Charities,** I have covered this in greater detail in chapter 19. This trek is in a different part of Brazil to the previous trek and is different in that each day we go up and over Mountains and come down to small Coastal fishing Villages that can only be accessed as we did by walking over the Mountains or by Boat from other Coastal Towns, on this trek I pulled a Muscle in the Calf of Right Leg and missed 2 days walking as a result. One day we had walked on a long Beach and had to cross a number of Streams which flowed down from the Mountains and across the sandy beach into the sea, we took off our boots when crossing the streams and could feel the Sand moving under our feet, when Niki was crossing one of those Streams the sand moved so much that it took her feet from under her and she was suddenly up to her waist in sand and water, she was helpless and was lucky that another member of our group Stephen Murray was standing right beside her when she went down Stephen grabbed Niki as she was being swept away, Niki was badly shaken but never complained, it was not her style to complain.

This trip will also be remembered because of another member of our group, I was introduced to Jane (not her real name) at the Airport as we checked in and my first impression was, my God this Woman must weigh about 23 Stone, (322 lbs or 146 kg,) how is she going to manage this trek, from my experience of previous treks I knew that unfit walkers suffered badly and often had to be rescued and were unable to complete the trek but I had never seen one that was about double their normal Body weight and I had a bad feeling each time I looked at her, my fears were well founded because on our first day walking we hit a steep hill almost immediately and Jane was in trouble from the start, she was stopping every few minutes and because a trek of this type can only move as fast as the slowest walker everyone was stopping constantly when there would have been no need to were it not for Jane. I gave her my 2 walking poles and showed her how to use them but it would have taken a Horse to pull Jane up the Hills. As the day progressed we were split into 2 groups, the slow group was Jane supported by Helen, a Guide and the Doctor who was staying with us for the whole 6 days walking, at one stage near the end of the days walking we had to wait for about 1 ½ hours for them to catch up, many of the group were furious and said, is it going to be like this every day. We were told later that on the Mountain Jane had seized up with cramps in her Stomach and could not move at all, the Doctor Gave her something that got her moving in more ways than one, she later called the Doctor a Witch Doctor and said he was trying to kill her, next day she would not leave her room and would not talk to anyone, a decision was taken that she could not be allowed to continue, she would have to be sent home, and she was. We learned afterwards that she had not turned up for any of the training days arranged but assured Helen by Phone that she was training a lot at home, she was one of the first to pay her €5000 and no one had met her until she arrived at the airport. With Jane out of the way the remainder of the 2nd Brazil trek was a very enjoyable one.

Jenny with her cousin Jillian O'Neill

Our son Phil in our back garden

Climbing Croagh Patrick l to r, Jim Smullen my
brothers John and brendan and Me, 2009

Me with my good friend tommy Kelly

Chapter 19

Thursday April 13 2006 Barretstown Vietnam Trek We all
Meet at Airport 1 pm and depart for LHR @ 3.35

Depart LHR for Seoul, South Korea at 9.30—as the Plane was coming
in to land in Seoul I looked for my Tickets and could not find them,
everyone was leaving the Plane and I had to go with them.

Helen O'Malley from Barrettstown was in charge and had gone ahead
and I could not get out to let her know what had happened. Stephan
Meigh from Action Challange was behind me and stopped to see what
was wrong. He wanted to bring me out to where he could arrange to
have new Tickets issued but they would not let us go any further. They
were saying I would have to buy new tickets but Stephan would not
hear of it, he kept saying to them, you must issue new tickets. The big
problem was that I had not only lost my Ticket from Seoul to Hanoi but
also my return Tickets from Hanoi to Seoul, and to London and also
to Dublin.

I kept saying the Tickets must be on the Plane because I had them all
when I boarded at London. Stephan asked if he could go back and
search the Plane where I sat but they would not agree. In the end, the
Korean Woman who was dealing with us agreed to go to the Plane and
ask the Cleaners if they had found my Tickets. About 10 minutes later
she came back smiling with my Tickets; we had to wait six hours for our
flight to Hanoi.

We had a four and a half hour flight and when we arrived in Hanoi I was
told my Bag had gone to Japan by mistake. They presented me with a
small overnight bag so I could have a shave and shower. They also gave

me $50 for the inconvenience. I had to borrow clothes from Mick Kelly and Socks from Susan O'Brien. We had a forty five minute Bus journey to our hotel in Hanoi City Centre. I had worn my Boots on the Plane just in case this would happen but I had no walking Socks, I had no spare Underpants or Shirts. It was 1 a.m. local time when we got to our Hotel, 2 a.m. when we got to Bed; we had to be up again at 6.30 am.

Day One in Vietnam

We were up at 6.30 a.m. We had Breakfast and got a Bus for a four and a half hour journey to our first Camp. We were shown to our Rooms; one big open Room for all 33 of us, men and women all in one room with a mattresses about one inch thick side by side on the Floor. They later put up a Mosquito net over each Bed which gave a small degree of privacy. For the afternoon, we had a 4 hour trek through the Village and out through Rise Paddies into the Hills. We passed some houses that could only be accessed by Foot or by Scooter. As we walked through the hills we heard loud music coming towards us. It was a man on a Scooter with a Shop on the back of his Bike. He had everything from Shoes to mobile Phones to CD's. That night we were told that one evening we could have a choice of Dog or beef for Dinner but we had to place our order now, four or five including me ordered Dog.

I had only taken four or five pictures when my Camera went dead. I have spare Batteries in my Bag which is now in Japan. I have to take Anti Malaria Tablets but they are also in Japan along with my Cap which has to protect the back of my Neck so I got sunburned for the first two days. I also have a problem that when I go for very long walks the insides of my Legs are rubbing against each other and they become very raw and sore. My solution to this problem would be to rub Vaseline on the insides of my Legs but that is also in my Bag in Japan. I did not want to ask anyone for Vaseline so I head off on the second day to take my chance that everything will be ok. As it turned out it was far from ok and the inside of my legs are feeling raw, that night local men and women put on a lovely show of singing and dancing for us.

Day Two

Our three flights Dublin / London, London / Seoul and Seoul / Hanoi, to hotel had taken twenty nine hours so I dumped the Underpants which

I had worn and borrowed a clean pair from my roommate Mick Kelly, my bag has still not arrived. I have been borrowing Malarone Malaria Tablets from Conor and will have to continue to do so until my bag arrives and I can then return them to Conor.

The razor I got in the overnight bag from Korean Airlines is only good for one shave and I cut myself several times before throwing it in the bin. I also have to borrow Socks, Mosquito Spray, Sun Block, Tee-Shirts before setting off for our long trek. It turns out to be the longest, hardest day of the whole trek, ten hours and 30 km over two mountain ranges. By the end of the day my Legs were raw and sore, I was walking with my Legs wide apart like a Crab to try and minimise the rubbing.

Apart from my sore legs it was a very enjoyable day. We went over the mountains and down into the Valleys where the Hmong people live in isolated houses that can only be reached by foot or in some cases by scooter. The Hmong are originally from China and came to this area about four hundred years ago to avoid persecution, they also went in droves to, Burma, Laos, and Thailand but there are still about 5 Million of them in China. They like to live in isolation at very high altitudes. They are very shy and get flustered if someone tries to communicate with them, even our Vietnamese guide who can speak their language has difficulty communicating with them. The women have very long hair but they wear it up in a huge whirl on their heads.

Kelly developed a bad Blister on her Foot and had to be helped to a location where she could be met by another guide on a Scooter who took her to a Jeep which has the supplies for the next Camp. We have a lady Vietnamese Doctor who stays with the slowest walker. She was with Kelly but she cannot cure a Blister. She can only give Kelly some relief and will see her in the Camp later on tonight.

I arrive at our new village to be told my bag is only arriving back in Hanoi which is 500 km away and cannot be got to us; in those villages everything is very basic. The Toilet is a Hole in the Ground outside our building. Our shower today is a Pipe which is really an overflow pipe from a water tank on the side of the Road at the edge of the Village. We have to be very careful because this Water is flowing constantly and has formed slime on the ground which makes it very slippery.

As it is on the side of the Road we need to have a quick Shower because there are Women and Children walking by and we pull a Towel around us until they have passed, The Ladies Shower is the same but at least it's in behind walls although there is no roof. Our water pipe comes out of the tank about 4 feet high so it is a bit awkward as you have to crouch or squat to get under the Pipe. I still have no batteries for my camera. I missed some great photo scenes today and a chance to take a picture of the Hmong people.

I told Colo about my Leg problems and that I did not expect to be able to walk tomorrow but I applied Savlon Cream to the affected areas and took ponston and voltorol so that I might have some comfort for the evening and get some sleep tonight, I took another Ponston when going to bed.

Day Three

I got a good night's sleep and woke up feeling much better so I decided to have a go but I borrowed Vaseline from Tim and applied a layer of it. I still have to borrow all other items until my bag arrives. Kelly cannot walk today so she will be taken by Scooter or jeep to our next Village. Fabulous scenes of Rice Fields in the Mountains but I still had no Camera. Very hot all day, thirty four degrees and very humid. About 11 am Conor from Kerry had to be rescued by Scooter. He had Blisters and was exhausted. At 12 noon Rhonwyn is rescued by scooter with Blisters and exhaustion.

I learn that there are two types of Rice, Wet Rice and Dry Rice. The Wet Rice is where the Paddy Fields are flooded with water all the time. Dry Rice grows without Water and depends on Rain for moisture. The wet Fields can produce two Crops each year and down in South Vietnam where it is much closer to the Equator they can get 3 crops a year. However, the dry rice is a better quality. I don't know which type we get in Ireland. In the villages where we stay the only form of transport is a bike or scooter and the scooter is used as a work horse. It's incredible what they get on to them. A regular sight would be a man and woman with one, two or three Children, Pigs, Chickens, Bananas, Corn, Timber or a man with twenty foot long by three inch wide Bamboo Poles on one Shoulder while riding the bike with one Hand. Children are on scooters as babies and they grow up on them so everyone has complete confidence while on them. We see Children two or three years old on the back of a Scooter holding on or in some cases just with their Hands resting on their Legs looking around them. The good thing is they don't go very fast but then they can't because the roads are just dirt tracks even in the Villages and they have to avoid the Holes.

Still on day three and twice during the day I have borrowed Vaseline from Tim and taken Ponston so that I can keep going. Every House seems to have a Cow or two with Calves, Pigs, Chickens and they also breed Dogs for eating. At lunch time we reach a Village where Lunch is prepared for us. It is laid out on the Floor and we all sit cross legged on the Floor to eat our Meal.

I get the good news that my Bag is in the Jeep so I get some clean Clothes and have a Shower before sitting down for Lunch. Everyone has been very good to me while my Bag is missing but it also gave rise to lots of jokes because I have lost both my Tickets and my Bag. Helen O'Malley said that when we are in the Mountains I should lead the way because if anything bad was going to happen it would happen to me and then everyone would be ok after that, Helen has a great sense of hummer and always knows the right thing to say to cheer people up when it's needed.

In most houses we eat from Tables about four inches high but today we have hit rock bottom and are on the Floor. When we are finished our meals the staff just pick up the Table with the Dishes still on board and carry them to the room that acts as a Kitchen. It is not a Kitchen as we would think of it. The Dishes are washed in a Basin under an outdoor Tap or in the River when there is one close by.

The food is all prepared by Women sitting on the Ground. No Table or Bench of any sort. We find it hard to understand why they do it in this way because most of us find it uncomfortable to sit like this for very long. The scenery gets better each day and now that I have my Camera back in action I can get more Pictures.

Today we have to cross some very rickety Rope Bridges. Being on a Rope Bridge forty feet above Water is un-nerving for most people but couple that with about every second Plank missing makes it a real challenge. Some Girls and some Men have to be helped across. Two people would not move without two people holding them by their Arms. It is just another example of how those trips make people do things they did not believe they could do and overcome their worst fears.

As we descended the mountain today a Log fell against Martina and gave her a large bruise on her Thigh. She was badly shaken up by it and we stopped about 20 minutes to let her get herself together again. In one village there was a Man, Woman, Child and Cat on a scooter weaving in and out between the Holes in the Road. A Waterwheel made from bamboo takes water from a River, dumps it in a Tray which is balanced and when the Tray is full it drops down dumping the Water into a Channel which is directed into the Rice Fields, this is a scene that probably has not changed for thousands of years,

At our briefing this evening, we were told that there will be no Motor Bike rescue available tomorrow because the Track is so rough, so anyone with Blister problems or any other problem that would prevent them completing 8 hours hard walking should stay with the Jeep or the Truck which has all our Bags along with our food and drink. If someone gets stuck on the Mountain and is unable to walk our guides would make a temporary Stretcher out of Bamboo poles from the Forest and carry them to where they would be met by appropriate transport. Niamh at 18 is the youngest; I am 62 and the oldest that's a 44 years difference.

Day Four

Ron, Kelly and Conor are out of action due to Blisters, Mary hurt her big Toe on our first night when she banged it against a Post. She managed to keep going but today with no Motor Bike rescue available she is afraid to take a chance. The other three are all people who did not prepare themselves properly by getting in plenty of training in advance. Kelly and Ron should have known better as they were both in Brazil with us and the same thing happened to them on that trip.

They missed the highlight of the trip as far as scenery is concerned. The rest of us are a bit dopey because we were awake most of the night. At 3.20 a Rooster started crowing under our House and continued non-stop until 3.50 when he was joined by Ducks going quack quack! Another Rooster joined in later but he was either very young or very old because he could only manage a squawk. This continued until we were called at 6.30. As the night went on and the noise got louder some men would shout "f . . . . off" or "shut up" or "go away". Then Mick Kelly shouted "alright I'm going"!

Day 5

We were almost at the top of the mountain at 3 p.m. when we came upon a group of about fifty Women sitting on the side of the Road with empty Baskets which they carry with a Strap over their Shoulders or over the top of their Head. They were there to carry our Rucksacks (which had not yet arrived) down to the Valley over one thousand feet below us. This was because the Road was as narrow as about three foot wide at some points with one thousand foot drop over the side. Not only did they have to carry our Rucksacks when they arrived but also the Food and Drink for our Dinner this evening and our Breakfast in the morning. We were all flabbergasted at this idea but it is extra Money for those women who would normally only work in the Rice Fields. We were told that the Jeep with the Bags was not due for another two hours so we set off down the narrow track to our Home for the night.

Normally the first thing we do is have a shower but without our bags we have no toiletries or clean clothes so we all just sat around and rest. Soon it started to rain and we were worried about the Ladies carrying our heavy Bags down the steep slippery Path. It got dark about 6.30 and still no sign of our Bags. We then got word that there was problems. The Truck with our Bag's, Food and Water was supposed to drive as far as he could up the mountain where he would be met by a Jeep which would have to make two or three trips up to where the girls were waiting on top of the Mountain. The problem was that the Truck could not manage the Mountain roads which were now in a mess from the Rain. It was stuck 125 km away from where it should have been. We all said that we did not want anyone putting their lives at risk for our sake as we could not imagine how those ladies could come down the slippery three foot wide path in the dark with a thousand foot drop on one side and their only footwear are flip flops.

We were told that there was no chance we would have our bags tonight and it was agreed there would be no point bringing them down in the morning just so we could have a change of Clothes. The people in the village were trying to put together a Meal for us but it was not ready until 9 p.m. It was a great Meal and everyone was in good form considering what had happened. After dinner we just sat around and talked. There was no Beer or soft Drinks so it was a dry night. Some people including myself went to bed early. At 12.30 am. I was woken by someone shouting "The Bags have arrived". I could make no sense of this so I just went back to sleep.

But indeed the Bags had arrived. The drivers of the Truck and Jeep who had refused to tackle the wet Mountain Road had changed their minds and made it up to where the Girls were waiting from about 2 p.m. in the afternoon. Then some men came up from the village on scooters and loaded the rucksacks onto them and the women carried the rest of them down the Road. We still can't believe it but we know it happened. It was about 11.30 p.m. when the last Bag arrived in our Village.

To look down into this valley it's the most beautiful site you could imagine but when you get down there it is the poorest of all the Villages we were in. Three hundred people living in about fifty houses. They have their own School and with all their own Animals and fowl and Rice would probably be close to self sufficient but my god they are so poor. We had a collection among ourselves and raised about $300. If our other group coming next week have another collection there should be enough to buy a generator for the Village.

Day Five

I had a wash with at an outdoor Tap using a Basin of Water and a Saucepan to wash the Water off myself. Then rub on Shampoo and Soap and then more saucepans of Water to wash it off. The Women who took our Bags down in the middle of the night are already waiting for our bags at 7 a.m. to carry them back up the Hill and out of the Valley. They are all smiles as if they were the ones having the adventure rather than us. When we were all gathered waiting to leave, all the people of the Village were there to see us off including the local Chief, Helen gave a short speech saying how much we appreciate what had been done for us and the Chief responded thanking us for supporting their Village, one of our Vietnamese Guides acted as interpreter during the speeches.

It took us about one hour to climb back up the mountain with our Bags on our back and we stopped to rest at the top. About ten minutes later the first of the girls arrived with loads at least twice as heavy as ours. Maybe three times as heavy and they kept on going to where they were to meet up with the Jeep. It rained half way up the Mountain for about half an hour and then stopped with the Sun coming out but not for long. It started to rain again and continued to rain heavy. We took shelter in a half built School and sat on heaps of Rubble to have our Lunch. After Lunch it rained almost all afternoon and when we reached our Village we were soaked from Head to Foot and covered in Muck.

4.20 am A Cow or bull started bellowing beside our house and continued at regular intervals until about 5.30, another night of broken Sleep. Some Vietnamese people don't want us to take their picture as they say it will take away their soul.

Day Six

This is our Last day of walking. It's supposed to be an easy Day. A Bus should collect us at 8 a.m. and drive for about one hour. Then we should walk two to three hours where we meet the Bus for Hanoi. (That was the plan) but no Bus arrived. As we leave the Village the Truck with all our Bags passed us and they will to take our Bags to the Bus for Hanoi. About twenty minutes later we saw our Truck ahead of us. It was half way across a wooden Bridge and the Wheels had broken through the Timbers and were well and truly stuck. The Bridge was blocked and it was only possible for us to pass it by walking sideways and clinging to the side of the Truck. Two of our Trekkers, Kelly and Connor, were in the Truck as they were unable to walk due to Blisters. They thought the Truck was going to fall into the River 20 feet below. When we saw what happened to the Truck we were glad the Bus had not collected us and tried to cross the Bridge.

Some of our group were afraid to try passing the Truck on the very narrow space at the edge of the Bridge. There was no Rope or Handrail to hold onto. Those people had to be helped to walk across the River which was about 3 feet deep and flowing quite fast. We waited about half an hour and as there was nothing we could do we continued walking not knowing what was going to happen to our Bags or to Kelly and Conor. However we know by now that the Vietnamese people are very resourceful and we are confident that they will find a way to get the Truck with all our belongings across the Bridge and moving again.

The next village was about an hour's walk away and we stopped for a rest and to have a drink, we were there about twenty minutes when we see our Truck rumbling up the main Street none the worse for its experience. As we waited in this Village a Carnival atmosphere developed. Our Barrettstown Lads were great at entertaining children. Hagi can do magic tricks and he always gets a crowd! Anthony is six foot and sixteen stone and he pretends to be a Monster and chases the kids. They scream with delight but keep coming back for more. The Buses were much further away than they were supposed to be and our planned 9k trek turned out to be about 18k. Eventually we get on our Bus set off for Hanoi with our trek completed.

As we travelled it occurred to me that even out on main Roads we still don't see any Cars, only Bikes, Scooters, an occasional Truck or Bus we are still in a very remote area. We had travelled one and half hours before we saw one Motor Car. We travelled another hour before we saw another Car. After about one and half hours it became clear the driver did not know the way when he stopped twice to ask directions. The second time he stopped he then turned the Bus and the other Bus which was following us also turned. We went back about three miles and took another route. It's a six hour journey. After two and half hours, we came on to Highway one which is the main Road to Hanoi. For the first hour on this Road traffic was 2 way on a single Carriageway, because there were almost continuous lines of heavy Trucks the traffic is slow moving and Trucks and Buses overtake in the face of oncoming traffic.

They always manage to get back in just in time to avoid a collision. It was even more hair-raising after dark. As well as Trucks, Cars and Buses you also have cyclists and Motor Bikes and at least half of those have no Lights, front or rear. **Just imagine, two Men on push Bikes, on a dual Carriageway with no Lights, in the fast Lane, and going the wrong way!!**

On the Bus journey I got a signal on my Phone and rang home but Puddin was in Arklow with her friend Roz. After dark we had a second Toilet stop. Ingi got off the Bus with her Toilet Roll thinking she was at a proper Toilet but soon found she was in a Field. Haji went into a Field to have a pee but was chased out by a Dog. He had wondered into someone's Garden.

On our way to Hanoi we stopped at two Toll Booths. The first is at a Hut and a man comes over to our Driver and sells him a Ticket. Then we stop at the Toll Booth and hand over the Ticket. While we were still in the Mountains we had to cross a River by driving our Bus on to a Barge.

Another time a Barge was in a fixed position across the River and we just drove on one side and off at the other side of the Barge. At this crossing there was a Toll for crossing and some delay, a man in a uniform was shouting at drivers, no idea what he was saying. We arrive in Hanoi at 9 p.m. after a six hour journey; we just have time for a Shower and go out for a Meal.

Day 7

It's a free day in Hanoi and twelve of us hire a Bus with a Guide for a tour of the City. We also had a chance to watch the traffic which on a first visit is the most amazing site you can think of.

There are probably about one thousand Scooters to each Car in Hanoi. Having observed it for a couple of days and taken a huge number of photos I come to the conclusion that while it looks absolutely crazy and out of control it is far from it. The main reason is that, because everyone literally grows up on a Scooter right from Baby stage they have complete confidence in themselves and the passengers have complete trust in the driver.

Imagine a situation where our bus is in very heavy traffic and behind two Scooters. On the back of each scooter are two well dressed Ladies having a chat at about 15 miles per hour. As our Bus overtakes them we can see a very small child on each bike in between the rider and the passenger fast asleep at 9 p.m.

As we overtake further we can see that each rider has another very small Child in front of them and sitting between their legs aged about two or three years old. Over our two days in Hanoi I realised that the scene I just described is not crazy but perfectly normal.

At junctions that don't have traffic lights it's everyone for themselves. Everyone seems to beep their Horn and keep going but then everyone gives way and everyone gets across in safety.

Outside our Hotel I heard a bang and looked around to see two Scooters on the Road and two young Men picking themselves up apparently uninjured. One of them picked up his Bike, started it and drove off. The other Guy seemed a bit dazed. He picked up a part of his bike which had broken off, then picked up his bike, started it and drove off. All the time this was going on the traffic had continued around them without stopping. Although I think I got some good pictures I know I missed the best of them because we were on the bus moving too fast or I did not have my camera ready in time.

We see a man using his mobile phone while on a scooter. A woman on the back of a Scooter with a Mirror putting on her make-up, a Woman on the back of the scooter holding an Umbrella to keep the sun off her, It was not raining, A Woman on the back of a Scooter with a Baby the same age as my Grand Daughter Abi which is one year old, asleep on her Shoulder. Many Women wear masks while out walking or on Bikes or Scooters. They want to keep their Skin as fair and white as possible.

We went to a Museum where there was a group of about five lovely Girls selling music CD's. Every ten minutes or so they would get up on a stage and perform on strange musical instruments and sing songs. When they had finished performing I asked one girl what type of songs were on the CD I had in my hand. She started singing one of the songs in a high pitched but beautiful voice. She sang the entire song while looking straight into my eyes. I bought 2 CD's of music and songs from her.

Vietnamese Children are just lovely; they laugh and giggle at everything. While we were stopped where the Truck broke through the Bridge there was one little Boy about 4 or 5 in a lovely outfit posing for everyone to take his picture and when you did that he came over and shook hands.

You would think that with all this traffic it would be a nightmare trying to walk across the road. Not so, you just walk out into the traffic and they slow down or drive around you. When one of our Vietnamese guides told us about it we could not believe it because even at a Pedestrian Crossing the Traffic might not stop. Owen was so amazed at this that he walked across a busy Road three or four times just to convince himself that it was perfectly safe to do so.

Perhaps the funniest event of the trip was our second night in Hanoi. We all met in the lobby at 7.30 to go out for dinner. Then Stephen said, ok lets go and we all went out to get on our Bus but instead there was thirty three Rickshaws lined up, one for each one of us, to take us to the Restaurant. The journey took about Fifty minutes but about half way there Anthony who is one of the Barrettstown Team and weighs sixteen stone decided it was not right that this little man should be pushing his sixteen stone so he told the rider to stop. He got out of his Seat and put his rider into it and proceeded to peddle to Rickshaw. He was not happy with the slow pace so he took off at high speed. When Stephan saw what was happening he stopped his man and took over. When Owen saw this he did the same thing. At this stage, it had developed into an all out race with Motorists beeping their horns and Pedestrians cheering us on.

I am sure the Rickshaw drivers in Hanoi will talk about it for many a year to come. At about 10.30 Helen had to leave along with our Vietnamese guide to go to the Airport and meet the next batch of trekkers who were only starting their adventure. We are going home to recover but Helen is Meeting another group at the Airport and will do the entire trek all over again with them, she did the same thing last year in Brazil, she is an amazing Woman and one who would become a good friend in the years ahead.

Scene outside a school

A Teacher with thirty children who were about four or five years old, she was leading the first Child by the hand and each of the other children held onto the Tail of the Dress of the Girl in front of her. They were all in white and all dressed the same, it was a beautiful scene but I was on a Bus and could not get my Camera in time to take a Picture of them.

When I had checked in at Hanoi Airport on our journey home a well dressed man came up to me. He bowed to me then shook my hand and said "Mr. Cummins, I am sorry for losing your bag". It was the man who looked after me at the airport ten days earlier when we arrived in Hanoi. There was four of our group who witnessed this incident otherwise I'm sure they would have found it hard to

believe. When we arrived in Seoul Airport Deirdre could not find her Passport. Eventually they searched the Plane and found it again.

The Vietnamese are lovely people, especially those in the remote areas. It was not unusual to be stopped as you walked through a Village or along a Mountain Track and to be invited into a House. You would be offered a Glass of Rice Wine which Helen had described as terrible but most of our trekkers got to like it. One Day about ten of our group were invited by a Man in to his House. He gave a drink to everyone. Some0 of his neighbours came and joined in the fun. No one had a clue what the other Person was saying, it was great fun and our crowd talked about it for days. They are also a very attractive people. Many of the young fellows and girls are stunning and look like they should be in the movies. To see such beauty among such poverty is difficult to get in perspective. Most Vietnamese people are happy to let you take their picture but many will not as they believe that if you take their picture their soul goes with it.

Vietnam, whether in the mountains or the
rice fields the scenry is stunning

trekking in Brazil

Pat on charity build in Lesotho Africa

Chapter 19

Lesotho Africa May 2007, this was another fund raiser for Barretstown where each participant had to raise €5000.00 and then go on a Mountain trek in one of the poorest Countries in Africa and maybe in the World.

My Son Rob collected me at 8 a.m. We met my Wife Pat and Liam Flanagan at the airport. They had just arrived in from New York where they had been attending a presentation to my Sister in law Marie who is married to my Brother Pat and live in New York; Marie was named Kildare/New York person of the year. Pat went on Home and I headed off to Africa

We flew to LHR, and then by SA airways to Johannesburg, then to Bloemfontein, then by coach to Malaya Laya in Lesotho which is an independent Mountain Kingdom but is completely landlocked by South Africa. We had a border crossing on the way. Lesotho is about the size of Wales. Our Coach journey was about four hours and we got there at 7 p.m. having left home thirty six hours earlier. After dinner we were entertained by a local Choir and a Band made up of young people who we were told was trying to make something of themselves rather than do nothing and have nothing. I had a room to myself (because I snore so much) and went to bed about 10.30.

Next morning there was no hot water so I had neither a shave nor a shower. Breakfast was good and we then had to pack all our clothes into heavy duty plastic Bags which were then put into another heavy duty plastic Bag which was designed for being carried by Horses with saddles specially designed for carrying those Bags.

The plan was that we were to cross a Mountain range, sleeping in Tents on the Mountain each night. All our Food, Drink and Rucksacks would be taken over the same Mountain range on Horses. It was a huge logistical operation requiring twenty eight Men and thirty Horses to carry everything including our Tents. There were two more Horses with riding Saddles to rescue anyone who might get injured or who was unable to complete the walk. All this was organised at the African end by a white South African called Volker who also walked every step of the way with his Horsemen and did all the cooking for our crowd which numbered thirty six and also his twenty eight Horsemen and Himself.

It seemed like an extraordinary operation and indeed it turned out to be just that from start to finish. In addition to our Tents for sleeping there were also three large Tents. One to cover the cooking area, one for all the Horsemen to sleep in and one for us to assemble in after dinner and have a sing song. Volker told us before we left on our first day of the trek that he had never had so many in one group before. The most he had was twenty in one group. This would have required less Food, Tents, Horses, Water, and he was hoping that everything would work out ok.

The first sign of things to come was when Volker told us that he was going to move us by truck to where we would start the trek. The truck was a Nissan cab star with an open body and sideboards about fifteen inches high. We all climbed on board and were squashed together to fit everyone in. We were not worried as we understood the journey would only be about a half hour in the truck.

One and a half hours later everyone's backside was numb from sitting on the hard Floor of the Truck or sitting on the edge of the Sideboard so we asked them to stop so we could stretch our legs and go to the Toilet. It was a dirt Road, full of Holes and large Rocks so we had been moving very slowly and had made very little progress. The driver thought it would take about another hour to get to where we were going so we set off again on the dirt road at about 15 mph.

After another hour the Truck stopped again although not at the point where we could start our climb into the mountains. The driver was not sure how much longer it would take, Helen knew we were all pissed off on the Truck so she said let's start walking, it can't be far.

Two and half hours later, we got to the point where the Truck was supposed to take us. Volker was already there with some of his Men and had a lovely meal of Pasta and Pineapple ready for us. However, we were still not near the point where we would start to climb the mountain.

Colo is our guide from Action Travel in London and he is an excellent guide and very experienced. He and Helen were depending on the African guides to know how long it should take. They always said "about one hour"

Colo said its 1.30 now and I'm told it will take us another hour to get to the start of the Mountain and another two and half hours to climb the Mountain. It gets dark at 5.30 so we need to go at a good steady pace.

As always there are slow people who hold back the main bunch. It was about 4 p.m. when we began climbing the Mountain and our African guide said it should take about one to one and half hours to get to the top so we were happy enough with that news. Things soon began to go wrong. Annette who is about five stone overweight developed a problem with her knee and could not continue so Helen had to move up to the head of the group and send back a horse for Annette to ride on. At this stage we were well into the mountains and a Horse was the only way to rescue anyone in trouble.

The sun was going down and every time we asked our African guide how far we had to go he would say 45 minutes or less than an hour. At this stage, we were strung out over a few kilometres and were worried that the people who were away from the main bunch would go off on the wrong track and get lost so Colo told the lead guide to take the fastest group and go on ahead while he would stay with the slow group. They also had an African guide with the Horse for Annette so it was safe to split us into two groups.

It is now fully dark as we struggle up a Rock strewn Path. Fortunately, almost half of our group had brought their Headlights for use in the tents otherwise we would have been in serious trouble. We are on a strange Mountain; the Track we were following was littered with loose Rocks and large boulders with a guide who we had lost confidence in who kept saying about 45 minutes or an hour. His name was Pakeny but Helen called him Pat Kenny and that stuck with him.

One of our group Tony who is 55, overweight and out of condition, was having a bad time and at about 7 pm his Calves seized up and he could not walk any longer. He was in front of me and when I caught up one of the Girls was trying to massage his Legs to get them moving again. I gave him Voltorol Gel and they rubbed that into his Legs. I also gave him a Voltorol Tablet and wanted him to take a Ponston for the pain but he would not take it. Tony is a wealthy business man and is used to being in control of everything. He was now embarrassed to be in a situation where he was not alone out of control himself but that he may endanger the entire group as we could not go and leave him.

After about 20 minutes we got him up and moving again. Then one of the girls fell over a loose stone and hurt her hip. She rested a while but we got her back on her feet and moving again. After that, Tony collapsed again and there was a crowd around him. I was bringing up the rear and when I arrived I was working my way around the crowd over loose rocks when a Rock rolled from under my foot and I went down on my right side. I put out my right hand to save myself and my middle Finger came straight down on a Rock and I could feel that something bad had happened. My light had fallen so I used my left hand to feel for what was wrong with my finger. It was L shaped. The top of my finger was pointing back rather than forward and it was very wet. I grabbed the top of my finger and tried to straighten it out. I could hardly believe it when it clicked back into its normal shape. I picked up the light I had dropped and it was only then I could see that it was bleeding badly and when I pulled the finger back to check if it really had gone back into place. I could see the bone so I pulled it forward quickly to close the wound.

The damage was not caused by a sharp rock but by the action of the knuckle being forced back in such a way that it split the front of my finger in two. By this time everyone had turned from Tony to see who had fallen. Two of the girls got some plasters from a first aid kit and I got them to tape it in such a way that it kept my knuckle pulled forward to stop or slow the bleeding. We got up and got going again but Tony was unable to keep going so we made him take his Bag off his back and I carried it for him. At the same time I was trying to shine the Light in front of Tony so he could see where he was going. He was sweating profusely and having a real bad time but we could not stop for long as he would start to get cold.

I heard the crowd ahead cheering because they saw some lights above them and thought it was our Camp; however it was some of the Africans with horses who had already set up our camp and came back looking for us. The reason they were above us was that we were on the wrong Track and had to scramble up through bushes and stones to where they were. I asked one of them where is our Camp and he said go up that way and when you find the road it's less than an hour away. I told him there was another group behind us who might need help and could they go looking for them. He said we have three horses and he and we will go find them.

Mark took Tony's bag to give me a break as I had my own bag as well as a busted finger. I concentrated on shining the light for Tony so that he would not fall over loose rocks and do himself more harm. In doing that I could not always see where I myself was going and I was stumbling and falling a lot. We reached our camp at 8.00 p.m. after walking for three hours in the dark. Caroline reminded me that when I got up with my Finger in plaster she had said to me Jim "Look where you fell down". When I shone my Light I could see nothing. I was about two feet from the edge of a Cliff and I don't know where I would have ended up if I had fallen a bit more to my right side. A broken Finger would have been the least of my problems.

Colo, Helen and the rest of the group arrived at 8.30. Volker was all apologies to everyone but we decided to leave it to Helen and Colo to sort things out. As usual the Doctor on our trek stays with the last of the group so she was late getting in and I suggested we have dinner first and she could then have a look at my finger. When Helen got into the camp with the last of the group she was very angry at the way things had gone all day and went right off to have a meeting with Volker to see what he had to say.

After dinner Alison, the Doctor, looked at my Finger and said it should be stitched but that there probably was no point in doing it as it would be impossible to stop it from being bent with me having to climb over rocks and God knows what in the days ahead. She tried to put on the tape stitches to keep my Finger from bleeding but she could not stop the bleeding long enough to get them to stick, in the end she just put a Bandage around it and then bound it to the next Finger to give it some support. I had been lucky that up to then I had felt no pain whatsoever. I decided to take a Ponston going to Bed that Night in case I rolled over on it in my sleep.

With my Finger bandaged up I went back to the Tent where the rest of the gang were trying to get a sing song going. I decided to try and cheer them by singing Jack the Sailor and it had the right effect.

Those who had been in Brazil and Vietnam were amazed to hear me singing as I had never sang on any of the other trips and of course I had to sing each Night after that. Imagine their reaction when I sang the Fatal Wedding. I thought that after us having such a brutal day we might have an easy day tomorrow but no such luck. We were to be called at 6 a.m. as usual. We were in the Mountains now and the only way out was up, and the same Mountains would still have to be climbed whether we delay it or not.

Our first night in the Tents

We had been told that temperatures would be about 25 degrees during the day and as low as 8 degrees or 10c degrees at night so I had my three season sleeping bag and my thermal top and bottoms and I thought I should be ok. It was very cold, about 3c below zero going to bed so I wore an extra Tee-shirt over my thermals. I had also bought a good Blanket which was on sale at the Lodge where we stayed for our first Night for $40.00 and I spread that over my sleeping Bag when I went to bed. I still woke up several times from the cold and decided that tomorrow I would wear more clothes going to bed.

Day Two

We had Porridge for breakfast and it was great on a cold Morning. We then had to pack our bags and leave them ready for the horsemen. We are learning by now that the black Africans love singing and dancing and it was while they were loading our bags and tents on the horses that one of them, a big fellow with a powerful voice, started a chant as he worked. Another one would repeat it and this went on for a while. Some more of them joined in as they worked and some started dancing around as they worked until all twenty eight of them were singing and dancing in circles. It was lovely to listen to and to watch and when they finished after about 10 minutes they got a huge round of applause from our crowd which they all loved. We would see more of those spontaneous outbursts from time to time and it was always lovely to watch.

The terrain is much better today. Much of it is over grass tracks and most of it along the top of the Mountain rather than uphill all the time. However, we are still climbing and each day we will reach new heights and camp at higher altitudes. Annette who had knee problems yesterday had finished on foot and today she is back walking again but when we get to a steep climb her Knee gives up and they have to put her on horseback again. She is about five stone overweight, never rode a Horse before and is very nervous on the Horse.

It is amazing to watch those sure footed Horses climb the rocky Paths where sometimes we are almost on our hands and knees. They move slowly but never seem to put a Foot wrong. It was nerve wrecking just looking at Annette up on the horse as she climbed up and down the rocky slopes. I can only try to imagine what it must have been like for her.

We stopped for a rest and Annette got down from the Horse to try walking but could not do so and when we were ready to go she was helped on board again. We had just started walking again when there was a shout for us to stop. Annette had fallen from the Horse and was lying motionless on the ground. Alison, the Doctor, was with her and was trying to get her to speak and find out where she was injured. Annette said I'm alright but it still took several minutes before it was clear that she had no serious injury. She had landed on one side of her Bottom and we were convinced that it was all her padding on her Bum that saved her from a broken Hip.

We got her to her feet and someone asked her if she wanted to get back on the horse again. She said I would slide down the Mountain on my Arse before I get up on that thing again. She was trembling and crying; I took her hand and linked her for about ten minutes. When she had calmed down, she was ok to walk on her own as long as she took it slowly. She came back to me later and thanked me. I said for what? She said for just being nice. I am fed up with people telling me I'll be alright, you just helped me saying nothing and that was just what I needed at that time. Another woman, Catherine, was also having knee problems and had to be put on the other spare Horse from time to time. But it was never more serious than that. The funniest part of it is that when it was all over about ten of our group went Horse riding from the lodge at Simonkong and Annette who had fallen from the horse was among them.

We were at our camp early in the afternoon and were beside a river so we were able to have a bit of a wash. The Toilets at those camps are a Hole dug in the Grass by our Horse Men, Then a fold away frame is opened across the hole with a toilet seat on it. When we move camp the hole is filled in with the soil that was dug out in the first place. There is a wind break placed around the hole for privacy. Kieran was sitting on the Toilet when the wind break fell down around him. Everyone stood there laughing but no one thought of going to help Kieran in his hour of need. Eventually three of the horsemen who had set up the Toilet went to his aid.

The food is very good and there is lots of it. After dinner, on our second night in Camp we had another sing song. Helen had heard about my singing and said I would have to sing again for her so I sang the Fatal Wedding. Helen's friend Ger Dunne said she never saw Helen laugh so much, they thought she would get sick from laughing.

When going to Bed on the second Night, I prepared for the cold by wearing my heavy socks and an extra tee-shirt but as we were at a higher altitude, it was much colder than the first night, about 5 below zero and I woke several times from the cold again.

Everyone was affected by the cold at night. Many of them were not as well prepared as I was with my thermals and the Blanket I had bought on day one. It is difficult in the morning when we are called at 6 a.m. as its still dark and very cold but we have to get changed into our day clothes which are much colder than what we had slept in. We have to roll up our sleeping bag and get it into the tiny bag and the same with the inflatable mattress using Hands and Fingers that go numb quickly.

Day Three

We are still climbing. We find it enjoyable as the tracks are mostly good and not too steep. There are times when we go for hours without seeing a House or a person. There are lots of villages which could be three or four houses or maybe a dozen houses. In most parts of the mountains, we see herds of Sheep, Goats, Cattle and sometimes Horses grazing. They always have a shepherd with them who just sits with the animals all day and takes them home and puts them in a Pen at night. In the really remote areas the shepherds have a Hut which they sleep in as it is too far to go home each night. The shepherd can be a Man or a Woman or even a Child. There seems to be a fairly good education system as primary education is free but secondary is not. Children who work as shepherds miss out on a School education,

We were surprised at some of the places we found schools and if we were passing at a time when the children were coming out of the School there would be great excitement as they would come rushing out to look at us. They would shake hands and loved to have their picture taken.

The higher we climb the more effects we feel of the altitude over 2,500 meters. There could be Blood on your Tissue when you blow your Nose; some in our group have swollen ankles and more have difficulty breathing and of course the cold at night is severe.

Our third night in our tent was the worst; the temperature was –9 or –10 degrees. No one knew it was going to be so cold and so most us were not prepared for it. Heavy frost on the ground, I got up to go to the toilet and the frost was glistering on the **inside** of the tent. Some people said it's better to wrap the blanket around yourself before getting into the sleeping bag but it did not work for me as I could not move when I need to change position during the night.

On the third night I went to bed with my thermal long johns, my thermal long sleeve top, and two tee-shirts, my hoodie with the top pulled up, a woollen cap, heavy socks, sleeping bag and blanket. I could not sleep for more than a half hour before waking up with the cold.

The cold was so intense that even a tiny opening in the Zip of the sleeping Bag was enough to wake me up. The sleeping Bag has a flap over the top and when you fold this over the bag is completely sealed. At first I worried that I would not be able to breathe with the Flap closed but the cold was getting to the top of my Head so I decided to take a chance and close it over. One Girl woke to find her Hair stuck to the inside of the Tent and when she tried to pull it free her Hair broke off and stayed stuck to the Tent.

The people from the local Village came out en masse and formed a soccer team to play against our horsemen and when that was over they all joined in singing and dancing to entertain us. They just love to sing and dance and will do it every chance they get. They all join in from the very youngest to the oldest Men and Women. They love to sing their National Anthem and they all know every word of it. They then ask us to sing our National Anthem which we did but only a few of us knew every word of it and it seemed very dull compared to the Lesotho National Anthem sung with gusto!

Each of us was given a Bowl to wash ourselves and Water to drink or clean our Teeth with. The only Water was in a River that passed near our Camp and we had to wash ourselves in the very cold Water.

At lower altitudes people use donkeys and horses but at those altitudes there are no donkeys, only horses for transport of people and goods. Some villages have modern houses built with concrete Blocks and galvanised roofs and windows, as there are no roads everything has to be brought up the mountains by the horses.

We met Women on horseback with tiny Babies strapped to their Back. They look at home and very relaxed on the horses and it's clear that everyone grows up on horseback so they have no fear even on the Mountain tracks. Some of the Houses and Villages would be two or three days away from where building materials or even basic items can be bought. To go shopping would be a big deal for those Mountain people.

Well, we had got over three nights sleeping in tents and our next night will be in a lodge in Semoncong. Tomorrow we go abseiling down what they claim to be the highest commercial abseil in the world. They give us a certificate which says we did it and a DVD with a few pictures of ourselves as we go over the Edge on our way down the 670feet (204metres) Waterfall. It took our crowd between eleven minutes and twenty minutes each to make the decent. I did it in six minutes. Everything went very smooth for me but I was amazed to hear I had done it in six minutes.

When you get to the bottom and walk away a bit to look back and see what you have done, you just can't believe that you came down all that way on a Rope about as thick as your Finger. Even still I find it hard to take in. The Photo of me which was taken from the bottom looking up just shows a white dot against the Rock face beside the Waterfall.

I was full of confidence while I waited my turn to go so I waited till last so I could give some encouragement to some of the others who were very nervous and up to the last minute were not sure if they could do it.

Teresa from Wicklow is a very strong Hill walker but she is so afraid of heights that she can go no further than the third step of her Attic Ladder. She really wanted to do this, so she could bring the cert home and show her husband and children otherwise they just would not believe she could have done it.

When you are going over the edge you do it backwards and they keep telling you not to look down. I was fine for about forty feet when the rock face went in and away from me. Then I had nothing to put my feet against and so I have no control and start spinning around. At that point I looked down and my Stomach went up into my Throat. I felt like I was floating in space.

I got moving again and soon came into contact with the Rock face and used my feet to guide me down, I felt I was in control again. A couple of times I slowed down to look at the Waterfall roaring down beside me and it was awesome to behold.

Sunrise in the Mountains,

One of the nicest memories was of the frosty mornings in the mountains as we had Breakfast and got ready for the days walking was waiting for the Sun to come over the mountains, wrapped in all our clothes and a Blanket to keep warm as the Sun rose above the mountains. The effect was immediate. You took off the blanket and heavy clothes, by about 8 a.m. when we started walking. We are down to shorts and tee-shirts in mid winter "June".

The area where we camped will soon be covered by a foot of snow and because the air is so dry at 3000 metres altitude there is no humidity even when the sun is out so the snow can last for weeks. I wonder how the locals cope in their round stone huts with the thatched roofs and how they manage to feed the goats, sheep, cattle and horses that are scattered over the mountains.

When the last of the abseiling was over we piled into our Coach and headed for Maseru which is the capital of Lesotho. The journey was really slow as almost the entire country is mountainous and a lot of the journey is with the bus in first gear going up and down mountains and around hairpin bends, the first three and half hours was on dirt roads.

We have been invited to dinner with the Irish Ambassador to Lesotho at his home in Maseru. The reason is that ours is the largest single group to come as tourists. There is a serious effort to make trekking a tourist attraction. Our arrival is seen as very important.

We checked into our Hotel in Maseru and had time for a shower before we were collected in a fleet of SUV's and taken to the Irish Ambassador's residence. His name is Paddy Fay from Ballyjamesduff in Cavan.

He had been called away at the last minute so we did not get to meet him after all but his Wife Dee was there and was a very good hostess along with her teenage son Niall and their dog and a half dozen staff. All black Africans.

They produced a lovely buffet and we all had as much as we could eat. We left there about 10 p.m. and went back to our Hotel. I went straight to bed as we were to be called at 4 am for our Bus jurney to Bloomfountain where we get a flight to Johannesburg but first we will be taken on a Safari.

We were met at the airport and taken by bus to a lodge at the edge of a national park which has all the African wild animals in abundance. I never thought I would enjoy going on safari and watching wild animals but when you see them walking free about twenty feet away it's only then you appreciate how impressive they really are.

Acara, Project Management for Charities.

One day as we were walking through the Mountains in Lesotho Colette O'Sullivan and I were talking about how poor this Country was when she told me that herself and Helen O'Malley were going to set up in Business together, they would be organising treks for all charities and Lesotho was on their list for treks, but their plans went much further than trekking, they were already planning a building project in Lesotho which would be centred on caring for Children. The principal of what they were planning was similar to the Niall Melon Foundation which is that they will seek volunteers to raise €5000 each and then go to Africa and work on the Project, this was the first I had heard of their plans and I was very surprised because as far as I knew neither of them had any experience in construction, Helen had been in charge of fundraising in Barretstown and although I had known Colette from previous treks all I knew about her was that she was a senior sales executive in Dublin. Lesotho became their main focus because in planning the Barretstown trek in Lesotho they got to know the Lesotho Ambassador to Ireland very well and also the Irish Ambassador to Lesotho and were almost overwhelmed by what they learned about the levels of poverty and the enormous number of children that were orphaned and homeless due to Aids and HIV which had spread through the country like a plague.

They got the new company up and running and their first trek was to Brazil which I went on, again in support of Barretstown, I have covered this trip in greater detail in Chapter 17. Helen and Colette knew very little about construction but that did not stop them from proceeding with their Plans; they recruited a team of professionals beginning with the Architect Katherine Kelleher, Andrew Gargan Quantity Surveyor, Peter Finn a Building Foreman and a team made up of tradesmen as well as women and men like me who were willing to assist anywhere they were needed.

The first project was to build a safe house for Orphans and homeless Children in the Town of Mafeteng and was undertaken in October 2008, about 60 Irish Men and Women spent almost 3 weeks there and were very proud to hand over a lovely new building for the Local people to manage, it had sleeping accommodation for 22 Children, a large Dining Room and playground for large numbers of local children to come and use, we also built a vegetable garden called a Keyhole Garden, this is a raised Garden surrounded by stone Walls about one Metre high and is built up with layers of, Soil, Cow Dung, Dead Grass and all kitchen waste, if maintained properly it should continue to produce crops year after year. We worked 12 hours a day from 6am to 6pm and everyone was exhausted but we left with a great sense of achievement. When the building was ready to be handed over to the local people the Local Chief and officials all came and made speeches and we mingled with the locals, one of our girls Geanne Boyle seemed upset and I asked her what was wrong, Geanne said she had been talking to one of the local women who was about 30, this young Woman said, "I have Aids, will you pray for me". Geanne was taken by surprise and was quite upset; I took a picture of Geanne with this young lady before we left.

The next project was in 2010 when we went back to the same town Mafeteng and built 2 new Classrooms in the local school, this time my Wife Pat came and did her share of the hard work. This was a new experience because we had a lot of interaction with the children and the School Teachers, we had just started work on our first day when we were called to where all the children were assembled and ready to say prayers and to sing the National Anthem before class began, but they were also going to sing a song which had been written to say thanks to us for coming to build new classrooms for them. There were over 1600 children in the School Yard and it was amazing how obedient they were for their teachers, it was beautiful to watch and very emotional to be part of. There was a funny side to it when one of our group Colm Quinn began clowning with some of the children, he would put his hands in the air and the children would do likewise, then he would put his hands out to his sides and the children would follow his movements, each time he did something more and more children joined in, this was happening as the singing teacher was trying to get the children ready to sing together and continued until all 1600 children were jumping to every move Colm made, there was great laughter from every one as the singing teacher waited patiently for Colm to conclude his show which he did to a big round of applause.

To get a feel for what life is like in Mafeteng which is a fairly large town let's just look at the School, the numbers of pupils varies between 1600 and 1800, there is a complex of single storey buildings, toilets consist of about a dozen buildings in a field about 200 yards from the school, there is no sign to say which is for boys and which is for girls, each toilet block consists of about 10 or 12 cubicles, neither the building or any of the cubicles have a Door, each cubicle has a dry toilet which is simply a hole in the seat, there is no water in any of the buildings so no way to wash hands after using the Toilet and no Toilet Paper to be seen, the only water available in the School for 1600 to 1800 children and teachers is a tap in the centre of the school yard, this was where we had to get our water supply for mixing concrete for our job, our drinking water was bottled and the children collected our empty Bottles to fill drinking Water from the tap in the School Yard, Colette and Helen are completely devoted to their project and intend to come back to do some more building. We arrived at the building Site at 6am each day and some children would arrive around that time although School did not start until 8am and children kept drifting in way ahead of the starting time, We never found out the reason why so many children came in so early, a group of about 5 women cooked meals for all the pupils each day, the meals were prepared in a Shed which had a dirt Floor, this was the same shed where we locked away our tools and Wheel Barrow's each evening and had to have them cleared out each day before the Ladies arrived for work, however we still had to use it as our Store for small tools and supplies that could not be left lying around the Site and so we were in and out of the shed all day while the Ladies did their work and they always had a smile for us no matter how many times we had to step over or round them to get our Tools, the cooking was done in huge pots on open fires outside the Building, I was told the amounts of food required but the only thing that remains in my head is 40 dozen boiled Eggs each day.

Everyone who went to Lesotho had to raise €5000 and everyone had different ways of doing it, for the first Lesotho project Colette's uncle Gerry who was over 70 years old cycled from Cork to Dublin one Saturday and cycled back to Cork the next day and raised €25,000 although he was not going to Lesotho, Gerry intended to go on the 2nd trip to Lesotho but he had a serious accident while cycling in Cork and was unable to come, his Wife Eileen came and filled the roll of Cook looking after the rest of us while we were there. Gerry is still recovering from his injuries and we wish him well in that regard.

Me in St Lucia with Mrs Paul, (right) Mother of 22
children and one of her daughters, 2003

people who had a positive influnce on me, top Paddy
Flanagan and bottom Eamon Brandon and his wife Ann

Good friends who are no longer with us, top Liam
Flanagan and bottom Packie Fitzpatrick

Chapter 21

The Inca Trail to Macchu Picchu In aid of the Make a Wish Foundation

November 8th 2007, we meet other trekkers at Dublin Airport. First time to use auto check in and it worked ok. We flew to Amsterdam and from there to Lima, the capital of Peru, nice Hotel. On arrival we were greeted by members of Peru Make a Wish Foundation and a TV crew who were making a Documentary about the Make a Wish in Peru, It was the first time I knew it was an international organisation.

The next day we took a City tour of Lima for a half day and then did some window shopping. Lima has almost nine Million people but as it is very spread out and scattered city, there are very little traffic problems. The Presidents House in the main Square is guarded by Armoured Cars and Soldiers with Machine Guns at each corner of the square. We flew from Lima to Cusco and had our first problem with altitude sickness as soon as our Plane touched down. Cusco is at 3300 meters altitude and our youngest Man Stephen was affected right away. The symptoms are many and include Stomach cramps, Headache, dizziness and breathing difficulties.

Out of a party of twenty five, eight would need a Doctor; some of them had a Doctor several times. One Man seemed to be having a Heart attack. A Doctor came to our Hotel at 1 a.m. with a mobile ECG Unit but fixed him up with medication. Machu Picchu is at 2450 meters and right on top off a mountain but there is a Road right up to it. (Buses and delivery trucks only) so everyone can get there, however we were taking the hard route. Even those in Wheelchairs can get up and around the site. We had six days walking altogether with four of them on the original Inca trail from Cusco to Machu Picchu.

One day we reached a summit at 4200 meters and this was my toughest day. We were climbing nonstop for over three hours and its amazing how much more difficult walking is at that altitude. We were moving at a fairly quick pace because when we got to the top we were going down the other side which was a much longer journey and it gets dark at 6 p.m. As we went through the Mountains, we passed the remains of Towns and Villages which had been built in the most incredible slopes but which were abandoned and covered in dense Vegetation. Those places had been abandoned hundreds of years ago but the sites have been cleaned and so it's possible to see what the houses were like and the agriculture terraces are still in good condition. We look in amazement at where they created the terraces and grew their cops one thousand years go.

On the day that we went over the 4200 meter summit all went well until we got to a certain point on our way down. On our descent the track became very steep, very narrow and dangerous with a sheer drop on one side; there was loose grit and stones on some of the really steep slopes. Many of the Women and some of the Men just froze on the spot and could not move. There was no point going back up as the only other way down was closed for Track repairs. Those of us who were not affected had to take people by the hand and move at a Snail's pace, the last part which should have take thirty minutes, actually took one and a half hours. It was dark by the time we got to where our Bus was waiting to take us to our Lodge for the night.

The last day climbing to the summit of Machu Picchu was tough and the last hour was the hardest, this consisted of a long flight of stone Steps which seemed to go on forever, what made it harder was each Step was about 18 inches or 2 foot high and we had to use our hands and feet to keep moving, eventually we reached the high point and entered the Sun Gate, this is the ruins of a temple and when you walk through it you are looking down on the **Lost City of Machu Picchu**. Getting to this point and looking down on the fabled Lost City had a strange effect on many of the walkers, many of them burst into tears and could not stop crying, I took some Pictures with Seamus Lynam and then I thought I might be Lucky enough to get a signal on my Mobile Phone to ring my Wife Pat, I got straight through to her and when she answered hello I tried to speak but could not get a word out, I was sobbing as I tried to tell her I was looking down on Machu Picchu but could not put 2 words together, this went on for some time until our group started walking down the track and I had to follow so I blurted out to Pat that I had to Go and cut her off, it took us about 40 minutes to walk the remainder of the journey and the phone rang twice as I was walking but I could not answer it because the Track was very rough and I had to concentrate on every step I took. It was Pat ringing back because she had been unable to make sense of what I was saying and was worried that there was something wrong with me and then I had just cut her off, later that evening I rang Pat and tried to explain my behaviour but it made no sense to her or indeed to me for that matter, we arrived at the site of Machu Picchu about 5pm and the site was empty, the normal entry Gates close at 4pm and all visitors were gone when we arrived so my photographs show the site completely empty which is something very few visitors get to see and the only reason we did so was because some in our Group had been very slow and we were about 1 ½ hours later than we should have been,

Next Morning we came back by Bus to have a much longer visit and take as many pictures as we wanted, we had an excellent Guide Pablo who knew the history of Machu Picchu very well, Erwin Gill who organised the trip for Make A Wish had us there at 7 am because as the morning wears on the crowds build up and by 10 or 11 am the wait to get through the Gates is more than an hour long. Of all the treks I have been on this is my favourite by a long way and I intend to go back and bring Pat with me next time. The most amazing thing about Machu Picchu and many other deserted towns in Peru is the quality of the Stone work that has survived, the Incas had discovered Bronze and Gold but not Iron so they had no metal tools to shape the rocks and yet each stone is cut to perfection and fits in with the other rocks on all sides so tight that you could not fit a sheet of paper in between them, they used no mortar to keep the stones together, windows and Doors were beautifully built in what is called trapezoidal style or architecture where in most cases the sides of the Doors or Windows slope gently in towards the top. The commonly held belief is that in the absence of hard metal tools they used Stone on Stone which makes it all the more amazing when you see such perfection in the finished product, most of the walls are in perfect condition with only the roof's missing and the walls that are collapsed are believed to have been damaged by earth quakes, they had a wonderful skill in creating water channels that directed water into a Fountain or Bath which would be directed into other Fountains, most of those would have been functional but many seemed to have been created for fun or as a thing of beauty, I can't wait to get back there.

Looking down on Macchu is a peak called Hynna Picchu which means "Young Mountain" in the quecha language, the cliff up to it is a further 360m (1180 ft) and is a almost vertical rock face on a very tight path, at the top of this peak are some beautiful stone buildings which were believed to be homes for the high priest and young girls who were to remain virgins.

It takes about one hour and is quite dangerous to climb and they only allow 200 people per day to do it. Our guide Boris told us that on average one person per year is killed while climbing this section. I asked Boris if anyone had been killed so far this year and Boris said yes so I said maybe it's OK for me to climb it now.

The matter was settled when the track was closed because of heavy rains the night before the track was slippery and dangerous so no one was allowed climb it that day.

Final Thoughts

Today is your day, your Mountain is waiting, so, get on your way, Dr. Seuss

Hill walking, before I took up Hill walking I had a variety of other hobbies, when our children were quiet young I bought a speed boat but with a wife that hates boats and the children were too young to share my past-time I soon got rid of that and took up wind surfing, my next hobby was water skiing which I kept up for a few years until my introduction to sailing and my Trans Atlantic Yacht race. My introduction to hill walking was for my first charity trek in aid of Barretstown in 2005 and I have been at it ever since, it's something I never get tired of, I may be exhausted at the end of a hard day but all I need is some rest and I'm ready to go again, if there is no one available to come with me I'm quite happy to go on my own, Pat also loves walking and will go anywhere I take her and the harder the challenge the more she likes it, many members of my family have also started walking with me, Brendan is naturally very fit because he is in a running club and runs Marathons and other races so climbing mountains is no problem to him at all. His wife Mary also likes walking but only on nice days. My sister Dolores and her husband Joe love walking and come whenever work allows. My brother John has also taken to the Hills along with me or his sons Paraic and Sean who also love walking and has trekked all over the world. My brother in law Tom Bourke (Mosney) and his daughter Veronica have joined our little group and, My hope is to get more and more of the family involved and that plan is moving in the right direction,

I was a founding member of the Acara Walking Club which was an offshoot of Acara project Management for Charities, the walking club was used to prepare volunteers for charity treks abroad and we have a lot to thank Helen O'Malley and Colette O'Sullivan for in that regard, Hill walking is something that anyone at any level of fitness can start, if you are overweight there is no better way to go about losing weight, get a pair of walking Boots and join a walking club, there are clubs in every County and they are looking for new members all the time, I guarantee you that each time you walk you will feel better than you did the previous Day, as your level of fitness improves so will the level of enjoyment that you get from it, in the Mountains total strangers say hello and are happy to stop and have a chat, there is the most beautiful scenery that can only be seen from on high so go for it, in the Wicklow mountains there are huge herds of wild Deer and wild Goats but you won't see them by driving along the road in your Car. Every Mountain has its own attractions and different wildlife, getting into the wide open spaces can help remove a lot of the negativity that's weighing us down during this recession, if you meet me up there please say hello even if I have my Head down watching out for loose Rocks.

The End

6088304R00150

Printed in Great Britain
by Amazon.co.uk, Ltd.,
Marston Gate.